Michael R. Davidson

THE INCUBUS
VENDETTA

Also by Michael R. Davidson

Harry's Rules
Incubus
Caliphate

The Incubus Vendetta

Michael R. Davidson

©2013

In the development of this novel the author was inspired in part by actual events connected with the dissolution of the Soviet Union and its aftermath that have been amply reported in the press and literature.

Having made this clarification it is important to emphasize the fact that this is a work of fiction and the situations described, as well as the characters and their actions are totally imaginary.

Having reviewed the manuscript, as required by law, the CIA required the following disclaimer:

"All statements of act, opinion, or analysis expressed are those of the author and do not reflect the official positions or views of the CIA or any other US Government agency. Nothing in the contents should be construed as asserting or implying US Government authentication of information or Agency endorsement of the author's views. This material has been reviewed by the CIA to prevent the disclosure of classified information."

THE INCUBUS VENDETTA
Copyright © 2013 by Michael R. Davidson.

MRD Enterprises, Inc.
PO BOX 1000
Mount Jackson, VA 22844
mrdenter@shentel.net

Library of Congress Control Number: TXu 1-888-417
ISBN 978-0-615-72390-7

Contact author at info@michaelrdavidson.com

Cover Design by M. Davidson

Printed and bound in the United States of America.

First printing 2014

ACKNOWLEDGEMENTS

To my family I give thanks for their ability to put up with me as I struggled to write the final chapters in the Harry Connelly/Ewan Ramsay saga. Gratitude also is due to my colleagues in the Spymasters Literary Guild, Clabe Taylor and Robert Morris, for their many kindnesses in helping me edit the book. And very special thanks are due to Mark V. Lonsdale for his insights into the military aspects of the story. Mark is the real deal, as they say, and is quite possibly the real "world's most interesting man."

CHAPTER 1

The hoary Russian tradition of exile was alive and well.

The long flight had afforded plenty of time for the former President of the Russian Federation to contemplate his ignominy. He was the private jet's only passenger and had remained in the otherwise empty cabin even during the refueling stops at Frankfurt and São Paulo. He dared not risk being seen; his face had become too notorious to permit a stroll in public. Now as he stared glumly out the window at his uncertain future rushing up to meet the descending aircraft, his thoughts turned unbidden to the past.

Vitaliy Mikhailovich Shurgin, erstwhile president of the Russian Federation of States, still missed his old comrade, General Yuriy Ivanovich Morozov. Had Morozov still been there to counsel him and provide the ballast to keep Shurgin's zeal on an even keel, he might have avoided his recent problems and preserved his place in history. But his friend had perished long ago in a squalid cell in the basement of Lefortovo Prison on Shurgin's own orders.

To be sure, it had saddened him at the time in the way a dog's owner is saddened when it becomes necessary to put down a loyal pet – a transitory pang before going to the pet store to find a replacement. The KGB had taught him that people either were loyal or disloyal, useful or not, disposable or not, and

Shurgin had learned the lesson well.

He had not thought of Morozov for a long time. He'd tucked the memories into a safe corner of his mind and walled it off, but events had conspired to allow the specter to escape, and it haunted his dreams, refusing to be restrained again.

CHAPTER 2

The Soviet Union - 1991

As the summer of 1991 drew to a close the tumultuous domestic political and economic plight of the Union of Soviet Socialist Republics reached a crisis point. Shurgin had just won his General's star and with it command of the KGB's Group North, based in Leningrad, now St. Petersburg. As a particular favorite of KGB Chairman Vladimir Kryuchkov he had risen quickly through the ranks of the Committee for State Security (KGB). Had it been only a decade earlier his future would have seemed secure.

But perestroika had brought country to the brink of chaos. Dissent was in the air, dissent from all sides, like a pack of wolves harrying a crippled animal, and only a fool could fail to realize that things must soon come to a head.

One must choose sides.

Dismay was widespread in the KGB ranks and among Party stalwarts as the rusted edifice of Soviet totalitarianism collapsed into pieces around them. Gorbachev, President and Chairman of the Central Committee of the Communist Party of the USSR, was an unmitigated disaster.

At the end of July Shurgin received an unexpected summons to the office of KGB Chairman Kryuchkov in Moscow.

"This is an unofficial trip, Vitya," Kryuchkov had admonished him, using the familiar form of his name. "As few people as possible should know about it."

Shurgin was intrigued.

Rumors were rife within the KGB that the Chairman was planning something big. The previous December he had called for a return to order in a televised broadcast and had not bothered to hide his contempt for Gorbachev. Perhaps the time had come for the opposing forces to form into ranks and face one another across the field of battle.

He chose to take the "Red Arrow" overnight train to Moscow, travelling in mufti. The night was warm and passengers had lowered the windows, as much to evacuate the acrid cigarette smoke that floated in blue layers the length of the train as to let the cool night air rush in.

He found himself seated next to a middle aged man carrying a heavy canvas satchel who displayed a trait uncharacteristic in the Soviet Union of speaking with perfect strangers on trains. Perhaps it was a sign of the times.

The satchel, he said, contained cuts of beef he had 'liberated' from a meatpacking plant in Leningrad. His sister, who lived in Moscow, knew a man who would trade oranges for the meat. Oranges were a rare delicacy in the peoples' paradise.

The man laid a finger alongside his nose and winked at Shurgin.

"Did you hear about the man who had been waiting so long in line to buy a loaf of bread that he became angry and declared to his friend, 'I've had it. I'm going to go and kill that damned Gorbachev!'"

"No," sighed Shurgin, "how does it go?"

"Well, the man takes off to kill Gorbachev but returns to the bread line two hours later. 'What happened?' his friend asks, and the man says, 'The line's longer over there.'"

The man with the satchel chortled while Shurgin considered the deeper significance of such jokes. Gorbachev, he decided, did not have much time left.

The train creaked into Moscow's Leningrad Station just before 8:00 AM Wednesday morning where he was met by a driver in a black Volga sedan. Fifteen minutes later they passed through the narrow vehicular entrance off Furkasovskaya Perekhod into the interior courtyard of the yellow brick Lubyanka building. He knew his way to the KGB Chairman's office in Lubyanka 1.2.

There was an unusual amount of activity in the narrow, half-paneled corridors. The Chairman's suite was somewhat more spacious than most, and when he entered the thickly carpeted antechamber, he was surprised to see Vladimir Zhizhin seated behind the receptionist's desk engrossed in something on his computer screen. Zhizhin had been Kryuchkov's deputy when he commanded the First Chief Directorate, the KGB's foreign intelligence arm. Shurgin's old friend Colonel Yegorov, stood behind Zhizhin peering over his shoulder.

Both looked up when he entered. He couldn't discern whether it was guilt or fright he read on their faces before they recognized him.

Zhizhin greeted him.

"Vitaliy Mikhailovich, I'm glad you could get here so soon."

"What are you up to? You look like a couple of conspirators."

Zhizhin and Yegorov exchanged a nervous glance.

"Tell him," Yegorov said.

Zhizhin pointed at the computer screen and said, "We just ordered delivery of 250,000 pairs of handcuffs and 300,000 arrest forms. Yesterday we ordered Lefortovo Prison emptied so there would be room for new inmates."

He grinned ruefully at Shurgin. "How's that for a conspiracy?"

His suspicions were confirmed. Something big was up.

"They're waiting for you inside, Vitaliy Mikhailovich." Yegorov waved an arm toward the padded double doors that led to Kryuchkov's inner sanctum. "Prepare yourself."

Shurgin braced his shoulders and passed through the doors.

Had he not trained himself never to evince surprise his jaw would have dropped when he recognized those gathered around Kryuchkov's conference table. The Chairman wore a baggy tan suit and no tie, his lanky hair drooping over one side of his forehead overlapping the oversized glasses with thick, plastic rims that he favored. He'd been KGB Chairman since 1988 and Chief of the First Chief Directorate before that, a long-time favorite of former Chairman Yuriy Andropov with whom he'd first worked putting down the Hungarian Uprising of 1956. No one doubted his hardline pedigree.

Grishkov, Head of the First Chief Directorate, was there, as was Prime Minister Valentin Pavlov, Interior Minister Boris Pugo, Vice President Gennadiy Yanayev, and, surprisingly, also in mufti, there was grizzled, mustachioed General Valentin Varennikov, Deputy Minister of Defense and Chief of the Soviet Ground Forces.

The old general was nearly 70 years old. He'd fought the Germans at Stalingrad and back across the Ukraine and Belorus all the way to Berlin where he'd participated in the capture of the Reichstag. Varennikov was not only a hardliner; the old warhorse was an unreconstructed Stalinist.

He supposed he'd find out soon enough why he was here. At the moment all the old men were looking at him in frank appraisal.

"Sit," said Kryuchkov, indicating an empty seat at the table.

He sat.

"Comrades," began Kryuchkov, "allow me to present General Vitaliy Mikhailovich Shurgin, one of the most brilliant officers I know, and a loyal son of the Motherland." He continued to extol his virtues while Shurgin sat stone-faced and silent.

Kryuchkov finally addressed him directly.

"Vitaliy Mikhailovich, yesterday President Gorbachev met in the Kremlin with Yeltsin and Nazarbayev to discuss how they might go about replacing us so-called 'hardliners' with more docile individuals. Luckily for us, the room was wired for sound." Kryuchkov compressed his thin lips in a smug smile. "As far as this group is concerned that meeting spelled the end of Gorbachev's tenure and the beginning of the end of all the mischief he's brought about. In a very few weeks we will be ready to replace him. This will require that we declare a state of emergency throughout the country while we round up unpatriotic and disruptive elements. A new president will be proclaimed."

Kryuchkov nodded toward Vice President Yanayev whose eyes had not strayed from Shurgin.

They were planning a full blown *coup d'etat*. And with the internal security apparatus, as well as the armed forces involved, how could they fail? They must have recruited deep into the ranks for this.

Shurgin anticipated the inevitable question.

"Can we count on your loyalty, Vitaliy Mikhailovich?" asked Kryuchkov.

The old men at the table transfixed Shurgin with cold, lifeless eyes -- sharks' eyes. There was no choice, really. No hesitation was acceptable.

"Of course, Comrade Chairman."

Kryuchkov nodded in satisfaction.

"This is my man," he said to the others. "This is OUR man."

He turned back to Shurgin.

"You will play a role, Vitaliy Mikhailovich, a dangerous but vitally important role."

"Yes, Comrade Chairman."

Shurgin burned with curiosity but mastered the desire to ask what his role might be. He would be told soon enough.

"You are to return to Leningrad today and turn your duties over temporarily to your deputy. In one week's time you are to report directly to me here."

"Of course, Comrade Chairman."

Kryuchkov's smile disappeared.

"You will be fully briefed upon your return to Moscow, not before. When you come, don't wear your uniform."

"Yes, sir."

"You may go now."

Shurgin rose to leave.

"One more thing," said Kryuchkov. "Not a word to anyone."

Shurgin was almost insulted by the admonition.

"Of course not, Comrade Chairman!"

That was how it started. He wouldn't have the first glimmering of the idea that eventually brought him to the most powerful position in Russia until sometime later. But it was from this moment that his path was set.

A week after his meeting with Kryuchkov he returned to the Lubyanka to find that the Chairman's office had taken on the appearance of a war room. Armed guards from the KGB's special group guarded the corridor, and Yegorov and Zhizhin were now supplemented by others among whom he recognized the uniforms of both the military and the KGB's own special forces. Large maps of Moscow, Leningrad, and other cities, as well as one of the entire country covered the walls. All were dotted with pins of different colors. Shurgin wondered if 250,000 pairs of handcuffs would be enough.

Yegorov waved him on into Kryuchkov's inner sanctum where he found the KGB Chairman, Vice President Yanayev, and General Varennikov studying a map spread out on the conference table. A quick glance told Shurgin it was a detailed map of the southern Crimean coast. Gorbachev, he knew, had been at his dacha in Foros since the 4th of August.

The men stopped talking when he entered and he stood awkwardly at attention just inside the door while Varennikov hurriedly rolled up the map like an adolescent who had been discovered looking at pornography.

Kryuchkov's watery eyes, magnified by his glasses, stared balefully at him for a moment, and his voice had no inflection when he spoke.

"Ah, Vitaliy Mikhailovich. You are punctual, as usual."

He walked behind his desk and punched a button on the intercom.

"Yegorov," he said, "tell them that General Shurgin is here."

He didn't invite Shurgin to sit. With a glance at his co-conspirators, the KGB Chairman sighed heavily, betraying his fatigue, and began.

"By the time another week has passed the country will be in a state of emergency following the removal of Mikhail Gorbachev and his so-called liberal reformers. Under these conditions the country will be temporarily under the control of a new State Committee we will form. There will be disorder, probably worse, which could take some time to quell, especially in Moscow and Leningrad, and we are prepared to undertake extraordinary measures to do so. The plans are all but complete. Report immediately to the office of General Morozov where you will receive your instructions."

Kryuchkov dismissed him with a wave of his hand, and Shurgin did an about face and stepped back out the padded doors that swung closed silently behind him.

He wondered if the conspirators knew that General Yuriy Ivanovich Morozov, head of the KGB's Department "S" Illegals Operations, was an acquaintance of many years. Morozov's office was on the same floor as Kryuchkov's suite, and he was there within minutes.

Morozov waited in the reception area to greet him, immense and bearlike in his uniform.

"Vitaliy Mikhailovich," he greeted him formally and ushered him toward the door to his inner office.

In a lower voice he continued, "Just listen politely and follow orders. We'll talk later."

Inside the office, 54-year old Minister of the Interior Boris Karlovich Pugo waited. The KGB was not subordinate to the MVD, but it was clear that Kryuchkov expected him to take orders from Pugo.

When the three were seated at Morozov's conference table, Pugo began, "In the days following implementation of the plan, there will be unrest, perhaps even a certain amount of chaos on the streets. Until the situation returns to normal it will be necessary to safeguard state assets to keep them out of the hands of counter-revolutionary elements. This is your task, one we would entrust only to officers of the highest caliber. Tomorrow morning you will board a special train that will carry the liquid assets of the CPSU and the State to Leningrad where the cargo will be transferred to a ship waiting in the Sea Channel at the port."

Shurgin uneasily shifted his weight in his chair.

"Boris Karlovich, what do you mean by the term 'liquid assets'?"

Pugo spoke as though addressing a slow-witted child.

"Foreign currency and gold bullion."

At his side, Morozov evinced no reaction to Pugo's extraordinary statement, and Shurgin guessed that the General was already briefed on the mission.

Shurgin contained his astonishment. "What are our orders, Boris Karlovich?"

"You, Morozov, and an armed squad of his most trusted men will take the ship beyond our territorial waters and await a signal from us to return."

The mission was straightforward enough, and Shurgin now knew why he had been chosen. As the commanding officer of the KGB's Group Nord, no one would question his authority in Leningrad.

"General Morozov will join you on this mission. He will be in charge of security. The General will tell you what you need to know."

The unstated intention was for Morozov to keep an eye on him, or more likely, they were to keep an eye on one another. Again he wondered if they were unaware that the two had been friends for many years.

They stood and Pugo left, presumably to join Kryuchkov and the others. When they were alone

Morozov trapped him in a bear hug.

"You did a good job covering your surprise, Vitya," he said with a chuckle. "For a second there I thought you might fall out of your chair."

"It's a mad idea, you know." Shurgin frowned, not amused.

"As mad as the putch those old men are planning?"

Shurgin flinched at his friend's words and glanced at the walls.

"Don't worry, Vitya. There are no bugs in here. I'm a lot more secure from Kryuchkov's prying than Gorbachev."

He opened his desk drawer and pulled out a bottle of vodka and two glasses.

Shurgin accepted the proffered glass and gulped its contents before speaking. He didn't often feel the need for alcohol in those days.

"Why is Pugo giving us orders? He has his own men at the MVD."

"I don't think he trusts them yet. Remember, before they named him Minister of the Interior he was head of the Latvian KGB. I think he still feels more comfortable with us. And my men are one hundred percent loyal. Tell me, what do you think of it all?"

Shurgin remained silent, and Morozov continued. "We'll either be heroes or goats, depending on how things go." Morozov harbored a deep streak of Russian fatalism.

"How deep does the plotting go out here?"

"It's fairly top heavy, I think. Practically everyone that matters in the First Chief Directorate is involved, and I know the Third Chief Directorate will play a big role."

The Third Chief Directorate, responsible for the political reliability of the Armed Forces.

Morozov continued, "Border guards are in it, of course, and the Special Forces. Kryuchkov is counting a lot on everybody following orders."

"These 'liquid assets' -- how much are we talking about?"

"Pugo told me he personally supervised the transfer from the Central Bank. The train is seven cars long, including the guards' car. The value, including the gold bullion is around fifty billion American dollars. We're not taking any rubles."

Shurgin whistled.

"How much of that is gold?"

"Only about 350 tons."

This surprised Shurgin. The USSR was one of the world's leading producers of gold.

Morozov explained, "I know, I thought it would be a lot more, but the Central Bank has been selling off gold reserves ever since the value began to drop a few years ago. This lot's worth around four billion dollars."

Shurgin processed this and asked, "So the rest is foreign hard currency?"

"About half, mostly dollars and deutschmarks. The rest is in bearer bonds. Otherwise, we would have needed an entire train. We needed three boxcars for the gold alone due to the weight."

"My guess is that you're supposed to keep the cargo safe and I'm to keep an eye on you," said

Shurgin.

"Of course."

"I'd better go and find a hotel room for the night."

"Not a chance. They don't want us outside the Lubyanka until we catch our train tomorrow. We're to stay at one of the guard rooms tonight."

"They think I might let the cat out of the bag?" Shurgin again felt his bile rising.

Morozov nodded. "I'm confined here, as well."

"So who's guarding the freight cars?"

"My men. And a company of KGB Special Group is watching them. Special Group doesn't know what's in the freight cars."

"Who guards the guards? How many people know the truth?"

"My best guess? Pugo, you, me, the squad of my men, and maybe some Central Bank people, but I doubt the Central Bank knows where the shipment is headed. Kryuchkov and the rest probably have an inkling, but you know Bolsheviks – they prefer to keep everything compartmentalized. Pugo seems to be the one in charge of this phase. The train crew, of course, doesn't know what's in the crates they're hauling, and neither does the ship's crew."

"We'd best get a good night's rest, Yura. We're going to need it."

"Not before we finish this bottle." He poured out two more measures. "Did you ever see the American film about Butch Cassidy and the Sundance Kid?"

Shurgin nodded.

"Well, my friend," said Morozov, "we're about to pull off the biggest bank robbery in history. Let's hope we don't end up jumping off a cliff."

CHAPTER 3

The coup so carefully planned by Kryuchkov and his allies failed in a matter of days. Military units vital to the success of the plot in the end refused to accept their orders, and the disgraced conspirators were arrested. Within months the Soviet Union would cease to exist.

The exception was Minister of the Interior Boris Pugo, the man who had dispatched Shurgin and Morozov on their mission. He and his wife committed suicide before he could be taken into custody, which proved fortuitous for Shurgin and Morozov.

"Didn't I predict we'd be either heroes or goats?" sighed Morozov, gulping down a half water glass of vodka.

The two sat alone in Morozov's cabin aboard the Vladimir Ilich class freighter *Anna Ulyanova* which steamed in slow circles in the North Sea. The wealth of the Soviet Union, packed in sturdy wooden crates, filled the cargo hold below guarded by a squad of the KGB's elite *Banner* unit.

Shurgin's mind had not been idle during the several days aboard the ship. Kryuchkov's failure changed everything as did Pugo's death. Those few who might be aware of the seizure of the country's foreign and gold reserves were unlikely to add to their crimes by admitting they had sacked the treasury. There was opportunity here.

"I do not intend to be a goat," said Shurgin.

Morozov, who had just broken the seal on a fresh bottle of vodka, gave him a peculiar look and carefully set the bottle on table without refilling their glasses, a sure sign he was paying close attention.

"You have a plan," he said, his tone flat.

After Shurgin finished telling him, Morozov picked up the bottle and poured them each a generous portion of vodka.

He raised his glass and said, "You're crazy, Vitya."

He drained his glass and poured himself another, larger portion.

"Yura, they've left us holding the bag – literally. The only question is what to do with it. We might return everything to the Central Bank and claim we took it out of the country to safeguard it from Kryuchkov. We might even be proclaimed heroes, but what's the use? The fact of the matter is that Russia is now in the hands of fools."

Shurgin drained his glass and held it toward Morozov for a refill. There was no possibility of success if Morozov did not buy into the plan. He needed the Banner unit, and those men were loyal to Morozov.

"We're in this together, old friend. Whatever happens to one of us happens to the other. It's a gamble, a huge gamble, but just think of the possibilities."

He couldn't read Morozov's expression. It was one of the big man's strengths, in contrast with Shurgin's mercurial character. He needed that strength. He needed for Morozov to buy into his insane scheme. It was all or nothing.

Morozov sucked down another draught of vodka, his eyes never leaving Shurgin's face. The wheels were turning behind that bland, bearlike façade, Shurgin knew, calculating their chances of success.

"You really think we could take over the entire country?"

Shurgin nodded, "Eventually. With time we'll succeed where Kryuchkov and his geriatric conspirators failed. If we act decisively and ruthlessly all will be ours."

Morozov suddenly reared back in his chair and threw his glass against the bulkhead, smashing it into glittering shards.

"I'm in," he said.

Chapter 4

Asuncion, Paraguay – Present Day

The G5 taxied past the terminal at Silvio Pettirossi International Airport across a tarmac that reflected the pale yellow light of morning from a surface still glistening from a pre-dawn shower. In the distance along the horizon beyond the security fences a shimmering, undifferentiated green showed through the thinning dawn mist -- an alien landscape into which he must disappear like so much flotsam cast upon the sea.

The events that had brought him here continued to circle his mind like a swarm of angry wasps that stung him repeatedly. Thirty-six hours earlier, Vitaliy Mikhailovich Shurgin, until recently President of the Russian Federation of States, virtually its modern Autocrat, had slipped out of the Kremlin in a closed car bound for Domodedovo Airport to board a clandestine flight out of the country -- forced to abscond to this fetid South American backwater that he imagined to be teeming with serpents and crocodiles.

Several hundred meters beyond the main terminal the G5 came to a stop with a slight jolt inside a private hangar where Shurgin could see a black Mercedes waiting to meet them. He unbuckled his seatbelt and started to rise as soon as the engines spun to a stop, anxious to escape his long confinement, but the cockpit door opened and Rus

Ismayilov stepped through and waved him back to his seat.

Ismayilov was overweight with a shaggy head of black hair and a walrus mustache. These days he favored trousers with elastic waists and baggy, untucked shirts. Shurgin remembered the man when he was a young and trim KGB officer under Soviet Air Force cover, but he had fallen easy prey to the excesses of new wealth, unlike the wiry ex-president whose only indulgence was the drug of power.

"Let me make sure everything is secure."

Ismayilov spoke over his shoulder as he rotated the lever to unlock the forward cabin door. He pushed it open and lowered the steps. The heat that seeped into the cabin did not improve Shurgin's mood. Ismayilov approached the car and had a word with the driver, a bearded, dark-skinned young man wearing a white *guayabera* and dark trousers. Ismayilov turned and stretched an arm towards the plane in a thumbs-up gesture.

Shurgin descended the steps, and the humidity engulfed him in a sticky embrace, a shock after the arid atmosphere in the plane. He was grateful for the air conditioning as he settled into the back seat of the Mercedes. Ismayilov piled in beside him.

"Where are we going?"

Ismayilov would have made arrangements for him to avoid immigration and remain incognito. The hangar belonged to Ismayilov's company, Rusavia, and was used as a transfer point for shipments in and out of Paraguay, as well as for passengers who required discrete transport and a place to cool their heels. It was one of many such sites operated by Rusavia in convenient Third World countries, and at each one Ismayilov ensured that his business would not be troubled by customs and immigration officials.

"I keep a house near-by. You'll like it, and it's well guarded. You'll be safe there until I can make the arrangements in São Paulo."

Shurgin shuddered inwardly. He did not look forward to the agonies of plastic surgery, but his world famous face had turned overnight into a disadvantage. São Paulo plastic surgeons were reputed to be among the best in the world and much more attuned to discretion than their European counterparts. Besides, there was no place in Europe that he could have escaped notice.

Their destination was a residential neighborhood in Luque, a suburb of Asunción, adjacent to the airport. The Mercedes carried them along narrow paved streets lined with purple jacaranda trees and tall palms. The orange tiled roofs of Spanish style houses, their fences and walls festooned with riots of bougainvillea, brightened under the rising sun. But Shurgin kept his head bowed in thought until the Mercedes turned into an entrance and stopped before a wrought iron gate. When he looked up he was under-impressed by the single-story white adobe structure guarded by a brick wall with electronically operated wrought iron gates.

Ismayilov took notice of his guest's sour demeanor. They had not spoken throughout the short drive from the airport. He had not seen Shurgin since before the disaster in the United States.

"Don't worry, Vitaliy Mikhailovich, it's really quite comfortable and secure."

Shurgin was gratified by the solicitous tone, but his dark mood persisted.

"Besides," continued Ismayilov, "this is only temporary until you are settled in São Paulo. Believe me, this is the safest place you could be right now.

A bearded, dusky-skinned guard in a white *guayabera* who could have been the driver's twin opened the gates as a motorcycle belching blue smoke stuttered past them and disappeared down the street. The guard carried an AK-47 slung casually over his shoulder.

"How many of these do you have here?" Shurgin jerked his head in the direction of the guard.

"Ten right now. The number varies, but it keeps them busy and sharp while they're here."

"Where are they from?"

"The current crop all are veteran Hezbollah fighters. I provide them with weapons and training, and they pay well. This region is actually a sort of rest and recreation center for them and there's a training camp near Ciudad del Este. There are lots of Muslims in the Tri-Border area, many from Lebanon, Gaza, and the West Bank, and these fellows melt right into the pot."

"Business continues to thrive?"

"There are always small jobs, but the Iranians are the mainstay, thanks to you, Vitaliy Mikhailovich."

Shurgin's long-standing covert relationship with the Islamic Republic of Iran, both before and after he was President, had proven highly profitable. While clandestine Russian support of the mullahs' nuclear weapons program which discomfited the West and the United States in particular served Russian political ends, the covert sale of arms benefited Shurgin financially. His choice of the clever Ismayilov to run that business had been a stroke of genius. The combination of his established pipeline to the mullahs and the Farsi-speaking Ismayilov managing day-to-day affairs had made it a "plug and play" operation.

"I need some help from our friends."

The plan had gestated and was born during the long flight from Moscow. With one exception he knew the identities of those who had contributed to his downfall, and he would have his revenge.

In the cool interior of the surprisingly well-appointed house he settled into a comfortable chair and outlined his plan to Ismayilov.

"I have a list of five people," he concluded, "one in Europe, two in the United States, and the fourth, whose whereabouts is unknown. I don't know the identity of the fifth, a woman, but I believe if you find the man who is her companion, you will find her, too."

CHAPTER 5

A drop of perspiration fell from the tip of Sergio Blanco's nose to the tiled floor. His wiry frame tensed as he bent toward the dim black and white image on the monitor, straining to discern what was happening at the Rusavia hangar. It had cost months of careful vetting to identify an airport safety officer with the proper access, but in a country where bribery was a way of life, success was inevitable, and the surveillance operation got underway.

The video camera was affixed to the hangar wall concealed in a fire extinguisher modified by the wizards in Tel-Aviv to house it and the battery pack that kept it alive, as well as a low power transmitter to send encrypted imagery across a distance of a thousand feet to the safehouse on the other side of the Autovia Silvio Pettirossi that served as Blanco's observation/listening post. Blanco's tame safety officer changed out the old batteries for fresh ones every three months in the course of his regular inspections.

Blanco had an excellent reason for being there, an eye for an eye reason.

On July 18, 1994 an explosive laden van detonated in front of the Jewish Community Center in a densely populated section of Buenos Aires killing dozens, including 12-year-old Sergio Blanco's parents, and wounding hundreds. The ensuing Argentine investigation, assisted by Israeli Intelligence and the

IDF, identified Iranian-directed elements of Hezbollah as the responsible parties.

Young Sergio was sent to live with his aunt and uncle, who emigrated to Israel soon thereafter. Now nearing thirty, he'd completed his mandatory service with the IDF and realized his dream of being recruited by the Mossad who found a very special assignment for him.

With his native Argentine accent, slender physique and long, black hair, he was indistinguishable from the inhabitants of the Tri-Border region. He was the latest in a string of Mossad operatives assigned to penetrate the so-called Triple Frontier, the tri-border area near where the confluence of the Iguazú and Paraná rivers created one of the world's most magnificent waterfalls. The area, with some 20,000 Muslim inhabitants, boasted two television stations that broadcast exclusively in Arabic. It was quickly identified as a "safe area" for terrorists of all stripes, including Hezbollah and Al Qaeda, as well as a ripe source of funding for Palestinian terrorists. Israel could not ignore it.

Israel was not engaged in a game of King's X where one's opponent could be permitted to commit atrocities and then claim sanctuary. The country's leaders had not attempted to excise the word "terrorist" from their political vocabulary nor turned a blind eye toward either its practitioners or those who supported them. Israel would have her revenge, and Sergio Blanco would be her enthusiastic instrument.

The ultimate objective was several hundred kilometers east of where Blanco now sat, but Rus

Ismayilov was a key player in a deadly network that extended far beyond the borders of Paraguay.

*****

The arrival of Ismayilov's G5 was a rare occurrence. Most Rusavia flights used older cargo planes from the Soviet era acquired on the cheap from the Soviet Air Force following the dissolution of the USSR. The sleek private jet meant that Ismayilov himself was in-country, and he had a passenger with him. Strain as he might at the screen Blanco could not make out the passenger's face in the hangar's dark interior, but Ismayilov's bulk and walrus moustache made him easy to identify before the two disappeared into the waiting Mercedes and left the area.

They were undoubtedly heading for Ismayilov's house, and Blanco made a snap decision. He raced to retrieve his motorbike from the garage and tore off in a cloud of blue exhaust. With a little luck he could beat the car to the house.

Ten minutes later he turned into the street and saw the Mercedes approaching from the opposite direction. Blanco activated the miniature high resolution, stabilized camcorder concealed in his helmet. He could just make out the profile of the passenger in the right rear seat before the car disappeared through the gate.

CHAPTER 6

Tehran, Islamic Republic of Iran

Rus Ismayilov stepped jauntily from the official car that had brought him from the airport and stood for a moment in the bright sunlight that flooded the forecourt of the now-familiar white headquarters building of VEVAK, the *Vezarat-e Ettela'at va Amniat-e Keshvar* or the Ministry of Intelligence and Security of the Islamic Republic of Iran. The lush gardens surrounding the heavily guarded complex were still in flower, offering a fragrant façade that concealed the obscenities regularly perpetrated upon dissidents in the underground torture chambers that lay beneath.

He spotted the familiar figure of General Adel Hatimi, the operational head of Iranian Intelligence, limping down the steps to greet him. The narrow-framed General suffered from arthritis.

"Rustum, my brother, it is good to see you again."

Born of an Azeri father and Russian mother in Soviet Azerbaijan, Rustum was Ismayilov's complete first name.

Hatimi had been the primary conduit between Moscow and Tehran for two decades, ever since he and Shurgin signed the first secret agreement that guaranteed covert Russian support for "Project Magush," the code name for Iran's active nuclear weapons development program. Ismayilov thought the General must be over sixty by now, his dark hair succumbing to an invasion of gray.

"Adel," said Ismayilov as he embraced the Iranian and kissed him on both cheeks as custom dictated, "it's always a pleasure to return to the land of my ancestors. I do not deserve such an honor as you greeting me personally."

He spoke in Farsi, learned at his father's knee and honed to perfection at the Soviet Military Institute for Foreign Languages. Although ethnically Azeri, Ismayilov was Russian at heart and fully inculcated in the ways of Russian intelligence operatives. He played the ethnicity card to good effect with the Iranians.

"You are our honored guest. Shall we go inside? Moslehi is waiting to see us."

Hatimi referred to Heydar Moslehi, the mullah appointed as head of VEVAK by Iran's Supreme Leader who had recently supported him in a dispute with President Mahmoud Ahmadinejad.

Moslehi would be curious about the reason for the visit, and Ismayilov was certain he would accede to Shurgin's request. Rusavia was a key component in Iran's strategy and would be difficult if not impossible to replace. Without it the groups supported and "owned" by them, such as Hezbollah, would be without the weapons they required. Hatimi, closer to day-to-day operations than Moslehi, would support him.

Once settled in Moslehi's office, spartan except for the rich Persian carpet, they were served hot, sweet tea and Ismayilov waited patiently through the formalities until the mullah at last inquired about the reason for the visit.

"We'd like some help from Hezbollah in Europe

and one of your sleeper cells in the United States."

Moslehi's salt and pepper beard was neatly trimmed. He wore the traditional black robes and white turban, and sat quietly as Ismayilov outlined the proposal. His intelligent, dark eyes behind rimmed lightly tinted glasses never wavered from the Azeri's face. The mullah did not speak for several minutes as he considered both the logistics and the implications of fulfilling the request. Then, "Europe will present no problem, but the United States is more complicated."

"We have time," said Ismayilov, "but not too long."

"We would have to risk exposure of valuable assets in the United States. Europe is much easier, and cheaper."

It was only natural that Moslehi would try to bargain. It was in their blood. But Ismayilov had his orders, and bargaining was in his blood, as well.

"The US part of the operation is vital and cannot be avoided. Consider it an opportunity to strike a blow at the heart of the Great Satan and settle an old score for your friend, President Shurgin."

Ismayilov had briefly considered and quickly discarded the idea of going to one of his Al Qaeda contacts with this request. In contrast to the fanatics hiding in mountainous caves or Pakistani safehouses the Iranians were models of professionalism with a first rate intelligence service that boasted disciplined agents.

Moslehi would not refuse because Hatimi would have convinced him that his and Shurgin's clandestine assistance to the Iranian nuclear weapons program made it possible for the Iranians to leapfrog ahead. That assistance would continue because Russia's new leadership would not abandon Shurgin's foreign policies. In the meantime RusAvia represented an irreplaceable supplier of weapons to groups that permitted Iran to project its influence.

Ismayilov watched the calculations flicker across the mullah's dark face. He and Hatimi would have to sell the operation to the Supreme Leader, but that was their problem. Both were seasoned movers and shakers in the bloody back alleys of the Islamic Republic.

CHAPTER 7

Brussels, Belgium

The warm afternoon sun felt good on Asafu's back as he crossed the great square. Directly opposite him the magnificent Gothic *Broodhuis*, known as the *Maison du Roi*, dominated Brussels' Grande Place despite the loftier tower of City Hall opposite. The many cupolas that adorned the *Broodhuis* reminded him of the minarets of a mosque. Every detail was etched sharply in the slanting afternoon sunlight: the ancient cobblestones underfoot, the bright yellows of the building facades, the red awnings and umbrellas where restaurants had set outdoor tables. It was a good day to be a *shahid*. Life was, after all, unimportant except insomuch as one obeyed the dicta of Allah, translated for man by Mohammed, Blessed be His Name. And what was death if not a short bridge to Paradise and the rewards that awaited the obedient?

Asafu had enjoyed few rewards in this life save Islam, and Islam promised transcendental happiness in death, which was not to be feared but welcomed, especially if one had had little happiness in life. They'd told him he would feel no pain, but it didn't really matter. Life itself was painful, especially for an unskilled immigrant, a Berber from the mountains of Algeria.

Work for the poor and unskilled in France, where Asafu had been but one out of thousands of North African immigrants, was difficult, if not impossible to find, especially during a period of economic stagnation. Crime offered an alternative, and he had accepted its inevitability, the more so as the victims of the gang he had joined in Clichy-sous-Bois, a poor neighborhood on the eastern boundary of Paris, were infidels. Among the economically disadvantaged and ghettoized Muslims of France the only source of pride was their religion that told them they were morally superior to their Gallic oppressors.

His happiest memories were of his enthusiastic participation in what the French termed *"les emeutes des banlieues de 2005."*[1] Only seventeen at the time Asafu and his friends torched cars and buildings igniting a virtual firestorm all over France that prompted the government to declare a state of emergency throughout the country.

In the frenzy of the moment they dragged a man from his car and kicked him to death. Although Asafu had not participated directly in the beating, he was rounded up with the rest and sentenced to five years imprisonment at Les Vignettes detention center in Normandy. It was there that he was recruited by one of the "bearded ones," Islamist militants, also prisoners, who taught Salafism[2] in simple terms to

---

[1] "The riots of the suburbs of 2005."

[2] "Radical Salafism is the ideology of Osama bin Laden's al-Qaeda organization. Its particular world view can be understood by looking at the roots of this ideology in Islamic intellectual history and by realizing that its teachings have been marginal to and opposed by mainstream Islamic thought ... Salafism's hallmark is a call to modern Muslims to revert to the pure Islam of the Prophet Muhammad's generation and the two generations that followed his. Muslims of this early period are referred to as *al-Salaf al-Salih* (the pious forefathers) whence the name Salafi.

uneducated inmates such as Asafu. His friends in prison were Samir the killer, Kaïs the rapist, and even Stéfane the gang member. French or not, Muslims or not, "the bearded ones" taught them and converted them, and by the time he was released Asafu was well-prepared for jihad. Life suddenly had a meaning that had eluded him before.

He wore a light windbreaker two sizes too large to conceal the vest filled with explosives that Hamid, the Hezbollah contact to whom he had been directed in Brussels, had strapped onto his body one hour earlier. Packed around the explosives were steel nails, bolts, and ball bearings laced with rat poison. The trigger, a simple button, was attached to the detonator by two thin wires threaded into the windbreaker's pocket. Asafu wrapped his hand around the trigger as he walked across Brussels' Grande Place toward his targets. Hamid, he knew, was at the other side of the square watching. He would make Hamid proud.

His destination was a popular restaurant, La Chaloupe d'Or, and Asafu concentrated all of his attention on its bright red umbrellas and the dozen or so tables arranged under them where his targets were seated among tourists and locals unfortunate enough to have chosen this venue on this day for their afternoon beer or coffee. People were all over the

---

Salafism's message is utopian, its adherents seeking to transform completely the Muslim community and to ensure that Islam, as a system of belief and governance, should eventually dominate the globe. " Radical Salafism – Osama's Ideology, by Bernard Haykal, DAWN, Pakistan Herald Publications, 2001.

---

square, strolling, taking pictures, laughing, but Asafu
didn't see them. He saw only the man and the woman
at the table under the umbrella. A waiter in white
shirt and black vest had just taken their order.

Ten meters, five meters more. The patrons paid
him scant attention as he walked among the tables,
and a great tranquility settled over him as he prepared
his soul to meet God. Had anyone taken note of him
they might have been struck by his beatific expression,
his fixed stare, or the fact that his lips moved in silent
prayer.

He stopped beside the table where the targets
were seated, and the man looked up at him with mild
curiosity.

He was an older man, probably in his seventies,
with a full head of white hair. Both he and his female
companion of the same age, were dressed casually, in
short sleeves that revealed the creped skin of their
arms, tanned as though they spent a lot of time out of
doors.

"Alahu Akbar." At first Asafu said it softly,
almost to himself, but the man heard him, and his
eyes widened. Then, more loudly, "Alahu Akbar!" And
he pressed the button in his pocket. His handlers had
told the truth. Unlike his victims, Asafu felt no pain.
Within milliseconds the blast compression detached
his head from his body. Investigators would find it
hours later on a near-by rooftop.

The explosion roared across the square and
windows shattered. Then a silence, as though the
world were taking a long, ragged breath, before the
screams of the wounded and dying, their bodies

brutally violated by shrapnel and flying glass, began to penetrate the smoke and devastation. Softly at first, then growing in volume as bewilderment became realization that turned into agony, the sound rolled in a wave across the square and spilled into side streets, and those who heard it did not want to look back at its source.

CHAPTER 8

The West Coast of Ireland

Ewan Ramsay sat cross-legged at the edge of the stone dock staring dejectedly at the deck of his whale boat across which were scattered the parts of its dismantled Westerbeke 4/108 Diesel engine. The dock projected into a small but deep inlet that lay beside his house. Late summer had blessed the west coast of Ireland with a string of magnificent, cloudless days. People lingered in the sunlight on the wide veranda of Oliver's, Cleggan's only pub, less than a half-mile from where he sat, and Ramsay was tempted to retreat there right now to wrap himself around the comfort of a cool Guinness.

He recalled some wag who described boats as holes in the water into which people threw money. The whaleboat was a purchase he had made several years earlier because his house was on the littoral of Cleggan Bay. Taking to the sea and bringing in fresh fish, his wife opined, would be a pleasant diversion, but he was a landlubber. He'd never taken the craft any farther than Inishbofin, the large island that sat athwart the mouth of Cleggan's bay. Before leaving his native Mid-West to see the world the largest body of water he'd ever seen was Kentucky Lake, and the memory evoked lazy summer days fishing off the side of his father's flat-bottomed bass boat. Handling a whaleboat in rough seas was quite a different experience. He loved the sea, the sight and smell of it, but he was most content to enjoy it from the shore.

A black Scots terrier sat a few feet away, its almond shaped brown eyes fixed on him in what might have been sympathy. It was high tide, and a light northern breeze rippled across the surface of the water.

I don't know a damned thing about engines, so why did I take this one apart? He knew the answer. He was bored silly, and the idea of getting to know the power plant of his 26-foot Navy surplus whale boat seemed like a manlier pastime than puttering in the garden with his wife. Most men, he knew, would have preferred his wife's company.

For a second he considered just cutting the boat's painter line and letting her drift along the shore until some deserving local fisherman rescued her. Any of these hardy Irish locals probably could dismantle and reassemble a diesel engine in the dark. For better or worse, Ramsay's talents leaned heavily toward a similar skill with weapons.

He had just resolved to hire someone to put his engine back together when the tinny notes of an electronic version if *La Marsellaise* sounded from the Blackberry in the holster on his belt. Fewer than a half-dozen people had this number, and one of them was Alain DeBlottière, a Frenchman who did freelance work for the DST, the *Dirección de Surveillance du Territoire*, French internal security. DeBlottière's assigned ringtone was the French national anthem.

Ramsay brought the phone to his ear. *"Zut, Alain! Comment vas-tu?"*

As Ramsay listened to the voice at the other end

of the call his expression changed from one of pleased anticipation to granite-faced.

"Thanks, Alain," he said, "I'll get back to you. In the meantime, please keep me posted."

He terminated the call and sat thinking for a few moments before standing to turn toward the single story native stone house that stood fifty feet behind on a rocky promontory that jutted into the bay. His wife would be on the other side tending her flowers, and he dreaded telling her the news.

He rounded the corner, the dog trotting at his heels, and there she was, her unbound ash blond hair glowing in the bright sunlight. After two decades of marriage her beauty still took his breath away. She heard him coming and straightened from the flowers, removing her gloves as she turned to greet him. The words died on her lips when she saw his expression.

"Ewan, what's wrong? What's happened?"

"Bad news. I just had a call from Alain. There's no easy way to put it. The Nelsons were killed in that suicide bombing in Brussels three days ago."

"Oh, my God! Nancy and Lawrence?" She lowered her eyes and shook her head. "I can't believe it – a suicide bomber in Brussels."

Ramsay knew his wife would not become emotional. Aleksandra Sergeyevna Turmarkina, Sasha to her friends, Russian immigrant to Israel, former member of the Mossad's *Kidon* unit, had lost friends to suicide bombers before.

"There's a French connection of some sort, and the Belgians brought the DST into the case. They sent Alain to Brussels."

DeBlottière was a well-known expert on international terrorism.

"I'm going to see him," he said.

Her reaction was predictable.

"Why, Ewan? Surely Alain will let you know what he turns up. He didn't ask for your help, did he?"

"No. But I'm going."

"You're just looking for an excuse to get out of Ireland and poke your nose where it doesn't belong. And you know the risk you run every time you set foot into Europe."

There were longstanding Interpol warrants for his arrest for "murders" that had taken place in Vienna, Austria, in the early nineties when his name had been Harry Connolly and he still worked for the Central Intelligence Agency. Since then clandestine missions for the *Kidon* unit had put him at risk countless times throughout the Continent. Ramsay was the only non-Israeli ever accepted into the Mossad's ultra-secret action unit, and his status was still a closely guarded secret in Tel-Aviv.

"It's been nearly 20 years, and they haven't caught me yet. They have more important things to worry about now."

"That's because you had Mossad resources at your disposal. You're retired now and on your own."

It was an old argument. Sasha wanted him to "enjoy" retirement, sit by the fire and read books, fish, work in the garden, and enjoy friends at Oliver's bar. Fifteen years his junior, she'd begun to fuss at him as though at 65 he already was well into his dotage. In fact, he felt great, still ran three miles every morning regardless of the weather, and retained the rugged good looks that reminded people of the actor Clint Eastwood.

He'd awakened that morning as he always did, with the rising sun, pulled on shorts, sweatshirt, and running shoes to for his morning jog along the coast road. When he returned a half-hour later Sasha was still in bed, as he knew she would be, and he set about making breakfast. He ground fresh coffee beans to a fine powder and loaded the Pasquini Livia espresso machine, frothed a metal pitcher of milk, toasted two extra thick slices of whole grain bread he had baked himself, and beat four eggs in a stainless steel bowl for an omelet. By the time he'd set the small table in the kitchen, Sasha came through the door, attracted by the smell of fresh coffee.

It should be an idyllic life.

The trouble was, this was how every day began, and it was increasingly difficult for him to find things to do that held his interest. He'd become an accomplished gourmet cook, and this gave him pleasure, but cooking was a mere avocation. The boredom inevitably caught up with him, and today it had persuaded him to dismantle his boat's motor.

There had been a time when he couldn't wait to get to this place and have Sasha there with him. In the beginning, when they were new lovers, each feared that the joy they'd discovered in one another was temporary, to be curtailed at any moment either by Mossad rules or a bullet. Later, through all the dangerous missions the knowledge that they would return here to their safe haven had sustained them both. But now, nearly five years after retirement, a fearsome restlessness gnawed at his gut and threatened to create a barrier between them. They had always shared everything, but it had become nearly impossible for him to share Sasha's contentment.

If he were truthful with himself, the Cold Warrior in him did feel like a relic. The West no longer focused on Russia, long his area of expertise. Nearly forgotten was the time when the possibility of mutual nuclear destruction overshadowed all other international considerations, when the threat could be identified, quantified and contained within clearly defined international borders, when the rivals were nation states and arms treaties could be signed and verified.

Today the fear of annihilation had been replaced by the threat of generalized violence conceived by obscure religious fanatics in locations like the mountainous border between Afghanistan and Pakistan, Yemen, Somalia, Tehran, and Islamist mosques in London, Paris, and Detroit.

And so, in a world where human beings strapped explosives around their bodies in order to massacre other human beings, where unspeakable crimes were committed in the name of God, Russia was lost in the white noise, demoted far down the enemies list. Russia had become a bizarre *cine noir* sideshow featuring gangsters, oligarchs, and chaos. No one cared anymore. Ewan Ramsay thought it was a mistake. Leopards did not change their spots.

"You're just looking for an excuse," Sasha repeated.

"I'm going. You can come along if you want, in case I fall down and can't get up by myself."

The hurt on her face made him immediately regret the sarcasm. She was right. He was looking for an excuse, anything to relieve the ennui.

"Look, I don't plan to do anything dangerous. Our friends died horribly, and I just want to hear the details first-hand from Alain rather than over the phone. Why don't you come along, really? We could both use a change of scenery."

"No, thank you. I've seen more than enough mayhem already. Unlike you, I like it here. And I haven't finished the landscaping."

She turned her back and bent to her gardening.

There was nothing he could do once she'd dug in her heels. He packed a valise and began the drive south to Shannon where he could catch a flight to the Continent.

CHAPTER 9

Brussels, Belgium

"Why did the Belgians call you in, Alain?" Ramsay had met DeBlottière years ago when the Mossad needed someone in a hurry to meet an agent in Moscow and a mutual friend suggested the resourceful Frenchman. They had been friends ever since.

They were at a table in the lobby bar of the Hotel Amigo, a block away from the Grand Place. The City Hall that stood between the hotel and the square had protected it from the blast. The Grand Place itself was still completely cordoned off as the authorities combed the site for evidence and body parts. Clean-up and restoration would not begin until that task was complete.

DeBlottière sipped his beer before answering. He was a thoughtful man -- an intellectual with a taste for adventure. Ramsay noted that his tousle-haired friend had put on a few more pounds. The Frenchman was ten years Ramsay's junior, but middle age was catching up fast.

"There's a French connection. These buggers always lose their heads, so it's one of the first things the forensic investigators look for. There's often enough left to make identification. In this case they found the bastard's noggin on the roof of the building next to *La Chaloupe d'Or*. Other than missing its body, the head was relatively unscathed, and they ran the face through photo identification and checked criminal DNA records. Turns out he was a former guest in one of our fine French prisons where the humanistic powers that be think it's a good idea to permit Salafists to recruit and radicalize other inmates. As a result, Islam is the most prevalent religion in French prisons. Our bomber was Asafu Zidane, a poor kid from Algeria, may he rot in hell. If he finds any virgins there I hope he discovers he left his dick here."

"What group was he with?" Ramsay had arrived in Brussels only an hour earlier and immediately contacted DeBlottière.

"*Ansar al-Fath*, 'the Partisans of Victory,' a home grown bunch of crazies founded by a Salafist in a prison in Normandy."

"Are they claiming responsibility for the hit?"

"No, not yet, at least. And that's a little unusual."

"Why would *Ansar al-Fath* stage an attack in Brussels?"

"In the past they've sent *jihadis* to Iraq and planned terrorist actions in France, so they have a record of loaning their recruits to other groups. In this case, the Belgians suspect it was Hezbollah that organized the bombing. At least their informants are reporting rumbles to that effect. Everybody's on edge here. Brussels is the *de facto* capital of the European Union, so it wasn't necessarily a strike at purely Belgian interests."

Ramsay was surprised. "That doesn't make any sense. And why would a Salafist work for Shiites?"

"It wouldn't be the first time, especially with the Iranians funding a lot of them. Anyway, they're all crazy fucks. I'm less concerned that Sunni and Shia terrorists are working together than puzzled that Hezbollah would have any interest in staging a terrorist act in Belgium. As you said, it doesn't make sense."

The Frenchman pointed at the door. "Want to take a look at the scene?"

DeBlottière's credentials got them past the cordon into the Grand Place where Ramsay was startled by the extent of the damage. The large square which normally would have been teeming with tourists on such a perfect day was a scene of devastation. *La Chaloupe d'Or* was a blackened shell and the buildings adjacent were severely damaged, as well, their walls pockmarked by flying shrapnel. Windows all around the historic square were boarded up where glass had shattered, and tell-tale dried smears of blood that would later be erased with high pressure hoses were still visible on the cobblestones. The blast had killed twenty-one people outright and wounded another 103, some of whom were expected to die from their injuries.

"Lawrence and Nancy were in the wrong place at the wrong time," said Ramsay. He and DeBlottière stood in the center of the devastation in front of *La Chaloupe d'Or*. He shuddered inwardly as he imagined the blast and shrapnel radiating in a circle at 4,000 feet per second from the spot where they stood.

"Yes. Bad luck," said DeBlottière.

CHAPTER 10

São Paulo, Brazil

He summoned the strength of his Russian stoicism to bear the pain of healing from the surgery, but he had been jarred by an unfamiliar sense of vulnerability and was grateful that it had been in the solitude of Ismayilov's Asunción safehouse where his security was assured. The Lebanese staff had not minded that he preferred to be left alone, and he saw them only when he required a meal. The surgeon visited from São Paulo regularly to change the dressings and cluck over his progress, only too happy to attend a patient who paid so well.

During Shurgin's recuperation Ismayilov found a comfortable condominium in São Paulo not far from Ibirapuera Park where the former President settled when he was completely healed. His staff and guards were all Ismayilov's men.

He now waited on the veranda under the unfamiliar stars of the southern sky, vaguely aware of the night birds' serenade from the park across the street. His scars had healed but his bones ached from withdrawal from the incurable addiction of power. São Paulo was a pleasant city, at least in this neighborhood, but it was as far away from the center of power as Pluto from the Sun. It was not Moscow. Shurgin chafed at being an anonymous face in a foreign land.

There was much to consider: the revival of the

Voskreseniye[3] network, the elimination of a certain *Russkaya Mafiya*[4] kingpin who would resent his bid to regain control of the far-flung *vory v zakonye*[5] organizations, whether to retain or replace a financial manager in France who had the temerity to use Shurgin's accounts to enrich himself. But a more visceral need eclipsed all of this -- the desire for revenge burning deep within, waxing hotter with each passing day until it became an all-consuming obsession. It was illogical, but it was what he needed if he was to begin to heal himself, and he had set the wheels in motion.

All that was important in his life had evaporated like morning fog dispersed by the rising sun thanks to a chain of events set in motion the previous year by an octogenarian retired KGB General who wanted to cleanse his soul by revealing a decades-old secret.

And still, Morozov's wraith lingered nightly just beyond the edge of consciousness like the gatekeeper to Shurgin's personal hell to remind him how far he had fallen. The vaporous presence was a constant reminder that the great, burly bear of a man who had been at his side along the path to power was no more.

He was grateful when a servant interrupted his reveries to announce Rus Ismayilov's arrival. He had no doubt that the Azerbaijan-born Rus could be

---

[3] Russian word meaning "Resurrection" or "Rebirth."

[4] Russian Mafia

[5] "Thieves in the code," a term describing Russian criminals, especially those who spent time in the Gulag.

trusted completely to carry out his orders. Ismayilov was clever, but he was not a leader. He was the kind of man who could flourish only under the tutelage of someone like Shurgin. And flourish he had.

The collapse of the Soviet Union found the young KGB officer under cover as an air force major. Shurgin plucked the graduate of the Military Institute for Foreign Languages out of the KGB for an assignment for which Ismayilov's Iranian heritage and fluency in Farsi made him ideal. With *Voskreseniye* funds Ismayilov set up a private freight company, Rusavia, registered in Belgium. Lacking fuel and funds for spare parts, hundreds of aircraft stood abandoned on Soviet military runways from which Ismayilov selected the best to build his cargo fleet.

Shurgin forged a secret arrangement with the Islamic Republic of Iran to supply advanced nuclear technology, and Rusavia was the ideal instrument to make the clandestine deliveries.

Other opportunities could not be ignored. In the chaos of the Nineties there had been ton upon ton of weapons and explosives, even entire advanced weapons systems, in scarcely guarded depots throughout the old Soviet territories and Bloc countries under the guardianship of poorly paid and disgruntled military officers. The weapons brought good prices in the illegal arms market from eager customers in places like the Congo, Liberia, and Somalia. But first among equals were the Iranians who needed weapons to supply their puppet clients in Lebanon and elsewhere. Even the Taliban and Al Qaeda benefited from Iranian largesse, and Ismayilov's operation rapidly expanded. He set up logistical and maintenance bases in the United Arab Emirates, Spain, and Paraguay.

Ismayilov's loyalty to Shurgin had a practical aspect: the profits from the arms sales enriched both men. But he was not Morozov who had not feared to contradict Shurgin or treat him as an equal. *Just as well*, he thought as Ismayilov appeared on the veranda.

Shurgin stood to take the Azeri's extended hand.

"Did you have a good flight?"

"The G5 is a wonderful aircraft, and it's gotten a work-out since you moved here. And to answer your question, there were no problems. Despite the attention I seem to be drawing from various Western intelligence services, the Brazilians don't give a damn. Did you know that Brazil doesn't even recognize terrorism as a crime?"

"Brazil is a sanctuary as long as you don't cause the locals any trouble." Shurgin smiled. "What are you staring at?"

"I still can't get over the change in your appearance. You could go anywhere and not be recognized."

"The plastic surgeon earned his pay. I don't like wearing the wig, but it's the best money can buy."

Shurgin now kept his head shaved and wore a custom made black toupee of real human hair. His eyebrows were dyed black, as well, and he wore brown contact lenses.

"Remarkable."

Shurgin sat and gestured for Ismayilov to join him. A bottle of iced vodka stood on the table with two small glasses. Shurgin filled them.

"Let's drink to success."

CHAPTER 11

Arlington, Virginia

Vicky Kondratieva was lonely, all the more so since her father's murder the previous year. The publication of the so-called "Andropov Memorandum" that her father had stolen from KGB files had led eventually to the fall from grace of Russian president Shurgin, and she had been gratified. But she was not glamorous or clever enough to parlay the transient fame into something more permanent. Given the state of the real estate market, money from the sale of her duplex in Falls Church had been disappointing, but she did continue to receive royalties from her father's book, as well as a few thousand dollars per month in alimony from her ex-husband who still lived in California with his trophy wife.

Vicky had moved into her deceased father's upscale condo in Arlington. CIA officer Robert Strachey and his wife, Amy, still visited her every couple of weeks. Vicky was certain they did so out of pity, and that made her feel all the more inadequate and at loose ends.

She was, after all, only 45-years-old, still in the prime of life, and not unpretty. Her traditional upbringing in Moscow as the prim and pampered daughter of a respected KGB general had not prepared her to be a modern, independent woman. She had always been taken care of by a man, first her father and then her husband. But with her marriage in ruins, and her father dead, she contemplated the rest of her life alone in a country where she still felt like a foreigner, and it frightened her.

She tried internet dating services, and was sorely disappointed. As her alcohol consumption increased, she became a regular at an upscale bar a few blocks from her condo where she could be found several evenings a week.

And that made it easy for Ghasem Esfahani to find her.

Esfahani lived in Los Angeles under the name of Mario Rodriguez. His father had been an Iranian diplomat, and thus Esfahani spent much of his childhood in Spanish speaking countries. He spoke the language like a native and even managed to tinge his English with a Latino accent. These were definite advantages for an illegal intelligence operative living in California, a State in which it was practically forbidden for any official to inquire about one's citizenship status.

A trusted member of the *Quds* Force, Esfahani was a VEVAK sleeper agent who already had completed a variety of missions in the United States – everything from casing targets of interest, human and architectural, to servicing dead drops. His dark good looks and ready supply of cash would have made seduction easy, but Esfahani had a problem with women.

Fortunately, in the case of Vicky Kondratieva he was only after information. Hers was the first name on the list sent to him from Tehran.

The woman's address was not a secret and it

was a simple matter for him to determine her pattern of activities, which seldom varied. Parked in a pool of shadow at the end of her street, he'd watched her exit the red brick condo and set out on foot toward North Fairfax Drive. Thinking she might be headed for the Ballston Metro Station, Esfahani locked his rental car and followed on foot. But she by-passed the turn to the Metro and crossed the street to continue south toward Wilson Boulevard.

She was a small woman with straight, black hair cut short. She wore a dark skirt that was a tad too short for a woman of her age and a matching, form-fitting jacket with a large handbag dangling from a shoulder strap. Esfahani wondered for an instant if she might carry a weapon in the bag but immediately discarded the notion. There was something hesitant in her carriage that screamed vulnerability to the Iranian's trained eye.

He waited a few moments after she turned into a hotel that faced Wilson Boulevard then followed her inside. The lobby was all white marble filled with uncomfortable looking stainless steel furniture upholstered in white faux leather. Esfahani followed her into an elevator with three other people, each of whom got off on different floors until only the two of them were left. She'd pushed the button for the top floor bar/restaurant. He thought at first that she might be meeting someone, but she headed alone to the terrasse and took a chair at an open air table under an umbrella. Esfahani lingered by the bar until he saw her order a drink, vodka on the rocks, which she downed in two swallows and ordered another. The bartender and waitress, he noted, treated her like a regular.

Esfahani decided to get a closer look. He walked onto the terrasse and took a seat at the table next to her, nodding at her politely with a greeting and a flash of brilliant white teeth. She acknowledged him shyly before averting her eyes and turning back to her drink.

She wore too much make-up, he thought, and through the shyness her eyes betrayed an introspective desperation that he recognized immediately.

He ordered a tequila sunrise and sipped it in silence as he continued his observation. His position permitted him to partake of alcohol, indeed often required him to do so, and the mullahs had assured him that God would look the other way. Was he not doing the work of God, after all?

His drink finished, Esfahani stood to leave. He again nodded politely at the woman and wished her a good night. In the hotel lobby he took a seat and picked up a newspaper. An hour later, she crossed the lobby to the exit on slightly wobbly legs, and he followed discreetly until she disappeared inside the condo.

Esfahani's opinion of women in general was low. They existed to serve men and please them as a receptacle for desire, a momentary relief from the pressures of life, and to bear children. Western women were even lower in his estimation, mere brazen whores, their revealing clothing an open invitation to lust. And Vicky Kondratieva, drunk in public, was worse, so worthless even that her husband had divorced her. In Esfahani's country such a woman would long ago have been strangled or stoned to death to preserve her family's honor. That made his assignment even easier.

*****

The next evening, Vicky again found a seat on the hotel terrasse. Summer was drawing to a close and the nights had turned from sultry to mild. She liked the hotel bar. It was so impersonal, so transitory; a place that people passed through but never stayed long. She was unlikely to run into anyone she knew here.

The terrasse offered a panorama of the neighborhood's clean, new buildings, the artificial world of brick and mortar that circumscribed her existence. Childhood in Moscow was a distant memory of hot summers on the banks of the Moskva River and week-ends at her father's dacha where he would grill shasliki and smoke fish for gatherings of family and friends. Russian winters were harsh, but so very Russian, with sleigh rides behind troikas of fine horses arranged for the elite of the KGB. She and her mother had never accompanied her father on his many assignments to the West. Had they done so she might now feel more comfortable in the United States. But instead, she yearned for Russia, a country to which she could never return.

She squeezed her eyes shut the better to recall the scenes of her childhood and so was surprised by a gentle tap on her shoulder. She looked up to see a handsome young man smiling down at her. It took her a second to recall where she had seen him before.

"I hope you won't think it impolite," he said, "but I remember you from last night. You're alone," he indicated the empty chair beside her, "and so am I, and I hate sitting with no one to talk to. Would you mind terribly sharing your table with me?"

He smiled at her again and she thought she had never seen teeth so white. It must be the contrast with his slightly dark complexion.

She hesitated only for a second, flattered that such a handsome man, obviously younger than she, would pay her such attention. She felt herself blush.

"No, of course not," she said. "Please sit down."

He introduced himself as a businessman from Los Angeles. His Spanish surname explained the dark good looks and slight accent. He seemed surprised to discover she was Russian, and he amused her by trying to pronounce a few Russian words.

By her second vodka on the rocks Vicky was feeling more confident, and she didn't object when her companion suggested they have another. Instead of motioning the waitress to the table he walked over to the bar and waited for the bartender to prepare the drinks.

Vicky did not see him empty a small vial of colorless liquid into her drink as he returned to the table. The vial contained gamma hydroxybutyric acid, known colloquially as liquid ecstasy. Half-way through the drink a feeling of relaxation and drowsiness washed over her.

CHAPTER 12

Robert Strachey was cautiously edging his BMW out of a parking garage on 'K' Street when the car's hands-free Bluetooth phone connection beeped. Annoyed, he punched a button on the leather wrapped steering wheel with his thumb to open the connection. He'd just escaped from a three hour meeting that should have taken no longer than thirty minutes and now faced a battle with Washington's infamous rush hour traffic, recently rated the worst in the nation. A light rain was falling which meant that Washington's heterogeneous mix of drivers of various nationalities and dubious talent behind the wheel would be even more skittish than usual. He'd be lucky to make it home to McLean before six P.M.

"Strachey," he said to the car's interior.

"Bob, it's Krystal." The familiar voice of Krystal Murphy, a detective with the Arlington Police and a good friend filled the car.

His annoyance forgotten, his voice mellowed with pleasure, "Krystal. It's good to hear your voice. Caught any crooks lately?"

"Not a social call, Bob. Something bad has happened, really bad. I thought you should know."

The tension was transmitted clearly through the BMW's Bose speakers. The stress she put on the word 'bad' was ominous.

"Tell me."

His first thought was that something had

happened to Amy, his wife, but he immediately discarded the possibility as highly improbable. She was still on maternity leave from the CIA and should be at home in McLean, Virginia, with their new baby.

Krystal continued, "It's Vicky. She was found dead in her condo this afternoon. Murdered."

Vicky Kondratieva's condo was in Arlington's jurisdiction.

"What happened?"

Strachey concentrated on the bumper to bumper traffic as his stomach did a somersault.

"It's too soon to be certain. CSI is still at the scene, as am I. Bob, it was messy. Very messy. Somebody cut her throat."

Vicky Kondratieva was a gentle, lost soul, lonely and with very few friends. She'd been through a lot of tough times. Driven out of Moscow by her father's political enemies, she'd suffered through a broken marriage, her father's death at the hands of an assassin sent by that bastard Shurgin, and her own kidnapping. More than enough trauma for anyone, let alone fragile Vicky. He and Amy had done their best over the past year to show her friendship, to let her know there were people who cared about her, people she could rely on.

He nosed the car into the traffic on Washington Circle and drove three quarters of the way around so he could catch 23rd Street to Virginia Avenue. From there he would merge onto Route 50 across the Theodore Roosevelt Bridge and make his way to Ballston.

"I'm on my way," he said.

"You can't enter the crime scene."

"I know, but I can meet you outside so you can tell me what you know."

Her answer did not come immediately. Strachey had no official license to become involved in the investigation, but he was confident that Murphy would talk to him. The detective cared for Vicky, too. This was personal for both of them. His instinct, honed by his years with the CIA, immediately conjured up a mental image of Shurgin.

"OK," she relented. "Meet me at First Down on North Fairfax."

She referred to a sports bar not far from Vicky's apartment.

"It'll take a while for me to get there. I'm just now crossing the Roosevelt Bridge."

"No problem. CSI should have some preliminary findings by then. And I'm not going anywhere."

"See you."

Strachey ended the call and punched the speed dial for home.

When Amy picked up he said, "I'll be a little late tonight, honey. Something's happened to Vicky and I'm on my way to meet Krystal Murphy."

He gave her the grim news and promised to tell her everything as soon as he got home."

*****

Murphy was nursing a coke when Strachey entered the bar looking out of place in his expensive navy blue business suit. He spotted her at a table in back, and she gave him a dispirited wave. Murphy was in her usual work clothes: a pair of jeans, a black Arlington Police Department polo shirt, and sneakers. Her Beretta 9-millimeter pistol was holstered high on her right hip, and her badge hung from a chain lanyard around her neck. Her auburn hair, damp from the rain, was pulled back into a ponytail.

When he sat down and got a better look at her there was no mistaking that she was agitated and angry behind the calm, cop demeanor.

Without preamble, she said, "It was bad."

Barely able to contain her anger, she continued in a low voice so the other patrons would not hear.

"Whoever did this was an animal. She was tortured for a long time before he cut her throat according to the CSI guys. I don't think we've ever had such a savage, sadistic murder in Arlington."

Strachey felt ice in his gut. "Was it a robbery, a rape?"

Murphy's response was cautious.

"Maybe. She was bound and nude on the bathroom floor. We won't know about rape until we hear from the coroner, but nothing was missing from the apartment."

"You're not telling me everything."

"Damn it, Bob, you're not a cop, you know. I'm not supposed to be talking about this with anyone."

"I know. But Vicky was our friend."

"Yes, but this is such a private thing, an intimate thing."

Strachey waited, knowing she would tell him. A

year ago circumstances had thrown them together in the aftermath of the murder of Vicky's father. Murphy had been investigating the General's murder, and Strachey was playing a more subtle role on behalf of Terrence Stoddard, the Director of National Clandestine Intelligence. They both had been with Vicky when Russian hit men sent by President Vitaliy Mikhailovich Shurgin invaded her house. They'd been friends ever since.

Finally she relented.

"The bastard took a broom handle to her."

Murphy's face infused with blood. Whether it was anger or embarrassment, he couldn't discern. She was as close to tears as Strachey had ever seen her.

"It tore her all up inside."

Strachey grimaced, and his stomach did another flip at the thought of how the woman had been brutalized. After a minute, the corners of his mouth still turned down in disgust, he asked, "Who found her?"

"The cleaning lady. She has a key to the apartment and comes by every Tuesday afternoon."

"Have you determined the time of death?"

"Sometime between two and four o'clock this morning."

"Witnesses? Someone must have seen her come home. They have a doorman in that building. Didn't anyone hear anything?"

"The doorman gets off at ten PM, and the post isn't manned again until seven in the morning. There's no security camera. The tenants like their privacy, and they all have key cards to open the front door. The night guy says he saw Vicky leave alone around 8:30 PM, but she hadn't returned by the time his shift ended. We're checking his alibi for where he went after work. All the apartments are pretty well sound-proofed."

"The estimated time of death fits then."

"It's still preliminary. What we don't know is when she returned and whether she was alone or brought the killer with her, or whether someone was waiting in her apartment or maybe jumped her outside the door and the forced her inside."

Murphy's face assumed a haunted expression and she shuddered.

"Bob, it looks like she was tortured for a long time before she was killed. The murderer did unspeakable things to her, things you don't even want to imagine. We'll try to reconstruct where she went and what she did. Given who she was and the fact she was in the national spotlight last year, news of her death will hit the papers tomorrow morning big time. Maybe someone will remember seeing her." A fierce Celtic fire gleamed in her eyes. "I'm going to get the sonuvabitch that did this."

"Someone must have seen something."

"I don't know. It was a Monday night. These government zombies get inside and go to bed early week-nights."

Strachey nodded in agreement. "What's next?"

"I'll comb through whatever CSI finds, run the DNA traces with CODIS, and wait for the coroner's report. With luck, something will turn up that I can use."

Strachey made her promise to keep him up to date. Death had begun to intrude into his life with uncomfortable frequency.

CHAPTER 13

Ghasem Esfahani had taken a room at the Marriot in Rosslyn, Virginia, just across Key Bridge from Georgetown. His window offered a panoramic view of Georgetown and on down the Potomac to the heart of Washington, DC, itself. He could see the obelisk of the Washington Monument in the distance. He'd never been to Washington before and planned take the opportunity the assignment provided to familiarize himself with the Great Satan's capital.

He'd slept into the afternoon following his return from the long night at the Russian woman's apartment. She had been such a waste of human flesh, so weak and frail that his disgust at her gender had manifested itself to such a degree that he had continued to mutilate her body long after she was dead, long after she had told him what he wanted to know. By the time his rage subsided only a few hours remained before dawn.

Esfahani had been nude while he tortured and killed Vicky Kondratieva, a condition he found both terrified his victims and led to pleasing physical responses from himself when he had finished them. More practically, it assured that his clothing remained clean. He took a quick shower to rinse off the blood -- there was always so much of it -- dried off and tiptoed around the pool of blood next to the body.

He was certain no one saw him leave the Ballston condo. He'd left the rental car in a public parking garage several blocks away. The streets were deserted as he walked to retrieve it, and the drive back to the hotel down Wilson Boulevard had taken but a few minutes in the pre-dawn quiet.

He'd taken another long, hot shower to remove the last of the woman's stench before closing the curtains and lying down on the king size bed. He remained awake for a while, letting the adrenaline drain from his system before drifting off to a dreamless sleep.

This was not the first time Esfahani's disgust with the opposite sex had driven him to murderous rage. Since assuming his covert assignment in Los Angeles, he'd killed three women in a similar manner, although those killings had had nothing to do with Iranian intelligence. They had been for pleasure. This imperiled his assignment, he knew. He was supposed to keep himself well under the radar, and if his VEVAK superiors back in their luxurious compound just south of the Hemmat Highway learned of his extracurricular activities they would be most upset. But Esfahani was clever, and no one would catch him. Besides, he had developed a taste for it now.

One of his earliest memories was of his father beating his mother, a poor wretched creature. And the beatings continued, along with verbal abuse that made clear his father's contempt. His father had been like a god in the home, and young Ghasem worshipped him and mimicked his attitudes. When he was only 10, he struck his mother for the first time and exulted in her meekness and his own power. His father had laughed and praised the boy.

The Incubus Vendetta

He told himself the reason he detested women was God's will. He had never been attracted to them or moved by them to any emotion other than disgust. In his teens, when the topic of his friends' conversations turned to feminine charms, he discovered he did not share their enthusiasm but instead found his feelings stirred by members of his own sex. His strict religious upbringing, however, taught that this burgeoning desire would lead to abomination, and so the only correct choice in God's eyes was to suppress it. He had seethed with self-loathing until he concluded that the fault lay not within him but was a failure of the opposite sex, a failure that he resented immensely.

He diverted his energies into academic pursuits and athletics. His friends attributed his rigid "self-control" and abstemious lifestyle to piety, and he embraced the excuse. It was this "piety" that had attracted the mullahs and led them to entrust him with such an important assignment. They could be certain of his loyalty.

But his detestation of women had grown into a dangerous obsession that he dared not express in Iran. The assignment to the United States at last provided an outlet. American society was ridiculously, even dangerously open. He could move freely with no one watching, judging, or reporting what he did. And American women were all of such easy virtue. It was ironic that they were so easily attracted by his dark good looks.

Vicky Kondratieva was the first female victim he had not picked completely at random, and when the details of how he had dispatched her became public, he would tell Tehran it had been necessary to cover the true nature of the interrogation. He would be rewarded.

And there was more to come. The Russian woman had not been able to tell him the whereabouts of the fourth name on the list or of the woman associated with him. But she had been in contact with them, and knew them as *M. et Mme. DuPont*. She recognized the other names on the list, as well. He would rest today, watch the papers and news broadcasts to see what was reported about the Kondratieva killing, and then begin to study his next target.

He was making progress.

CHAPTER 14

"You were right about the media," Strachey said.

The three of them, he, Amy, and Detective Krystal Murphy were gathered at the Strachey home on Meadowbrook Avenue in McLean, Virginia. It was a relatively modest neighborhood in tony McLean terms with narrow paved streets lined with a variety of smaller, older homes and larger, newer ones. The Stracheys occupied the former variety, a house he had purchased several years earlier when his Agency salary had reached the point where he could afford it. Before their marriage Amy had rented a small townhouse nearer the village center. Despite the recent improvement in Strachey's income they didn't want to leave the comfortable, bucolic neighborhood. If they had another child, Strachey would have to give up his office/den that he'd set up in the spare bedroom, so perhaps there would be a move in the future. For the time being Amy relished the fact that it still took her only twenty minutes to drive to CIA headquarters where she would return to work after maternity leave.

News of Vicky Kondratieva's brutal murder had made the front pages of every local paper that morning, and both local and national telecasts had picked it up.

"Yes, and actually it's a good thing," said Murphy. "I'm still hoping it turns up a witness or two."

Amy sat with their month old baby, Robert Thomas, "R.T." for short, on her lap. Their conversation over a light dinner had been muted, all of them preferring to postpone discussion of Vicky. Strachey poured them each a couple of fingers of Lagavulin, a peaty single malt Scotch whisky for which Amy had taken a long time to develop a taste.

After a contemplative sip of the strong drink, Strachey asked, "Did forensics turn anything up?"

Murphy looked uncomfortable and shot a sidelong glance at Amy.

Reading her thoughts, Amy said, "Don't worry about shocking me, Krystal. Remember I'm an intelligence analyst. I've seen enough atrocity reports and pictures out of the Middle East that it takes a lot to shock me about what one human being can do to another."

Murphy considered this a moment before continuing.

"OK. As a matter of fact, forensics did turn up some pretty bizarre stuff. For example, there was DNA all over the place. The killer apparently got his rocks off at some point and wasn't too picky about cleaning up. Except that he took a shower before leaving – with his victim's body right there! That left more DNA in the drain. And there were fingerprints all over the place, too. Either the perp is abysmally stupid or he's never seen an episode of CSI on TV. I guess that qualifies as relatively good news."

"What about the coroner's report?"

Strachey wasn't looking forward to the autopsy

details, especially after a meal, but they could not be ignored, no matter how unpleasant.

"Yeah, the coroner's report ... You know the body was mutilated."

Strachey noted that she purposely used the word "body" rather than naming their dead friend. It was an insulating pace toward objectivity and away from personal involvement.

"If it's any consolation, the worst mutilations were post-mortem. Everything before he cut her throat appears to have been intended to inflict maximum pain without killing her. It was very methodical. But after she was dead, the perp just went berserk. That's when he used the broom handle and started slashing. The Coroner says it reminds him of pictures of the victims of Jack the Ripper, although no organs were removed."

Strachey drained his glass and reached for the bottle. He offered to top off the women's drinks, but they declined, and he poured himself another two fingers of the Lagavulin.

"You used the word 'methodical,'" he said. "That's another way of saying torture. Maybe it didn't start out as a crime of passion."

"Hard to say, but we're clearly dealing with a first class sadist, here, someone really twisted. But torture before killing is not uncommon."

Strachey knit his brows and stared into space for a couple of beats. "It could have been an interrogation."

Murphy considered this.

"I don't know, Bob. You would know more

about that sort of thing than I, but this guy was just crazy. Nothing about this says it was a professional job. And what could Vicky have known that would justify such an attack?"

"The Russians did try to kill her last year."

"The Russians? But she'd already made public everything she knew. She was no longer a threat to anyone."

"How about revenge?"

"I know you CIA guys see a conspiracy everywhere you look, but Shurgin was behind everything that happened last year, and he's gone. The last thing Moscow would want now is to stir the whole, ugly affair up again, especially now that Shurgin has left the scene."

"Some of the media reporting speculates on Moscow involvement."

"The media," Murphy made a sour face, "those assholes don't know any of the details ... yet, and when they do they'll change their tune. They're just looking for sensationalism so they can sell more advertising. Some of the details will inevitably leak."

"There's a connection you might not have made yet, Krystal. Vicky is not the only person connected with the Andropov Memorandum who has recently died violently."

Her eyes widened as the realization hit her.

"Lawrence Nelson and his wife? You see a connection?"

"Maybe. It's too early, but even though I'm no longer a 'CIA guy,' as you put it, I still don't believe in coincidences."

"But the Nelsons were just two among many people who died in the Brussels bombing, and everything we've seen points to some crazy Islamist group as the guilty parties there. I don't see a connection."

"Yes, they've traced it to Hezbollah." *Ewan Ramsay had filled him in on the details.* "But I wouldn't dismiss the possibility that the incidents are related."

"Bob, I have to go with what I know, with the concrete evidence, not with speculation. Conjecture doesn't cut it in a court of law, and that's the sandbox I have to play in."

"You're a good cop, Krystal, but remember, I've seen you go with your gut and play outside the rules."

"You've got me there, but in this case, right now, there is nothing that twitches my gut other than disgust at what that creep did to Vicky."

CHAPTER 15

After Krystal Murphy left Amy fed the baby and settled him in his crib with her favorite lullaby while Strachey cleared the dishes and loaded the dishwasher.

His domestic chores complete, he poured himself a third Lagavulin, a large one, and stretched in his favorite chair. He closed his eyes and listened to the sound of his wife's voice floating down the hall from the nursery.

Hush-a-bye, don't you cry,
Go to sleepy little baby.
When you wake, you'll have cake,
And all the pretty little horses...

He knew Amy would remark the third whiskey when she rejoined him. He seldom overindulged, but he needed an extra drink this evening.

He was worried, deeply so. The manner of Vicky Kondratieva's death was ghastly. Nobody deserved such a fate, and he could not put away the thought that she had not been selected at random. Vicky had a controversial past that had proven a magnet for trouble. That may have been enough for some murderous thrill seeker to kill her, but the Nelsons' had been connected intimately with Vicky, and they were dead, too. And if the two events were connected, no run-of-the-mill punk could have been responsible. On the other hand, he could not logically connect Hezbollah and the Andropov Memorandum.

Amy's voice dwindled to silence, and he heard her close the door to the nursery. Strachey opened his eyes to see his wife standing beside him staring at the glass of whiskey in his hand.

But instead of the scolding he expected she sat on the arm of the chair and ran her fingers through his hair.

"You're really worried about this, aren't you?" she asked.

Strachey sat the glass on a side table, leaned back and closed his eyes again. Amy's soft touch was more comforting than the whiskey.

"Yes, I have a bad feeling. But that's all it is, just a feeling. Krystal has every reason to believe Vicky's death had nothing to do with last year."

Amy sighed and slid into his lap, snuggling her head into his shoulder. The scent of Amarige filled his nostrils.

"Daddy called today," she said, changing the subject.

Her father, Thomas Jefferson Dawson, lived in Charlotte, North Carolina. Amy's mother had died when she was still very young, and Strachey thought that Thomas had done a splendid job raising his remarkable daughter on his own.

"How is he? You didn't mention any of this business, did you?"

"Of course not. I asked him again about coming to live with us."

Thomas was in his mid-70's, and they had been trying unsuccessfully for months to convince him to leave Charlotte and move in with them. It would mean moving to a larger house, and with Strachey's new income that would not be a problem. But the old man was stubborn and valued his independence.

"What did he say this time?"

"Oh, you know, he'll 'think it over.'"

"I'd really like him to be with us."

"I know."

Strachey wanted his bi-racial son to know and in later years remember his black grandfather so he could fully appreciate his heritage.

"We'll have to work on him some more. Why don't we invite him for a long visit? Once he spends some time with R.T. he'll be easier to convince."

"Maybe, but he's so attached to Charlotte."

"We could move down there, you know. I could work out of my uncle's office there."

This was a sensitive topic. As much as she loved her home town, a move would be difficult for Amy. Her work at the CIA was important, both for her and the Agency. She ran the top secret Palantir program for Deputy Director of Intelligence Harvey Grant, the Agency's top analyst. Palantir, a computer program of startling complexity, was a major factor in breaking down the barriers between the nation's multitude of intelligence collection organizations. Amy did not relish the idea of becoming a stay at home wife, and he didn't blame her.

"Let's leave that one as a TBD," she murmured.

Despite the many frustrations and its ups and downs, working for the CIA was a seductive experience.

"I miss it, you know."

She understood immediately.

"The Agency? I know it was hard for you to leave."

"I had no choice."

"Ramsay would have done it for you."

"I know, but Terry Stoddard was my friend. It was my obligation to take out the man who killed him, not Ewan's And there was no way I could remain in the Agency after that."

"You're a stubborn, difficult man, Robert Strachey. So is Ewan Ramsay, but I wouldn't want you to become what he has become."

"No chance of that. I'm a filthy lobbyist now. And don't forget that Ewan's had some hard choices to make. What he 'became' was thrust upon him."

"So he says."

"He was set up by his best friend in the CIA to be killed by the KGB."

"He had a different name then, didn't he?" asked Amy. "And wasn't his former 'best friend' murdered in the end?"

"That's right," he said.

"All the old-timers at Langley think Ewan came back and killed him for his betrayal. The story has assumed mythic proportions."

Strachey had never coaxed the full story out of Ramsay, but he had his suspicions.

"I wouldn't blame him if he did."

"See what I mean? You could be just like him. You've already shown you have it in you."

Strachey knew it had been difficult for Amy to

accept that the man she loved and had married had killed a man in cold blood.

"Maybe, but like I said, my spook days are behind me, and I can't undo what happened. It's just as well, really. If I stayed in the company until retirement I'd be too addicted to leave and I'd probably become one of those pitiful green badge types who can't imagine life without Mother Agency."

Agency retirees who were re-hired as contractors wore green rather than blue badges at Headquarters.

Even as he said it, somewhere deep inside Strachey knew he was not being completely honest with Amy or with himself. Like it or not, men defined themselves by what they did. At heart, when he allowed himself to think about who he really was, he saw a spook. And that was what he always would be at his core. Being an intelligence officer was not just a job. It was a calling, a craft, almost an art form, and in Strachey's experience the modeling clay was human. He wondered if he would ever escape its grasp or if in the end he would be drawn back in.

Stay with it long enough to understand it and thus understand the way the world really works, and it became addictive. Those green badges, veterans of the intelligence wars, were addicts who could not break the habit, and Strachey understood their ache.

Amy said, "It's a good thing we have some retirees coming back. Most of the new people don't know anything."

"That's because too many of the new ones have no intention of staying and leave for private sector money before the Agency mind-fucks them. And that's another thing about Ewan: he was locked in by what happened. He never had a choice. He was never given the choice to leave the life, and as a consequence he doesn't know anything else. He's going crazy with nothing to do. Sasha worries about him because he's getting older, and I think he must feel like he still has something to prove."

Thinking more of himself than Ewan Ramsay, he concluded, "It has to be frustrating."

"I like Ewan and Sasha, but I wouldn't want their life with half the world looking for them. There are so few people they can trust, let alone call friends."

"We're fortunate to be in that select group. If there weren't people like them the world would be a much more dangerous place."

She nuzzled his cheek.

"I prefer you as a filthy lobbyist."

Strachey stood, lifting her in his arms.

"Let's turn in."

The third glass of Lagavulin remained on the table, untouched.

CHAPTER 16

Ghasem Esfahani prepared his report on his laptop, encrypted it with the built-in program Tehran had supplied, and transferred it to a memory stick. He did not use the hotel's wireless internet connection, but rather found an internet café on 'M' Street in Georgetown, just across the Key Bridge from his hotel, where he e-mailed the report to an address in Frankfurt. From there it would be re-transmitted twice more before arriving at VEVAK headquarters.

The Russian woman had told him enough before she died to suggest that there was a reasonable chance for success. Yes, she had met the fourth man and his blond female companion, whom she knew only as *"M. et Madame DuPont,"* obvious aliases. They had rescued her from Russians who had kidnapped her when she had sought refuge with her father's friend Lawrence Nelson in Belgium. Later they'd arranged her safe return to the United States. She'd never seen the woman after that, but she did know that she spoke Russian like a native.

Even better, she had confirmed that the others names on his list were more likely to know where to find the couple. One was a CIA officer, and that gave Esfahani pause. Going up against a trained intelligence officer, especially one who reportedly knew how to use a gun, entailed certain risk, although there was no reason to believe the man would be on guard. Esfahani also was well trained and did not fear an armed encounter.

But there was another target better suited to his taste, also presumed to be armed, but with the attraction that she was a woman. This one would not be as easy to capture as the Russian woman. He would have to plan carefully.

*****

The front pages of the next morning's papers carried lurid headlines about the murder of Vicky Kondratieva. The accompanying stories re-hashed the suspicions of SVR involvement in her father's murder the previous year and her role in making public the infamous "Andropov Memorandum." That hoary document, long hidden in the KGB archives until her father removed it, laid bare the KGB's role in the Kennedy assassination.

Esfahani read the news accounts with intense curiosity. As usual, he was carrying out instructions but was not privy to the reasons for them. He perceived no connection between his current assignment and the Islamic Republic of Iran. There was clearly a Russian connection, but why were the mullahs interested? He turned the question over in his mind several times, but could not puzzle out an answer. It would have been interesting to know, but in the end, it made no difference to his task, and he had spotted something else in the news stories.

The next person on the target list, Krystal Murphy, was identified as the lead detective in the Kondratieva murder case. Even better, there was a photograph of her, taken as she briefed the media. A plan began to take shape in Esfahani's mind.

*****

August had passed the baton to September, and Washington's oppressive summer was fading from memory. The trees were beginning to add color to the alabaster architecture of the nation's capital, and people were pulling sweaters out of mothballs. It was still not nearly cool enough to encourage them into heavier coats.

In Krystal Murphy's case the only wardrobe change was a light windbreaker over her Arlington Police Department polo shirt. However, with the temperature dropping into the forties at this hour, one o'clock in the morning, she regretted not having worn something warmer.

The call had awakened her only fifteen minutes earlier, and she had thrown on the same clothes she had worn during the day and rushed out of her apartment.

Her destination was a large garden apartment complex on Walter Reed Drive. The white and red brick buildings were old, dating from the 50's or even earlier, but they had been nicely renovated to justify the $1,400 per month rental fee. Most of the occupants were young, low-ranking government workers seeking accommodation as close as possible to the Pentagon, Rosslyn, or D.C., and the majority of them were single.

The particular ground floor apartment to which

Murphy had been called contained two bedrooms, a single bath, a galley kitchen, and a large combination living/dining room. The furniture was mostly odds and ends of second-hand store vintage, and the posters on the walls indicated that the occupants were young and female. One of them now lay sprawled on the floor at Murphy's feet. The beige wall-to-wall carpeting had soaked up most of the blood and the room reeked of copper and offal.

Murphy forced herself to look at the nude, mutilated body, and she felt unspeakable sorrow, both for the victim and the human race that it could spawn such atrocities. The girl might have been anywhere between 18 and 25. It was hard to tell. She was lying on her side. Her throat had been slashed from ear to ear, but the killer had not been satisfied merely with his victim's death. Nose AND ears had been hacked off, and breasts mutilated. A long, clean slit down the front of the body from breastbone to pubis had allowed internal organs to spill out onto the carpet. Murphy didn't think anything was missing. Her gorge rising, she could not escape the conclusion that a serial killer was loose in Arlington.

From one of the bedrooms the sobs of the victim's roommate could be heard. The body on the floor had been identified as Teresa Haines. Her friend and roommate, Sandra Barnes had discovered the carnage upon her return shortly before midnight. Outside the door along the hallway, neighbors who had been awakened by Sandra's screams sat behind closed doors discussing in horrified whispers what had happened as uniformed police and EMT's went back and forth on their errands. Murphy would have to interview them all separately before she left. She didn't anticipate getting any sleep until the following evening.

Murphy instructed the CSI team to cover the body and headed into the bedroom where a female uniformed officer was comforting Sandra Barnes. It might be days before the distraught girl could give a coherent account, but Murphy had learned that it paid to interview witnesses as soon as possible following an incident, before their minds began filling gaps in their memory with imagined details.

The uniform was sitting on the bed with her arm around Sandra Barnes, who appeared to be in her mid-twenties, petite, blond hair in a pixie cut that accentuated large, blue eyes, now red from crying. She was dressed informally in jeans and a Georgetown sweatshirt. Murphy waved the uniform away and replaced her beside the girl on the edge of the bed. There was little other furniture in the tiny room besides a chest of drawers and a folding chair against the opposite wall. The wall behind the bed was adorned with a large poster of a shirtless Matthew McConaughey, the actor.

Murphy introduced herself and took the girl's hand. "I need you to tell me what happened."

"I came home just before midnight. The front door was unlocked, and when I opened it ..."

She gushed more tears.

"I need to you to be calm so we can figure out who did this to your friend. Let's start at the other end. When was the last time you saw your roommate."

"Tonight. We were both at the Lost Dog Café having pizza with friends." Murphy knew the establishment a few blocks away on Columbia Pike.

"You saw her leave?"

"Yes, she had to go into work early tomorrow. New fiscal year stuff. Teresa was a bank teller."

"Did anybody leave the café with her or leave immediately after?"

"She was alone."

"On foot?"

"Yes, it's only a few blocks."

Murphy thought about the route the victim would have taken. It would only cover a couple of blocks along Walter Reed Drive, a boulevard with a grassy median. The Arlington Career Center was on the side opposite the apartment complex, which covered several acres. There was ample street lighting along Walter Reed, but once inside the apartment complex which consisted of several buildings it would be darker.

"Do you recall what time she left the restaurant?"

"Around ten, I think. I'm not sure."

"I'll need the names of everyone who was there."

This would go on for hours, Murphy knew. It was like pulling teeth to gather witness information and then more hours to piece it together until a reasonable picture emerged of the victim's movements prior to death. Police work wasn't neat, and it certainly wasn't quick. She almost wished she had accepted Executive Assistant Director Enoch

Whitehall's offer to enter the FBI, but it would have required a long training period and being a rookie again. Whitehall had been impressed by her work on the Andropov Memorandum case, but she'd worked too long and too hard to achieve the rank of detective, and she wasn't about to give it up. She was good at what she did. That was why the Department had assigned the Kondratieva case to her.

There were too many similarities between the Kondratieva case and the murder of Teresa Haines for it to be coincidence. And now she faced the likelihood that Vicky's murder had not been an isolated incident, but was the work of a serial killer.

If this scene was anything like what she'd found at Vicky's condo, there should be plenty of physical evidence, including DNA, that would tell her if she was dealing with the same killer. The lab reports on Vicky's case should be on her desk by morning, only a few hours from now. She shot a weary glance at her Casio G-Shock wristwatch. She would order expedited processing of the evidence from the new crime scene.

The preliminary interviews were finished by 7:00 AM, and Murphy drove home for a quick shower and to change into fresh clothing before heading for Headquarters.

CHAPTER 17

America was, indeed, the land of opportunity! In his own country never would a woman have been permitted on the street alone so late at night. He followed her into the apartment complex and came up behind her at the door where he flashed his dazzling smile and told her he was a new tenant in the building. She'd been surprised when he appeared, but after an instant of alarm she'd taken in his dark good looks, and he could tell that she liked what she saw. Slut!

The fact that her apartment was on the ground floor just a few steps from the entrance was a stroke of luck. As soon as he saw her unlock the door, he struck her on the back of the neck with the edge of his hand, driving her onto the floor inside the apartment. After that, he made quick work of her, first slashing her throat and then setting about his work on her body. There had been no time for finesse, no time to remove his own clothing or take a shower afterwards, he dared take no more time than was needed to clean his hands and face in the bathroom washbasin. It took more mental effort than he expected to stray from his routine, and he had to remind himself that this was an "operational" kill, a means to an end.

He made it back to his rental car unobserved and removed his jeans and dark shirt that he stuffed into a plastic garbage bag. It wouldn't do to return to his hotel in blood spattered clothing. But as he began to pull on the change of clothing he'd brought along, he was overcome by a familiar sexual urge. Although he had been able to restrain himself at the murder scene the fresh memories of his victim's body caught up with him, and he gave in and began stroking his already erect penis. A few moments later he ejaculated into the plastic bag and leaned his head back, gasping. Calmer now, he pulled on the change of clothing and waited, watching the entrance to the apartment building.

He watched the entire parade of events. The arrival of the roommate, the screams followed by lights coming on throughout the building. And then the arrival of the police. At 1:00 AM, his heart beat a little faster when he saw Krystal Murphy get out of a big, black Ford, obviously an official car, and enter the building. He recognized her from her picture in the papers and settled back to wait. The woman was taller than he had imagined, probably 5'4", just a few inches shorter than Esfahani, and she dressed like a man in tight fitting jeans and a dark windbreaker.

He was getting uncomfortable as dawn approached, concerned that he would be noticed in the light of day, but shortly before 7:00 AM the policewoman came out of the apartment building and entered her car. He followed at a comfortable distance well concealed within the rush hour traffic until she turned into the parking lot of a large apartment building on North Barton Street. Esfahani cursed. He might well have attempted to grab the woman then and there had the day not fully dawned. Other tenants were coming out of the building and heading for their cars. He would have to wait and set it up. Timing would be critical, but he knew now how to draw her out under cover of darkness. The outdoor parking lot right off the intersection of 10th Street North and North Barton Street, he noted, was unguarded.

CHAPTER 18

"Los Angeles? Are you sure?"

Krystal Murphy's phone had been ringing when she arrived in the office. The first call was from Chief of Detectives Marty Jefferson to give her the unwelcome news that their presence was required immediately in the office of the Chief of Police a few blocks from where she worked in the building the Department shared with the county jail. Word of the second slaying had travelled fast.

The meeting with the Chief was not a pleasant affair. The murder rate in Arlington, Virginia, was normally low, only one or two per year, and now two women had been killed in the vilest manner possible within just a few days of one another. The Chief made it clear that he expected a resolution in short order.

Sure, Chief, and standing here listening to you state the obvious while work is waiting really helps speed things up.

Murphy fumed beside Jefferson as the two drove back to the Police Station on North Courthouse Road.

"Present company excepted," she said, "do people just get dumber the higher they climb? Does he really just think we're sitting on our hands? Christ, the second murder was only a few hours ago."

"But it's been longer since the first," said Jefferson.

"What? Now you're on my back, too? I'm still

waiting for the DNA results from CODIS." The Combined DNA Index System administered by the FBI.

Jefferson's handsome brown face remained impassive. "This is a big deal, and you know it. It's bad. I want you to set up a task force. Pick anyone you want."

"Sure." Murphy fell silent while she considered the options.

The second call, the one she had just answered, was from FBI Executive Assistant Director of the Counterintelligence Division Enoch Whitehall who had tried his best to recruit her into the Bureau last year. According to him there were three CODIS hits on the DNA from the Kondratieva condo, all related to similar murders in Los Angeles.

"... So it looks like we have four murders by the same person, and he's moved from one coast to the next," he finished.

"Make it five," she said. "We had another one last night here in Arlington. Same M.O."

There was silence at the other end of the line while he processed this information.

"Then he's speeded up. The killings in Los Angeles were months apart."

"Why are you calling about this, Enoch?"

Whitehall was a bit high on the Bureau totem pole to be dealing with this sort of case, and as far as she knew there was no intelligence connection.

"This is quite an unusual case, don't you agree?"

She thought about it a moment before answering. "A serial killer is rare enough, but they usually stick to well-defined geographic areas. They have their comfort zones. But this guy has moved from coast to coast."

"There's something else."

"Tell me."

"Vicky Kondratieva was a key player in a matter of extreme national security."

Where is he going with this? She recalled Robert Strachey's suspicions.

"But we're dealing with a serial killer here, not an SVR hit man."

"They are not necessarily mutually exclusive."

"And the latest victim was a 22-year-old teller at Wells-Fargo. I don't see a connection. Did any of the Los Angeles victims have a national security tie-in?"

"No. They seem to have been selected at random – all young girls." He changed tack. "Have you formed a task force yet?"

"We're setting one up, yes. Given your info about Los Angeles, I'd better get in touch with LAPD, too."

"Right. Would you like some help from the CIRG?"

The Critical Incident Response Group, headquartered at the FBI Academy in Quantico was a law enforcement jewel. CIRG managed the National Center for the Analysis of Violent Crime.

The investigative capabilities of the Arlington Police Department were limited, especially in matters of this magnitude. Whitehall's offer of the nation's premier crime investigative unit was generous.

"Absolutely," she said without hesitation.

"OK, it's yours. And there's one more thing."

He wants to attach strings to the investigation. Typical FBI.

"Yeah?"

"I'd like your concurrence to run some additional tests on the DNA you recovered from the crime scene."

"What for? You've already confirmed that it's the same guy from Los Angeles. Obviously his DNA isn't on file anywhere, or you'd have i.d.'d him already."

"There's an outfit in Florida that CIRG has quietly worked with before. They've developed a method to identify ethnicity from DNA. It's a little tricky politically, but I'd still like to do it."

"Tricky politically?"

She wasn't sure what he meant.

"There are those who see it as a kind of racial profiling."

"How the hell could it be racial profiling if the donor has already committed a crime? Wasn't there a case in Baton Rouge where everybody thought the perp was a white guy, but some DNA expert insisted he was black. When the cops changed the search criteria they caught the guy within days."

"Correct, but it's still politically sensitive. I wouldn't do it if you didn't agree."

"Hey, every little bit helps, but if we find a witness who saw the perp, that test won't tell us anything we won't already know."

"We'll see."

Whitehall gave her the numbers to contact the

CIRG and promised to give them a heads up that she'd be calling.

But two hours later she got the break she'd been hoping for. The media coverage of Vicky's murder paid off in the form of a call to the hotline from the bartender at the Westin Hotel at Ballston Square. Vicky Kondratieva was a regular, and the bartender remembered seeing her the night she was killed. More importantly, he could describe the man who had accompanied her out of the bar.

Murphy set up a meeting. She grabbed Jefferson on her way out, and the two of them headed for Ballston Square where they found the witness waiting for them in the bar. They moved to a corner table.

The bartender was a 30-something part-time student with too much mousse in his hair told them his name was Ronnie Scoville. He said he'd worked at the Westin for over two years, and Vicky Kondratieva had become an evening regular over the past several months.

"She'd come in three, sometimes four times a week. Almost always alone. Always drank the same thing – vodka on the rocks. Guess it's a Russian thing, huh, vodka? Too bad about what happened."

"Tell us about that night, Ronnie," said Murphy.

"Well, she came in alone, as usual, and took a table out on the veranda. Then this dude walked over and sat down with her, and they started talking. I remembered that he'd been in the bar the night before, too, and thought maybe he was a hotel guest."

"Did he pay his tab with a room number?"

"No, he used cash. Left a good tip, too."

Murphy made a mental note to check the hotel register.

"Can you describe him?"

"I sure can. He came to the bar to get a round of drinks to take back to the table. Real nice looking guy, kinda Latino looking, and he spoke with an accent. Maybe mid-30's, dark skin, and he had teeth that you could see from a mile away."

"What happened then?"

"He took the drinks to the table, and a little while later left with the lady. She looked a little wobbly, you know what I mean?"

"No, I don't know what you mean. Why don't you tell us?"

"Like maybe she'd had a little too much. But come to think of it, she'd only had a couple of drinks, and I've seen her pound down more than that and still act sober as a judge."

"Could she have been drugged?"

"You mean like a ruffie? Jeez, I don't know."

"But the man picked up the drinks at the bar and carried them back out to the veranda?"

"Yeah."

Murphy's and Jefferson's eyes met as they shared an 'aha' moment.

"OK, Ronnie," she said, "You've been very helpful. We'd like you to come to our offices and have a sit-down with a sketch artist."

"Wow, just like on TV?"

"Just like on TV. As a matter of fact, we need you to do this right away. The sooner the better.

You'll have to find someone to sub for you this afternoon."

CHAPTER 19

Picking up the Russian woman in the hotel bar had been clever and effective, but it risked being seen. And that was evidently what had happened.

The drawing, along with a physical description that appeared in every Washington area paper and television news report surprised Ghasem Esfahani. The artist's sketch was not a perfect likeness of his face, but it was close enough to make him realize that remaining in the area would be unwise. He checked out of the hotel in Rosslyn and drove north on Interstate 70 until he found a small motel on the outskirts of Frederick, Maryland.

On the plus side this resolved the problem of where to interrogate the policewoman. The motel was shabby enough that there were few guests, and he checked into an end unit. Once he had the woman in hand, he would bring her here where he could finish the job at his leisure and then indulge in his personal pleasures.

On the negative side, finding another victim in Arlington might not be so easy with the public alerted to a killer on the loose. But a solution quickly came to mind. A dead body was a dead body, after all. Why take an unnecessary risk to find a decoy?

The plan was simple: kill another woman and make certain the body was discovered, and then lay in wait in the policewoman's apartment parking lot. When she came out, he would knock her out, tie her up, and drive back to the motel.

*****

"So this is what the Iranians call 'finesse?' Two women murdered, butchered according to the press, and every law enforcement agency in Washington looking for the killer?"

Shurgin gave Ismayilov a look of disbelief across the table. He'd flown to Asunción the same morning for the meeting.

The Azeri shrugged. "Hatimi's agent thinks it's a necessary part of the plan."

"It's too public," grumbled Shurgin. "He's attracting a lot of attention."

"So did the Brussels affair."

Shurgin was mildly annoyed that Ismayilov was defending the Iranians.

"That was different. It was part of the plan to camouflage the real targets."

Mass murder did not bother him so long as the objective was achieved. But in Washington he would have preferred a more surgical approach.

Ismayilov said, "Unfortunately the Kondratieva woman did not possess the information we need. But Hatimi's agent is making progress. According to Hatimi the strategy in Washington is the same as Brussels – to hide the real target."

"Yes, yes. The policewoman and the CIA officer, Strachey."

"As I understand it, Strachey left the CIA. He now works for his rich uncle as a lobbyist."

This was new information, and Shurgin looked up with sudden interest. His old KGB instincts came into play. "A man interested in money?" There might be another way to get at the information, one that is not so messy."

"It would seem so, but we're committed to the Iranian agent now."

"That's so, but it's something we need to keep in mind. The closer we get to the final names on the list, the more likely it is they'll figure out what we are doing."

"But your hand is nowhere to be seen."

"That's not what I mean. If the next one can't answer our questions, there is a chance that her death will flush them out of hiding."

"It's possible. With luck, we might pick up an indication of where to start looking."

"Find out what you can about Strachey in case we have to change tactics."

*****

Shortly after midnight the lights started going out inside the restaurant on the other side of the street. Esfahani padded across to the parking area which was nearly empty except for the cars he assumed belonged to employees. He picked one that was further from the building than the others. It was an older Japanese model of some sort that was more likely to belong to one of the young waitresses than the manager. He hoped he had chosen well. If not, he would repeat the procedure tomorrow night and the night after until the right opportunity presented itself.

He slipped into the shadow behind the car to wait.

*****

An hour later he crossed over the American Legion Bridge into Virginia and took the George Washington Parkway exit toward Washington. The girl in the shiny orange shorts and cotton jacket over her white T-shirt was stirring in the trunk as she recovered from the blow he had delivered. But she was securely bound, and Esfahani's thoughts were concentrated now on the next step. For this particular task he needed a site that combined two factors: private enough to emplace the bait, but public enough to ensure it would be found before too much time had elapsed.

He took the Key Bridge exit from the parkway and drove in the direction of the policewoman's apartment hoping an opportunity would present itself. It was nearly 2:30 AM by the time he found a suitable spot and pulled to a stop at the edge of a large, mostly empty parking lot. Making certain no one was watching, he went around the car, opened the trunk, and dragged the girl roughly to the ground behind the car where he showed her the knife, holding it in front of her eyes. He was particularly proud of the "tool" he had selected. It was called a "Chive" and it was made in Oregon. It had a snap open blade that was only two inches long, but razor sharp. It was not a fighting knife, to be sure, but it was a fine cutting instrument.

He'd used duct tape to bind the girl, legs together, hands behind her back, and to gag her. Esfahani regretted deeply that he would have so little time with this one, but the success of his plan depended on swift action. He slipped the knife under the T-shirt and cut the cloth completely open down the front, also slicing the front of her bra, exposing her breasts and abdomen. She began squirming, trying to wriggle away and kicked at him with her bound legs, catching him on the shin. He snapped her face sideways with a hard slap, and laid a knee across her legs to keep her quiet. In a practiced gesture, he buried the blade just below her bare rib cage and slashed downward, laying open her abdominal cavity all the way to the pubis. There was not so much blood because he avoided arteries by only opening he skin and underlying membrane. The girl's eyes bulged in surprise and sudden pain and she looked down to see her insides begin to spill out over her belly. She tried to scream, but the duct tape prevented her.

Esfahani stood and surveyed his work. He could slash her throat as he had done the others, but if he did not it was more likely that someone would see her moving or hear her. There were only a couple of other cars in the lot. He had not been there more than five minutes, and could see people inside the supermarket across the way, perhaps getting ready to come out.

He made a tactical decision to leave her as she was. Getting to the policewoman's apartment in time to set up properly would require several minutes if this one were discovered quickly. He wiped his hands and the blade on a rag in the trunk before stooping to rip the gag from her face. Her screams were high-pitched, keening like those of an animal dying in the forest. He drove quickly back out onto the street and turned toward his next stop.

CHAPTER 20

Shurgin shivered in the damp chill of the cell. He wore only the thin cotton uniform of a prisoner. The weak light of the bare bulb that dangled from the vaulted ceiling revealed walls of stone -- ancient looking walls in which were implanted iron rings. His wrists were entrapped in iron bands attached by a strong chain to one of the rings. He felt weak, and his knees sagged, leaving his arms to carry all his weight.

The lamentations of other prisoners were faintly audible even through the thick walls. The door to the cell was of solid metal with a small observation slit at eye level through which someone watched him. He couldn't remember being brought here, but he knew precisely where he was – the basement cells of Lefortovo prison.

A key turned in the lock, and the heavy metal door scraped against the floor as it was pushed open, the rusting hinges squealing in protest. Shurgin raised his head and squinted through the dim light at the burly figure now framed in the doorway. The man wore a uniform with blue collar tabs denoting KGB. But the shadow from the brim and wide crown of the uniform cap obscured his face.

The man was big and grew huge as he drew nearer. Something dangled from his hand.

"Hello, Vitya. Are you ready to come join me?"

The voice was familiar -- the resonance in the lower register, the hint of a growl in the throat. He squinted again, struggling to focus. A shock of joy *coursed through him, a sensation he had not known for a long time. His old comrade, General Yuriy Ivanovich Morozov had come to the rescue!*

"Yura ..." he started and then remembered. His friend, his best friend, had died in the basement of Lefortovo, died because Shurgin had ordained it to save himself. The decision had been logical and unavoidable.

And yet here was General Morozov holding something in front of Shurgin's face. Again, he struggled to bring the object into resolution with his aching eyes. A wire? A wire with a wooden handle at each end – a garrote.

"Are you ready to come join me?" Morozov repeated the question and grinned malevolently.

The meaning was unmistakable. Morozov had been garroted, perhaps in this very cell and then his body hung from one of the rings in the wall to make it look like a suicide. Shurgin was unable to speak as his old comrade slipped the wire over his head and pulled the ends tight until it bit into his neck. Morozov's face was inches from his own.

Shurgin gulped air into his lungs and let loose a howl of sheer terror.

"Nooooooo ..."

The sound of his own scream awoke him, and he lay still for a moment, heart jack-hammering, as the panic washed over him in successively smaller waves until it subsided. After so much time why were thoughts of Morozov invading his sleep? The dreams still came every night. Sometimes the General appeared as a huge bear with a man's head that chased him through a dark forest until Shurgin's feet felt like they were encased in glue and he could run no more. But instead of attacking, the beast roared with laughter as it pointed a huge paw in his direction. In another, Shurgin was a fox chewing through his own leg to escape from a cruel trap.

Something gnawed at a place too deep to reach. He would rip it out if he could -- if he could identify the source of the pain. Emotion was unfamiliar to him. Over the years he had isolated emotion behind a barricade of calculation. The KGB taught him ruthlessness just as the dialectic shaped his thought process.

He had long ago ceased to believe in Communism. Cold-eyed logic led to the realization that the Soviet system could never create the new Soviet man of which it boasted. Men were driven by more than mere thought, and political theory would never supplant basic human desires. Men would survive by whatever means available, would forever seek to dominate other men, and would forever seek power for its own sake.

CHAPTER 21

Two days had passed since the Teresa Haines murder, and for that Murphy was grateful. Maybe the bastard had gone back to Los Angeles. No more witnesses had come forward, and the media had taken to the idea of a serial killer loose in the Capital area with all the enthusiasm of a school of piranhas after a bloody piece of meat. A long summer filled with stories of a recession and political stalemate had left them hungry for something more colorful with which to entertain the masses.

Though the craven mavens may be hoping for more mayhem, Murphy nevertheless welcomed the media frenzy. As long as the story was hot, people would be more vigilant. Maybe no one else would die. Arlington nightlife, such as it was, was considerably muted. There would be no more ladies' nights at local bars until the murderer was caught or had ceased to be of concern.

Murphy was on her way to the J. Edgar Hoover Building for a meeting with Enoch Whitehall. He'd called just after lunch to let her know that the results were in from the supplementary DNA testing at the private lab in Florida. She'd almost forgotten about it as calls had begun to come in to the hotline, and the bartender had identified the suspect as most likely a Latino.

She surrendered her weapon and cuffs to the guard at the security checkpoint, who placed them in a numbered cubby hole and handed her a metal tag with the corresponding number and a visitor's badge. Five minutes later she was sitting in Whitehall's office across the desk from him while he explained the document he had just handed her. The office was austere, even though it boasted a window. Everything in it was in shades of Government gray.

Whitehall, she noted, had no family photos on display or anything else that hinted at his private life. Maybe he didn't have one. He wore no wedding band. His office also lacked the Washington staple "vanity wall" of photos with the famous and high and mighty.

The man himself emanated an aura that could only be described in neutral tones like his office. He was tall and thin almost to the point of emaciation, with deep set gray eyes set in a hatchet face on either side of a long blade of a nose. His voice was calm, and he measured his words carefully, probably borne of a lifetime of investigative work that demanded assiduous objectivity. Murphy had learned to respect the man's incisiveness and to heed what he said.

He was just finishing a long recitation of the FBI's criteria for DNA testing. "... And so, the genome of most humans is identical across a broad spectrum, but there are certain measurable variations, in what are known as short tandem repeats, or STR'S. I won't go further into alleles or genotypes, but suffice it to say that CODIS relies on thirteen core STR's in its tests to connect a suspect with a crime, the officially accepted purpose of DNA testing. But here are other tests that are not accepted. Several private sector companies claim the ability to determine one's ancestry, depending on whether it's traced through the Y chromosome or mitochondrial testing. Given the random nature of human mating throughout history, as you can imagine this is not an exact science. Law enforcement is reluctant to get into genetic testing for ethnicity."

Murphy snorted and elicited one of Whitehall's rare smiles, which consisted of a subtle elevation of the corners of his mouth.

"I know," he said, "and I agree that testing crime scene DNA for ethnicity could be useful in identifying the perpetrator, but there are many who fear that the science could be turned on its end and used to PREDICT behavior on the basis of genetics."

Murphy snorted again. "That's crap. But is this all a build-up to telling me the supplemental test didn't reveal anything useful?"

"Not at all. Quite the opposite, as a matter of fact. There are certain regions where one can identify pure gene pools. We seem to have stumbled upon a product of one such region."

Murphy was becoming impatient. She'd been in Whitehall's office for nearly a half-hour listening to him expound on the science of DNA testing without learning anything relevant to her case. This is what FBI guys do, she thought, lay out all the evidence before telling you what the hell they're talking about.

"Could we get to the point, Enoch? Please? I have a very impatient Chief of Police across the river in Arlington."

Was that a twinkle in the gray man's eyes? Murphy wasn't certain he was capable of amusement.

"What we have here," said Whitehall pointing at the document he'd just passed across the desk, "is a rare definite proof of ethnicity. Your killer is of Persian or Azeri lineage."

"An Iranian?"

"Or an Azeri."

"You're certain?"

He pointed at the document again.

"As certain as science can be."

She stared at him as though he'd just pulled a rabbit out of a hat.

He let it sink in for a moment and then asked, "Do you draw any conclusions from this information?"

"If we know where he's from we can check immigration and travel records." This was banal, but it was the first thing that came to her mind.

Whitehall shook his head. "He might not have entered the country legally or he could have been born here of Iranian parents."

"True, but we should check nevertheless."

"Agreed. But there is an inference that can be drawn."

She gave him a blank stare.

"You probably weren't aware of this," he said, "but the suicide bombing in Brussels was traced to a Hezbollah cell."

There it was again, this notion that the Brussels atrocity and Vicky's murder were somehow connected. Hezbollah was a bought and paid for cat's-paw of the Islamic Republic of Iran.

She shook her head.

"I see where you're going, but I still think it's a

stretch, Enoch. That theory still does not account for three murders in Los Angeles and two here. I don't see any possible Iranian national interest."

She couldn't gauge his reaction to her comment.

"Nevertheless, Krystal," he said gently, "it's something you should keep in mind. You were involved with both Vicky Kondratieva and the Nelsons, too. Don't discard a theory until it's been disproven."

She smiled and stood, extending her hand across the desk.

"Of course not, Enoch. Thank you for all your help. The CIWG folks have been super."

He took her proffered hand and stood, as well. Murphy scooped the documents into her bag and left, turning at his office door to raise her fingers in a "V" for victory.

His "be careful out there" floated after her down the hall.

*****

On the way back the office she considered the DNA finding and Whitehall's speculation about its significance. She respected Whitehall's opinion, but surely he was off the mark in this instance. So why was he so insistent? Both he and Strachey had arrived independently at the same conclusion. Well, Whitehall was a Fed and Strachey was CIA, or ex-CIA (did they ever really quit?), and they were trained to look for conspiracies. It was the nature of the shark-filled sea in which they swam where if you didn't always assume the worst, bad things would happen.

But Murphy was a cop, and she wasn't paid to chase wild geese. She'd follow a hunch if she had good reason, but that was not the case here. The major flaw in Whitehall's argument was that the second Arlington victim, Teresa Haines, had no connection whatsoever to the Andropov Memorandum affair, and neither had the three vics in Los Angeles. Murphy had a serial killer on her hands and damned few real clues to his identity beyond a physical description and now the fact of his ethnicity. What she needed to know was who he was and where to find him.

Her responsibilities might not be as exalted as those of an Executive Assistant Director of the FBI, but she kept the streets safe for citizens. She worried that she had not been doing a particularly good job of it lately. Murphy knew she should not berate herself, but she had built her career overcoming obstacles, especially the misogyny that still ran strong in police departments, and this was her first big case. Okay, so the affair of the Andropov Memorandum last year had been a big deal, too, but her role had been minor. She would find this shithead, and it made no difference whether he was an Iranian or an Eskimo.

CHAPTER 22

It was mid-afternoon, and Strachey drummed his fingers on his desk at his firm's "K" Street offices. His concern about the possible linkage between Vicky Kondratieva's murder and the events of the previous year refused to dissipate, and it had been impossible to keep his mind on business throughout the day. Krystal Murphy's common sense doubts were justified, but years in the CIA's Clandestine Service had taught Strachey to trust his intuition.

He could prove nothing, of course. Tying the Brussels suicide bombing to a serial killer in the U.S. was a stretch even considering the common connection between three of the victims.

He was counting on Murphy to keep him informed of progress in the investigation, but he did not expect her to broach professional discipline. There was always something the police wanted kept from the public. Like it or not, since leaving the Agency he was now just another civilian.

The second murder in Arlington flew in the face of his tenuously founded suspicions and made it more likely that Vicky had been a random victim of a deranged murderer. Nevertheless, he could not shake a feeling of impending disaster.

These gloomy thoughts were interrupted by the buzz of the phone on his desk. He punched the lighted button and his secretary asked if he would accept a call from Sam Worthington.

Worthington was one of a burgeoning number of ex-CIA officers who had left the Agency for more lucrative jobs in the private sector. After benefitting from the half-million dollar training and security clearances provided by the CIA, these people shopped their clearances and arcane skills to various private security firms or government contractors, known affectionately as "beltway bandits." It saved the firms the cost of clearances and provided a steady inflow of experienced employees.

Strachey had been Worthington's supervisor in Santiago during the latter's one and only foreign tour as a case officer. The man was competent and smart and had developed considerable respect for Strachey. They'd not remained in regular contact, and Strachey wondered what could have prompted this call. The last he'd heard, Worthington was working at Flackermann Security, one of the largest private security outfits in the world.

He asked his secretary to put the call through.

"Hi, Sam. Nice to hear from you. What's up?"

"Are you looking for a job?"

"I have a job. Why do you ask?"

"We received a request to run a background check on you."

Strachey didn't like the idea of strangers poking into his private life without his knowledge. In Washington it was not unusual for employers to run background checks on prospective employees.

"Who's the client?"

"I shouldn't be telling you any of this, but I thought you should know. And if you are looking for a job, we could always use you in my shop."

"I'm not looking for a job. What kind of information did the client want?"

There was a hint of disappointment in Worthington's voice. "I heard you left the Agency and hoped we could entice you to come to us before anyone else. You're really not scouting for a new place to work?"

"Like I said, Sam, I have a job. I'm not interested in leaving. How about that information?"

"Just a minimal check, you know. Previous employment, marital status, credit, addresses ..."

"Has the report been sent to the client?"

"Yeah, last week. Sorry. It just now came across my desk."

"Sam, can you bend the rules and give me the client's identity?"

"Sure, no problem. You're family." Strachey heard the shuffle of papers. "Here it is ..."

The name Worthington provided was that of a telecommunications company in Florida that rang no bells with Strachey. That was the way it was these days: practically anyone could commission a background check on anyone else without their knowledge. Credit companies did this every day, and it was absurdly easy to anonymously get one's hands on credit reports. In this instance he'd been lucky that whoever was checking on him had gone to Flackermann.

That evening he told Amy about Worthington's call.

"I don't like it," he concluded, "on top of

everything else that's happening. Can you check on this Florida outfit with Palantir?"

"That system's not for personal business, you know. And I'm on maternity leave."

Strachey knew that his wife did not completely share his concerns about Vicky's death. Amy was an optimist, a fact which proved to him the adage that opposites attract, and preferred Krystal Murphy's interpretation of events. He hoped she would not dig her heels in on this.

"It could be important, and it would take me weeks to get to the bottom of it on my own. You could go in for one day, just to see how things are going. I'll take a day off and stay with RT. You could you ask Harvey. He won't object to a one-time peek."

Harvey Grant, the DDI and Amy's boss at CIA, was a close personal friend to them both and would deny nothing to Amy.

"I guess," she said, "so long as Harvey agrees."

She returned to the house the next day at noon just as Strachey finished feeding the baby. He threw a towel over his shoulder and carried RT into the living room, gently patting his back, to meet her at the door.

From the look on her face he knew she'd found something and wasn't happy about it, but her expression softened when she saw him with the baby.

When RT spotted his mother he stretched his chubby arms in her direction and gurgled happily. She flung her coat onto the back of a chair and reached for the baby.

"Better take the towel," said Strachey, "He just finished a bottle."

The baby and towel having safely changed hands, Amy sat and rocked back and forth, cooing into RT's ear until he was asleep.

"I'll put him in his crib. Then we can talk."

Strachey paced impatiently until she returned. She obviously had news, and not necessarily the good kind.

"Harvey agreed to let me do a search. It took me about two hours, but I got results. The Florida outfit is just a front company. I traced ownership back through several other entities until I got to the end. The real owner is RusAvia, that gun runner's air cargo company."

And there it was – the connection with Vitaliy Shurgin. Strachey walked instinctively to the front window and peered out, half expecting to see a gang of Russian thugs in the front yard. Suddenly feeling foolish he turned to see Amy staring at him.

"What does this mean, Bob?"

"I don't know, but I'm sure it's nothing good."

"I told Harvey what you think about Vicky, and he became very worried." She hugged herself as if hit by a sudden chill. "Bob, I'm scared."

He stepped from the window back to the sofa and sat beside her to put his arms around her.

"I'm glad you told Harvey. I'm going to let Krystal know, too. Maybe it'll change her mind."

CHAPTER 23

Carmela Rodriquez' job as a night check-out cashier at the 24-hour Giant Foods grocery was perfect for her. With two kids at home and a husband who worked days, the night shift allowed her to be at home in time to fix the children's breakfast and see them off to school. Then she could sleep until afternoon and be fresh for them when they came home and for her husband when he arrived a few hours later. Carmela couldn't think of a more convenient arrangement and had let the store manager know that she wanted to be on the night shift permanently.

2:30 AM was Carmela's smoke break time, and she asked her co-worker, Linda Polk, to watch the register while she went outside. The nights were getting cooler, and she would have to start bringing a sweater to work pretty soon. There was a slight breeze tonight, and Carmela had to shield the flame of her disposable lighter as she brought it to the tip of her cigarette.

It was then that she heard the noise, faint at first, and then rising and falling in a chilling ululation. Later, she would tell the police that her first thought was that it was the mewling of a cat, but that almost immediately she got the impression that whatever it was, it was in pain, maybe dying. She searched for the source of the sound, turning her head one way and another to determine the direction from which it came. There was something white lying at the far side of the parking lot, just visible at the edge of the illumination from the overhead lights. The object seemed to be moving.

Carmela was suddenly frightened as the outline of the object came into focus. She dropped the cigarette and ran back inside the store to summon the night manager.

*****

Murphy was almost grateful when the phone beside her bed rang. She'd returned home late, showered, and gone to bed immediately but had tossed in a middle ground between troubled sleep and wakefulness despite her weariness. A glance at the illuminated dial of the clock radio showed it was nearly three A.M., and her heart sank.

There must have been another murder.

She grabbed the receiver. "What is it?" But she knew what she was going to hear.

"Detective Murphy? Sorry to wake you. It's patrolman Sam Hurley. Dispatch said to call you first thing."

Murphy was by now sitting up on the edge of the bed. She could feel her heart thudding against her ribs.

"Tell me."

"Well, ma'am, we're at the 24-hour Giant at Washington Boulevard and North Lincoln. Received a call about a half-hour ago from the manager reporting a stabbing in the parking lot. The vic was dead by the time we arrived. The paramedics got here at pretty much the same time. It could be one of yours."

By 'one of yours' he meant the serial killings.

"What do you mean 'could be?'"

"Well, the vic's a woman, early twenties wearing a Hooters uniform. You know, shiny orange shorts and a T-shirt. Somebody slit her belly open, and I mean all the way. Pretty grisly. Doesn't completely fit all the parameters for your guy, but close enough to call you."

"There are no other wounds? Her throat wasn't slashed?"

"Nope. CSI's on the way, and the ambulance guys are here waiting for the body to be released."

"Witnesses?"

She could always hope.

"Nah. One of the employees spotted the body lying in the parking lot when she came out to have a smoke. According to her the vic was still alive. You gonna want to see this before we clear the scene?"

Murphy was bone tired, but she was worried. She dreaded the idea that some demented copycat had decided to join in the mischief. In none of the previous five reported murders had the victim been left alive. Maybe something had spooked the killer before he could finish. But why would he have chosen a public parking lot in the first place? That was out of pattern, too.

"I'd better get out there. Don't let anyone touch anything until I'm there."

She calculated it would take her ten minutes to reach the scene at this time of night. Maybe something had happened to break the perp's normal routine and he had left more clues. Maybe it would be another dead-end.

She hung up the phone and went into the bathroom to splash some water on her face before pulling on the change of clothing she'd left on the chair next to the bed.

Ten minutes later she was in the elevator headed for the lobby. A Hooters waitress? Another random victim. Random selection of victims was the serial killer's strength. Other than the geographic area in which he was operating and the fact that all of his victims were female, no discernible pattern had emerged that would point to his identity, unless Strachey's and Whitehall's suspicions were correct. Her heart sank with the elevator as she anticipated that there would be more innocent victims. Why had this creep chosen Arlington?

She made a bee line for the outside lot where she'd left her unmarked police car, pulling the keys from her jeans pocket as she went, her head bowed as the thoughts raced through her mind.

As she bent to open the car door she sensed someone rapidly approaching even before she heard the sound of feet close behind and knew instinctively that she was in trouble. Had retreat not been blocked by the bulk of the car she might have fended off the assault or even subdued her assailant. As it was, she had only enough time to half-turn, one hand going for the service pistol at her waist as she raised the other to block the blow she knew was coming. She felt the crunch of metal hitting bone more than she heard it, and her left arm went numb. She knew instantly that one of the bones in her forearm had been broken by whatever weapon her attacker wielded. Struggling to hold a grasp on consciousness she had the pistol half-way out of the holster when she received a stunning blow to the side of her head that drove her to the ground beside the car and everything went black.

CHAPTER 24

Nice, France

V.I.P. arrivals are common at the Business Aviation Terminal at l'Aeroport de Nice. The Côte d'Azur is a magnet for the rich and famous, after all. But this was no common visitor. He was rich, certainly, but he shunned fame.

Those who were present when his private jet landed saw a slim, blond man of average height and indeterminate age, impeccably dressed. Had the three grim-faced bodyguards permitted closer inspection, attention would have been drawn to the man's glacial blue eyes and the premature roughness of his skin that bespoke a harsher life than his obvious wealth might suggest. On his right hand, just below the first knuckles of his fingers were faint tattoos of Cyrillic letters. The fine clothing concealed more crude tattoos that covered his upper body and arms.

Those familiar with the old Soviet penal system, universally known as the *gulag* would recognize him as a former denizen. And more, the cryptic prison tattoos identified him as a true *vor v zakonye*, a "thief in the code" in the arcane jargon of the Russian underworld.

The man's name was Ruslan Lomonosov. For the nearly two decades since the violent death of his brother, Zhenya, he had headed the "Brotherhood." The organized crime family had its origins in the northern precincts of Moscow and had grown rapidly to dominate crime in post-Soviet Russia. To do so they had fought pitched gun battles with the Chechen mafia, murdered crusading reporters, and bought politicians. His organization controlled money laundering, drug trafficking, sex slave trafficking, and owned interests in several well-known "legitimate" businesses.

Ruslan controlled the Brotherhood's worldwide operations from the same villa in Zürich where his brother had died. Zhenya Lomonosov had formed an alliance with a former KGB officer named Shurgin who had used his own mysterious wealth and Brotherhood muscle to rise to the top of the new Russian political system.

The disappearance without a trace of the disgraced Vitaliy Mikhailovich Shurgin months earlier had sent ripples of disquiet throughout the Brotherhood. The funding Shurgin provided was vital to several of the Brotherhood's operations. This was the reason for Ruslan's travel to France. There was one person here who might know the deposed President's whereabouts and the disposition of his great wealth.

Two cars, a limousine and a chase car for the bodyguards waited at the exit to the Business Aviation terminal. As they left the airport Ruslan's attention was drawn to a huge, crude figure of a man comprised entirely of boulders held together by iron bars. This was "Le Voyageur," by the artist Max Cartier. Ruslan was unimpressed.

Fifteen minutes later they made the U-turn off the D-33 into a narrow, two-lane street which they followed up the hillside to a set of ornate gates where two obviously armed men waited to check their documents. The formalities completed, Ruslan's two cars were permitted to enter the lush, park-like grounds, preceded by a Land Rover that led them to a parking area at the side of one of the world's best known villas.

To use the term "villa" with reference to the Villa La Leopolda was to do it an injustice. Built by King Leopold II of Belgium in 1902 for his mistress, Caroline Lacroix, it was in actuality a palace with extensive grounds commanding a spectacular view of the Côte d'Azur. Its present owner was international financier Edmond Salmen.

If the truth be known Salmen was apprehensive about the *vor v zakonye's* visit. He had known the man's brother, Zhenya, with whom he had had business dealings in Zürich. Zhenya, despite his background, had at least made a show of refinement. But Ruslan was another story. Unlike his brother, he made no attempt to adapt to the usual conventions of polite Western society. Salmen had doubled his guard force in advance of the visit.

There was a minor *contretemps* when Salmen's men demanded that the Russian's bodyguards surrender their weapons and wait outside, but Ruslan ordered them to obey and entered alone.

Salmen waited just inside and greeted his visitor with an uncertain smile.

"Welcome to my home, Monsieur Lomonosov. It is a pleasure to see you here for the first time. Your brother was a great friend."

Ruslan ignored the greeting and the lie, as well as Salmen's extended hand.

"Where can we speak privately?" He spoke in correct German with a heavy Russian accent.

Momentarily taken aback, Salmen suggested they use the sitting room just off the entrance foyer. Lomonosov obviously didn't expect a guided tour.

Ruslan glanced over his shoulder at the guard that stood just inside the door of the sitting room.

"Does he understand German?" he asked.

"No."

"Very well. I am here to inquire whether you have been in contact with Vitaliy Shurgin since his disappearance."

Salmen raised his eyebrows.

"Why would Shurgin contact me?"

"Do not take me for a fool, Salmen. I know that you're Shurgin's money man and have been from the beginning. Now please answer my question."

"But these are confidential matters, M. Lomonosov. I'm sure you understand."

Salmen looked at the Russian hopefully, but was met only by a reptilian stare that frightened him profoundly.

When he finally spoke, the Russian's tone was flat and uncompromising.

"Mr. Salmen, you must understand this is a matter of considerable importance to me and my organization. For that reason you will cooperate in any way I ask."

He looked over his shoulder at Salmen's guard, then back at Salmen.

"You are well-guarded here in your little palace. If you plan ever to leave these grounds again and live to return, you will answer my question."

Edmond Salmen was a man accustomed to wielding enormous influence, but it was the influence of wealth, the possession of which could make lesser men grovel. Ruslan Lomonosov, on the other hand, relied on the currency of fear and violence to achieve his ends. He'd grown up in a world without mercy where failure to back up threats with violence could mean death.

That such a man would come into his beloved Villa La Leopolda and make such a threat angered Salmen. Had he been a man like Lomonosov, he would have ordered his guard to shoot his visitor there and then. But he was not like Lomonosov. He was quite capable and willing figuratively to stab a rival in the back, to ruin a man completely. But he had no experience with literal murder.

As though reading his mind, Lomonosov said, "If you are thinking of killing me right now you should consider the fact that my organization would exact revenge; not only on you personally, but on every member of your family, no matter where they are, no matter how long it takes. And I mean EVERY member of your family. There will be no *zhid* Salmens left in the world."

The magical light of the Riviera spilled through tall windows into the room decorated by Renzo Mongiardino illuminating its antiques and priceless art. This was a setting which should bring pleasure to any who entered, but Lomonsov's presence drained every iota of joy from the atmosphere, and suddenly the only color Salmen could see was the icy blue of the man's eyes. The memory of this moment would be so traumatic that Salmen would avoid entering this room in the future.

Lomonosov had not moved a muscle nor had his face shown any emotion while he spoke. With his eyes still skewering the banker, he now said, "I will repeat the question: Have you been in touch with Vitaliy Shurgin?"

Salmen could feel the flush rising from his neck to heat his face and the sweat breaking out on his forehead. He was acutely embarrassed by the physiological reaction to fear, but he found himself unexpectedly under the control of this Russian butcher. He had no choice but to capitulate.

"No. I've had no direct contact with him for months."

"This is the truth?"

"I swear."

The Russian examined the cowed banker for a long moment, deciding whether he was telling the truth. Salmen's hands began to tremble.

Then the hint of a smile lifted one corner of Lomonosov's mouth.

"I believe you, Salmen. I think we shall be great friends now that you understand me."

"I ... I hope so, M. Lomonosov."

"Now that that we have been properly introduced, I think we should have a frank discussion about Vitaliy Shurgin."

CHAPTER 25

Edmond Salmen had been born in Beirut, Lebanon, into a Jewish banking family with its origins in Syria where it had thrived as gold traders and bankers in the Ottoman Empire. He entered the family business at a very early age and in time built a financial empire stretching from Lebanon, to Brazil, to the United States and Europe. By 1980 he was one of the world's most influential gold traders and bankers, and a very wealthy man.

Shurgin had been aware of Salmen's past dealings with the KGB and the Russian *Mafiya*. Indeed, the American FBI had investigated Salmen in connection with money laundering for the *Mafiya* through his bank. While still in the KGB Shurgin even had used Salmen's connections to finance clandestine arms sales to various "revolutionary" groups and terrorist organizations.

In that fateful August of 1991 following the failed coup, the Anna Ulyanova put into port for refueling at Rotterdam, where Shurgin went ashore to make a phone call. The ship then passed through the English Channel and around the Iberian Peninsula where she entered the Mediterranean and hugged the shore all the way to the French coast where she dropped anchor a mile off Saint-Jean-Cap-Ferrat.

Leaving the *Banner* squad's commanding officer in charge, Shurgin and Morozov went ashore in a motor dinghy piloted by the First Mate, alighting in the small yacht harbor of Villefranche-sur-Mer just east of Nice. Shurgin made another phone call, and a half-hour later a chauffeured Bentley fetched them to the Villa La Leopolda, the magnificent estate of Edmond Salmen.

Salmen was by turn astonished, intrigued, and captivated by what the Russian suggested. Could he discreetly handle fifty billion dollars in gold, cash, and bearer bonds? *Of course, my dears.* The handling fees fairly danced in his head. One of the world's wealthiest men, sums that staggered the imagination of mere mortals did not faze the financier.

Logistics presented the most difficult problem. They moved the ship to stand off-shore opposite Monaco where the crates were transferred to one of Salmen's bonded warehouses, where half of Dimov's men were stationed. The operation cost the better part of a week.

They were dealing essentially in cash, and while physically moving it was uncomplicated, ensuring that control of it remained in the two Russians' hands was another matter. Salmen was a past master at handling funds of questionable origin, and another day was required for the paperwork while Morozov's men stood guard over the treasure. By the end of the day Shurgin and Morozov had control of the former foreign currency and gold reserves of the Soviet Union. The account eventually would be divided into many others and spread around the world in the form of investments and holding companies.

The transfer complete, Shurgin and Morozov ordered the Anna Ulyanova's Captain to return to

Leningrad. They remained behind when the ship sailed carrying the crew and the *Banner* squad. Twenty-four hours later in the dead of night, the squad returned in the motor dinghy. The Anna Ulyanova disappeared forever.

CHAPTER 26

Interstate 270 North, Maryland

The throbbing pain in her forearm and head dragged Murphy out of the dark pit into which she had fallen. She groaned and opened her eyes only to find that she was gagged and bound hand and foot, lying in a fetal position. She could see nothing except a faint red glow that puzzled her until she realized that she was in the trunk of a moving car. The red glow came through small openings in the recesses in which the tail lights were mounted. She had no idea how long she had been unconscious.

She tested her bonds and gritted her teeth at the pain in her left arm. Her ankles were bound together, as were her hands behind her body. From the taste she guessed it was duct tape covering her mouth.

A male voice came to her from the front of the car. "Are you awake, Detective Murphy? How is that arm of yours?"

He must have heard her moving in the trunk.

She didn't answer.

"I hope you are awake," the voice continued. "I want you to be alert. We have a long day ahead of us, and I wouldn't want you to miss any of the action." He laughed. "Before we reach the end, you will tell me what I want to know. You will tell me where to find Harry Connolly and his blond bitch."

Murphy still didn't answer, not really registering

what he was saying as the realization blossomed that she'd fallen into a trap that could only have been set by the serial killer. There was no knowing how long she had left before they reached the killer's destination. The only certainty was that once there, she would have no chance against him. Grisly images of his previous victims flashed unbidden into her mind, and she fought to hold back the panic. She would have screamed had it not been for the tape over her mouth. Escape was the only option, and modern cars had inside trunk lid releases.

She could loosen the gag simply by licking the adhesive from the back of the tape, but with her hands behind her back she would still be helpless. She needed to have her hands in front of her body so she could remove the gag and tear the duct tape around her wrists with her teeth. Murphy was physically strong, and she was lithe. The question was whether she possessed the requisite flexibility. She'd managed the feat during escape and evasion training in preparation for her Army Reserve tour in Iraq, but that had been four years ago. It would have been easier if her captor had used zip ties because the technique for breaking out of them was much easier.

The fact that she already was in a fetal position, she knew, was a plus. The trick was to slip her bound hands under her hips and over her feet, but with no slack in the duct tape this would be doubly difficult. She hoped she wouldn't have to dislocate her shoulders in the process. The broken arm would make the maneuver agonizing, but she had to try.

Murphy stretched her arms as far downward as

possible and began to wriggle them around her hips. The pain in her arm was blinding, and she let loose a stream of curses that penetrated even the duct tape as she fought the waves of nausea that swept over her. But stopping the pain meant giving up, and she persevered as she felt the tape around her wrists loosen ever so slightly. She put the weight of her body over her right arm and wrenched her shoulder out of its socket.

CHAPTER 27

Donnie Strickler pulled his big rig onto the off ramp from Interstate 270 North. He'd driven up out of the Shenandoah Valley well before dawn with a load of live turkeys destined for a slaughterhouse in Pennsylvania, and the truck stop at this exit offered generous fare to hungry drivers. It had become Donnie's favorite breakfast spot on this particular run. A faint gray line over the eastern horizon promised dawn in another hour, and judging from the number of trucks leaving the highway here, a lot of other truckers had the same idea as he.

There was a traffic light at the top of the exit ramp that had just turned red, and Donnie pulled to a stop behind a couple of other rigs and a car. He was mentally going over the breakfast menu, weighing the relative merits of pancakes to steak and eggs, when his attention was drawn to the car in line directly in front of him.

The trunk lid had popped open and as he watched, a red-headed woman dressed in jeans and a dark T-shirt rolled out and sprawled to the ground. She looked like she was hurt. In the glare of his headlights he could see there was blood on her face, and she was having trouble using her arms to get to her feet. As Donnie looked on, the driver's side door of the car flew open and a skinny guy that looked like a Mexican leapt out.

Whatever else Donnie Strickler might have been

he was quick enough on the uptake to recognize a nasty situation when he saw one. Nice guys didn't carry girls around in the trunks of their cars. Valley guys, on the other hand, were good old boys with their own code of honor, a penchant for guns, and a general disregard for intrusive government regulations that offended their Second Amendment sensibilities. And when the situation called for it, even a pot-bellied 250 lb. part-time truck driver could move pretty fast.

Donnie reached under his seat to retrieve the Ruger .44 Magnum he kept there and stepped down from the truck's cab at the same time the Mexican rounded the rear of the car to where the woman still struggled to get up.

Donnie stepped to the front of his rig. "I'd leave her be, if I wuz you," he said.

His deep, booming voice matched his bulk and carried easily above the engine noise.

All of the Mexican's attention had been on the woman, and now he belatedly became aware of Donnie, who measured six feet and wore work boots, denim bib overalls over a checked flannel shirt, and a greasy Harley Davidson cap topping a shaggy head of hair and a broad, bearded face. Backlit as he was by his rig's headlights, his appearance was supremely scary.

"Stay away!" The expression on the Mexican's dark face was one of increasing fury. "This is none of your business."

Donnie narrowed his eyes and calmly raised the big revolver to point it at the Mexican, pulling back the hammer as he did so. He was only feet away from him by now. He couldn't miss.

"I'm makin' it my business, amigo."

There was definite, growling menace in his voice now. Donnie figured all Mexicans were illegals, and he sure as hell wasn't taking any lip from this one.

"Now you step back away from that girl."

Donnie took another step forward.

In the headlights' glare, he was gratified to see the Mexican's eyes grow round as he registered the large bore of the barrel pointed directly at his head. Donnie scowled darkly to emphasize the threat. Valley boys can be very convincing, and he left no room for doubt that he would not hesitate to pull the trigger.

The traffic light at the top of the ramp changed to green, and the rigs in front of the car began inching forward. Donnie's truck blocked the view from behind, and a few horns began to bleat.

With a lingering, malevolent look at the woman, the Mexican retreated back around the car, his eyes never leaving the revolver in Donnie's hand.

From the ground, the woman screamed, "Shoot the bastard!"

With a last glare of black rage, the Mexican got in and sped away. Donnie would have fired had the Mexican tried to harm the girl, but the immediate danger had receded, and killing an unarmed man who was backing off, even if he was a damned wetback, would bring more trouble than he was willing to risk. For all he knew he was dealing with some sort of domestic situation. And he still had to deliver the turkeys to Pennsylvania.

Donnie bent to help the woman who was still

struggling to stand. She was obviously in great pain, but she was cursing like a sailor.

CHAPTER 28

Murphy's pride was as battered as her body, and she was furious at herself. Her mood was not improved by the fact the she had just gotten off the phone with her parents. They still lived on the farm just outside Terre Haute. Murphy had called them, having decided that news of her ordeal would be best heard from her directly than from some snooping reporter.

Her mother had begun blubbering immediately and surrendered the phone to Murphy's father. Both of them, she knew, had been disappointed when she left home to join the Army, and even more upset when she became a cop. The path she had taken totally incomprehensible to them. But she could not envision a life that revolved around the price of milo and corn.

Her parents had always planned for their daughter to marry some nice, vanilla local boy and start popping out grandchildren. At least they had her older brother, who had married right out of high school and efficiently provided a grandchild six months thereafter. To his credit, he was still married to the same woman, and had produced two more children.

Unless her brother and his wife were still burning up the sheets, three grandchildren would have to suffice for her parents. Murphy certainly had no plans in that direction. She had yet to meet a man that stirred any deep emotion. As a matter of fact, she was ambivalent about romance and marriage, something that worried her more than she could admit to herself.

And now her pride had been grievously wounded. It didn't matter that she had escaped. What mattered was that she had allowed herself to be ambushed in the first place. What was worse, the sonuvabitch had taken her weapon. What would have happened, she wondered, if her captor had thought to grab it before he got out of the car and confronted that truck driver? On second thought, if he had, that country boy certainly would've taken care of business and the murdering Iranian wouldn't have gotten away. He'd be in the morgue with his spine blown apart by the truck driver's .44.

EMS had administered first aid at the scene and taken her to Frederick Memorial Hospital, just off the Interstate, where they'd x-rayed and set her fractured ulna and forced her into the bed where she now lay. She was still seeing double from the concussion, but the doctors said that would pass. Her arm was immobilized in a cast, and they'd popped her shoulder back into place and dressed the nasty cut on the side of her head.

Murphy had identified herself as a cop to the Maryland State Trooper who responded to the truck driver's 911 call, and he'd promised to notify Arlington. Her failure to appear at the Giant Foods crime scene had set off some alarms, and the discovery of her car still in the lot with blood smeared on the door triggered an all-points bulletin to every police department in the Washington, D.C. region, including the Maryland State

Police. A nurse told her that Lieutenant Jefferson was on his way to the hospital.

She'd seen the truck driver replace his big gun under the seat in the cab of his rig before the cops and EMS arrived, and she had said nothing about it. He might have a carry permit in Virginia, but the Peoples' Republic of Maryland frowned on concealed weapons. She'd get the guy's name from the police report so she could thank him properly.

In the meantime, what would she tell Jefferson? What could she tell him? She'd glimpsed her assailant only for a split second before he slammed her in the head with what she thought must have been a tire iron. She was lucky he hadn't split her skull. She was convinced that her assailant and the serial killer were one and the same. But she had no proof to offer other than intuition and the circumstances of the ambush.

Like any cop, Murphy had made her share of enemies among the criminal classes, but none she could think of would go to such extremes. With luck, the truck driver's description would match that of the serial killer and vindicate her suspicion.

She would share all of this with Jefferson, of course, but what about motive? It still didn't make sense – all of those murders in California and then in Arlington, all leading up to an attack on her. She had not forgotten Strachey's unease following the death of Vicky Kondratieva or Enoch Whitehall's similar inference that something more might be at the bottom of it all. But how to make sense of the facts? The killer's victims in California appeared to have been selected at random, as had at least two of the killings in Arlington. But three people connected with the Andropov Memorandum were now dead, and a fourth, Murphy, had been attacked. In the case of the Nelsons in Brussels, if a mass murder by suicide bomber had been conceived to conceal the true targets, could the same be true of this killer's victims? She and Robert Strachey had spoken only briefly on the phone before her abduction, and he'd told her about the Russian-instigated background investigation that seemed to lend credence to his theory. But why would the murders have begun in Los Angeles? And how was all this related to Iran and Hezbollah?

It was later, when she replayed the events in her mind that she recalled her assailant's strange reference to "Harry Connolly and his blond bitch." The name meant nothing to her.

The only person who might be able to make sense of it all was Strachey. She resolved to see him as soon as she was released from the hospital.

And there was another reason. If there was truth to the Andropov Memorandum connection, the Russian investigation meant Strachey would be on the list, too.

CHAPTER 29

Murphy's account of her abduction was chilling, and for the first time since his resignation wished Strachey wished was still in the CIA.

He'd arrived at her Arlington apartment an hour earlier and she'd told the uniformed policewoman assigned to stay with her to take a break.

Both the Chief of Police and Lieutenant Jefferson had insisted on assigning a personal protection detail after she was released from the hospital the day before. A black and white patrol car was stationed outside her building, as well.

Murphy was stretched full length on the couch with a bed pillow under her head, still suffering the residual effects of the concussion. She wore an old terry robe over flannel pajamas, and big floppy slippers on her feet. The doctors had shaved a swath of hair from the side of her head where they'd sutured and dressed her wound. The fingers of her left hand where they showed at the end of the cast were purplish and swollen, as was the left side of her face. She'd taken a real beating, and Strachey could see that she was ashamed of it, and he knew it wasn't her appearance that bothered her so much as the fact that she had been bested in a fight.

He'd known Murphy for nearly a year but this was the first time he'd been to the apartment. It was small and neatly kept, with one bedroom, a living/dining area, and galley kitchen. She'd decorated it in a schmaltzy country motif, including a collection of cow figurines that surprised Strachey until he remembered she'd grown up in rural Indiana where the taste in furnishings was similar to that in his own native North Carolina mountain country. There was a framed photo of a pigtailed teenage Murphy in jeans and a plaid shirt hugging a German shepherd with what looked like a barn in the background, as well as pictures of her in military uniform – the archetypical tomboy. He knew she'd been an MP and finished college on the GI Bill before joining the police.

He guessed she was in her early to mid-thirties, and she was very attractive when she decided to dress up. But for the most part she preferred jeans and practical cop shoes. Strachey recognized the signs of someone dedicated to their job.

He'd been the same himself and had two divorces to show for it. His marriage to Amy would be different, not only because they had a child, but also because he intended to devote himself to his new family, something he could now do without matters of national security interfering. The Fates had conspired to bring together two North Carolinians of wildly divergent backgrounds: he from the rustic western mountains and Amy, the African-American daughter of a Charlotte bus driver. Strachey couldn't remember being happier.

He wondered if Murphy had any romance in her life. She was at an age when most women hoped to be settled down with kids. Given the joy he'd found with Amy, he hoped Murphy would realize what she was missing before it was too late.

When she told him about her abductor's reference to a "Harry Connolly and his blond bitch" the unease he'd felt ever since the Brussels bombing jelled into certainty. Until the occurrence of certain incidents in Vienna, Austria, some two decades ago, Ewan Ramsay had been Harry Connolly, a senior CIA operations officer.

Murphy caught his reaction. "You know who it is, don't you?"

There was no reason to deny it. "Yes."

"The woman is the person who came here masquerading as a Russian cop, right?"

At the behest of the late DNCS Terry Stoddard, it was Strachey himself who recruited, actually blackmailed Ewan Ramsay aka Harry Connolly and his wife, Sasha, to investigate the suspicious death of General Kondratiev, Vicky's father. His relationship with them started badly but ended on good terms. Better than good terms. Ramsay had actually begun to like Strachey by the time the affair was over.

But Murphy's tale had just confirmed that it wasn't over, at all.

Probably fewer than a half-dozen people knew the true identities of Ewan and Sasha.

Murphy was waiting for a more complete answer, and given what she had gone through she deserved one. But Strachey couldn't provide it. The less anyone knew about Ramsay and Sasha the better. He trusted Murphy's discretion, but she was, after all, a cop, and it wouldn't be fair to test the limits of her loyalty.

"I can't say any more than that, Krystal."

"You don't trust me."

He caught a green flash of Irish anger in her eyes.

"It's not that, at all. There are some things it's best you not know for your own good."

After a moment's contemplation she said, "You CIA types are all alike."

He felt like crap.

"Knowledge can sometimes be dangerous and a burden you don't want to have to carry. I made a promise to these people that I can't break. You'd do the same if the situation were reversed."

Her eyes held an expression he couldn't fathom.

"Well," she said, "whoever they are, they could be the reason all this is happening, the reason all these people are dead. The question is why."

Strachey couldn't disagree. "I have an idea why," he said.

Murphy sat up on the couch, wincing from the pain in her head, and gave him a withering look that said, *you'd better not leave me dangling now.*

He had to give her something or risk their friendship. She deserved at least this much.

"Who was hurt the most by the Andropov Memorandum?"

"Besides everybody who died?" It took only a second for the light to dawn. "Shurgin?"

"'Fraid so. I think he's out for blood."

Her chagrin forgotten, Murphy asked, "But how could he do it? The Russians threw him out, didn't they?"

"Shurgin still has a lot of resources at his disposal. He's an extremely wealthy man with a lot of international connections."

"There's something I haven't told you," she said, "and I shouldn't because it's evidence that's not been made public. But I'm not a pissy-assed CIA puke, so I'm going to show you some trust."

Strachey grinned because the insult meant he was forgiven.

Murphy continued, "The FBI did some extra work on the perp's DNA. Turns out he's Iranian."

The Brussels *Hezbollah* connection was the first thing that flashed into his mind. This forged a stronger link between Vicky's murder and the Brussels bombing.

"It ties in with Brussels, doesn't it?" she asked.

"Shurgin has close ties with the Iranians."

Ramsay needed to know about this pronto.

Murphy said, "And here's something else you need to think about. That Iranian motherfucker is still out there. If Vicky and I are on some cockamamie death list of Shurgin's, so are you."

A sadistic serial killer was bad enough, but a sadistic serial killer who was also a trained Iranian operative was even worse.

The serial killer had dropped completely out of sight after Krystal Murphy's escape. He may well have returned to Los Angeles to avoid the spotlight the Washington area authorities were shining on him. That would have been the smart thing to do. The descriptions provided by the bartender from the Westin Hotel and the truck driver who had rescued

Krystal, had made it possible for the FBI artists to produce a very lifelike rendering of the killer's face.

But despite the ensuing publicity, the unidentified subject remained at large. Strachey attributed this to the killer's training as a professional intelligence operative. The FBI could not have failed to recognize this, not with Enoch Whitehall personally involved.

The Assistant Deputy Director of the FBI must be just a little frustrated by the still unanswered questions surrounding the previous year's affair of the Andropov Memorandum. The murder of Vicky's father, the revelation of the existence of a document that proved direct KGB involvement in the assassination of an iconic American president, and ultimately the unmasking of the current President's "Intelligence Czar" as a Russian agent of influence guaranteed the downfall of Vitaliy Mikhailovich Shurgin.

These events were of enormous political significance, and the catalyst had been an unknown "blond woman" masquerading as an investigating officer of the Russian FSB. What neither Whitehall nor anyone else in Washington knew, was that the woman was in fact Aleksandra Sergeyevna Turmarkina aka Sasha, wife of fugitive CIA officer Harry Connolly aka Ewan Ramsay, or that their involvement had been at the personal behest of the late CIA Director of National Clandestine Intelligence Terrence Stoddard.

The thought of Terry Stoddard called up the bitter recollection of the DNCI's violent death one fine August morning when an improvised explosive device detonated next to his car on Washington's Chain Bridge. Shurgin had ordered the murder, and while the Russian President was out of reach, his SVR assassin was not, and Strachey eventually had put a large caliber bullet through his skull.

Violence begat violence, and now a year later, one by one, first the Nelsons in Brussels, then Vicky Kondratieva in Arlington, and now the attempt on Krystal Murphy, Shurgin was eliminating the people who had brought him down. His intent was clear – revenge.

This was a fight to the death.

A frigid worm that he recognized as fear squirmed deep in Strachey's gut. So long as Shurgin lived his new family and his friends were vulnerable.

"How soon before you're up and around, Krystal?"

"Another day or two, but they won't let me back to work with this." She pointed at the cast on her arm.

"As soon as you're able I'd like you to move in temporarily at our place. Amy would love to have you, and you know she's a great cook. I'm going away for a while, and I can't think of anyone better to protect my family. Your gun hand isn't injured."

Murphy's face screwed up with emotion that seemed to surprise even her for just a second as she realized the level of trust implicit in the request.

CHAPTER 30

Ireland

Three days later Strachey steered the Hertz Ford Focus carefully into the roundabout at the exit of Shannon International Airport doing his best to get re-accustomed to the car's right hand drive. Past experience told him he would over-compensate toward the left margin of the road until he was well into the three hour journey north and west through County Galway.

Cleggan was a coastal village perhaps best known for the Cleggan Disaster of 1927 when 25 local fishermen drowned in a sudden gale while fishing for mackerel in the bay. But today the village held a secret of which even its oldest inhabitants were unaware. The handsome native stone house perched on a rocky finger that jutted into the bay on the northern edge of town was the unlikely home of two former agents of the Mossad's elite *Kidon* unit.

He'd been there twice before. First to convince the occupants through less than honorable means to help Terry Stoddard determine the true reason for the murder of General Pavel Kondratiev, and the second with his wife for a much more pleasant visit. In fact, it was on the second visit with Amy, then five months pregnant, that the two couples had celebrated their triumph over Shurgin. Ewan and Sasha had pampered Amy like a princess throughout the visit while wintry gales pounded the sea into white foam outside and the warmth of peat fires and good company prevailed within.

One evening when the women had left them to their stories and drink the two men sat before the fire enjoying the last dregs of a local bottle of *potcheen*, strong Irish moonshine. Ramsay took advantage of Sasha's absence to light a fat Habano.

Had it not been for the drink Strachey might not have asked the question, but he had been fascinated from the beginning by Ramsay's trajectory from rogue CIA officer to Mossad agent to retirement in Ireland.

"I know it's none of my business," he said, "but you could have been cleared of all charges had you returned to the States after the Vienna operation. Why didn't you."

The fragrant blue smoke from Ramsay's cigar wafted toward the hearth to find it's way up the chimney, and he was silent for so long that Strachey thought he was not going to answer. He knew the question was intrusive.

Ramsay finally spoke.

"There is a lot you don't know about what happened in Vienna and afterwards, things I'm not going to share, but I'm not so sure about the charges being dropped. Suffice it to say I was shoved over the edge by the circumstances. I met Sasha, and the rest is history. I found working with the Mossad quite liberating. I did consider returning to the States, more than once, but there were too many uncertainties, and besides, I was happy here. I'd re-started my life."

"How did you decide to settle in Ireland?"

The Incubus Vendetta

"Things were a little different twenty years ago. The violence was coming to an end in the north, and Dublin had opened the economy in the south. Anything was possible in Ireland then, and it was incredibly simple to establish an identity and settle down. Sad to say, by my observation America was in danger of crumbling, destroying itself, just like the Soviet Union, but for different reasons. Society was disintegrating, devolving into separate groups with special interests that had nothing to do with love of country. Today America's a different place from the country I grew up in. It's only a matter of time before things go seriously off the rails. Ireland seemed as good a place as any from which to watch the sun set on the American century."

Strachey recalled these words now as he drove through the Autumnal Irish countryside. It was difficult to refute the logic that brought Ramsay to such a conclusion, but Strachey hoped the older man's pessimism was misplaced, the product of advancing age and nostalgia for a simpler past. A new baby was reason enough for Strachey to hope for better, and a country that had survived the ravages of a civil war and triumphed in two world wars surely had a chance to survive the errant philosophies that threatened it today.

Strachey had notified Ewan of his arrival from a pay phone at the airport. He was one of a handful of people who possessed the number. Reflecting on his first visit when he had been received at gunpoint, he smiled at the dissimilar welcome that awaited him now.

He'd considered bringing Amy with him and leaving her in the relative safety of Ramsay's Irish hideout, but the baby was too young to travel. Murphy was with Amy now, and a police cruiser was parked outside his house. He felt reasonably secure on that front.

An hour into the journey he was getting the hang of driving on the wrong side of the road, and he picked up the pace, slowing only when he hit the narrow, twisting by-ways of western Galway where four-lane roads were supplanted by narrow, winding country lanes. It was still early afternoon when his tires crunched to a stop in the gravel parking area in front of the stone house.

He stepped out of the car and stretched. The afternoon still held some warmth under a clear, azure sky, and he took a deep breath of sea air as he admired the island-dotted bay that provided a picture postcard backdrop for the house. The front door opened, and there were Sasha and Ewan coming out to greet him, their Scots terrier, Angus, at their heels. Even Ramsay was grinning, and Strachey wondered how the man who bore an uncanny resemblance to Clint Eastwood coped with the bucolic lifestyle of the small fishing village after such an eventful life. There would be no tales of derring do that he could relate safely to friends at the local pub.

As usual when at home, both Sasha and Ewan wore old jeans and light cotton pull-overs, and despite the plain garb Sasha would still have turned heads. Strachey guessed she must be nearly fifty, but her striking Slavic good looks remained intact, marred only by a hairline scar that began just above her left eye and ended high on her cheek. He'd learned that she'd lost that eye under desperate circumstances many years ago and replaced it with a prosthetic one. Although he had not wielded the knife, Vitaliy Mikhailovich Shurgin had been ultimately responsible for the disfigurement. Now the ex-Russian President wanted to finish the job.

Despite the cooling air Ramsay had laid out a late lunch on the flagstone veranda behind the house that provided an unobstructed view of the bay. Grilled prawns, a local sheep's milk cheese, a simple salad, and a loaf of white bread from Ramsay's own oven were washed down with a fine Galician Albariño, undoubtedly selected in Strachey's honor because of his well-known penchant for all things Spanish. He'd once been DCOS of the CIA's Madrid Station, an experience he'd never forget.

He regretted dampening the Ramsays' pleasure at having a rare visitor by recounting the reason for his trip. Sasha was not so much horrified to learn that she and her husband were the ultimate targets of the campaign of mayhem as at the multitude of violent deaths it had provoked.

Ewan Ramsay barked a bitter laugh.

"So," he said, "it's come full circle. We tried to destroy Shurgin for years and finally succeeded, and now it's his turn to try to destroy us."

He went to fetch a second bottle of wine while the other two waited in silence.

When Ramsay returned and had recharged their glasses, Strachey said, "I no longer have the resources to put an end to this thing. I'm just a civilian now. I hoped that maybe you still had access to certain capabilities."

Ramsay turned to his wife. His bearing had changed subtly, like a lycanthrope under a full moon, into something wolfish and feral. Strachey had seen the man like this before, had seen him kill.

Sasha's shoulders sagged under the weight of undeserved guilt and resignation. Strachey knew that this was the last thing she wanted. But she had no choice. Either they dealt with the problem or they would live the rest of their lives looking over their shoulders. And the senseless killing had to stop.

She stood and placed a hand lightly on Ramsay's shoulder. Strachey watched a single tear trace its way down her right cheek. "I'll make the call," she said and turned toward the house.

CHAPTER 31

Tel-Aviv, Israel

The white towers of the high-rise apartment buildings at Or Yehuda flashed past the wing tip as the El Al flight from London touched down at Ben Gurion International Airport. The last time Sasha and Ramsay had been in Tel-Aviv was five years earlier for Ramsay's formal retirement ceremony. It had been a highly secret affair. He was the only non-Israeli ever to have served in the Mossad, although he had always seen it more as collaboration than an employer-employee relationship.

Whether the service would give them what they wanted now was in the hands of the *memuneh*, as the Head of Mossad was known, and in that regard Ramsay had good reason to hope.

A driver waited for them in a silver Audi A6 outside the main terminal building, and twenty minutes later they turned off the busy Ayalon Highway into the northern suburbs and within minutes pulled up at the gate of a non-descript five-story building situated on a low hill. There was no plaque or sign advertising this as the headquarters of the Institute for Intelligence and Special Operations, the official name of the Mossad.

The complexity and effectiveness of the operations that were devised inside this building belied the plain façade. Despite its sprawling Langley campus with its two immaculate buildings and thousands of employees the CIA envied certain of the Mossad's capabilities. The Israeli service was still a relatively informal organization, run almost like a family business. Bureaucracy was kept to a minimum, as were practitioners of the legal profession. As a matter of fact, Ramsay couldn't recall ever meeting a Mossad lawyer. That was one way to insure that operations remained opaque.

Just inside the entrance they were surprised by the sight of the *memuneh* himself in shirtsleeves waiting for them with a huge grin on his broad, sunburned face. Eitan Ronan had succeeded to the Directorship five years earlier. Ramsay estimated his current age at somewhere around 75. Ronan's wrestler's body had grown wider and his head was encircled by a white fringe with a faint memory of once thick black hair. Despite his age, the man was still a force of nature.

The 'force of nature' descriptor fit Ronan well. Besides its usual connotation of "boss," the religious meaning of the word *memuneh* is an angel in charge of dreams whose purpose is to translate the will of God for Man. Ronan was the last person Ramsay would have suspected of having a direct line to the Creator. The tough Israeli would question too many of God's decisions for them to have anything but a stormy relationship.

In his day Eitan Ronan, former head of the *Kidon* squad, was the quintessential field man, so ruthlessly efficient that his actions had horrified Ramsay on their first mission together nearly 20 years earlier. But time and Sasha taught him to respect the burly Israeli.

The *memuneh* and Sasha had a history, one that bound her to him and therefore did the same for Ramsay, like it or not. Ronan had served as a substitute parent and mentor for her since she was 12. And if there was a single tender spot in Eitan Ronan's heart, it was for Sasha.

Ramsay and Ronan each in their own way vied for her affections, but in the end she brought them together, and Ramsay now had to put up with the *memuneh* as an ersatz and highly irascible father-in-law. His clandestine visits to see them in Ireland had grown scarce since he'd taken over The Office, and Ramsay was gratified to see the happiness now infuse his wife's face as Ronan engulfed her in his burly arms. The old man shot him a mischievous look of triumph over her shoulder.

A still smiling Sasha finally managed to disengage herself from Ronan's gorilla grasp, and Ramsay and he exchanged a handshake during which each tried to crush the other's hand.

"Come on, let's go inside and talk. It must be something big to bring you two all the way here from Ireland."

They rode a creaking elevator to the third floor and followed Ronan's broad, wrestler's back down a hallway to the office at the end. The old man still had a spring in his step. His assistant had laid out tea and cookies on the plain conference table that occupied one end of the room, and Ronan attacked the latter with crunching gusto as soon as they sat. Cookies were his weakness, especially the Belgian variety, and Sasha had not forgotten to pick up several tins at Heathrow.

She sat mutely as Ramsay told the *memuneh* why they were there. At the end of the recitation, Ronan exchanged the cookies for one of his favorite Gauloise cigarettes. Ramsay noted that the old man still smoked the stronger, unfiltered "Gauloise Brune," identical to the original first produced in 1910.

Ronan pushed away from the table and walked to his desk leaving a trail of pungent smoke that belied the tobacco's Turkish and Syrian origins. He punched an intercom button.

"Moshe," he said to his assistant, "bring me that film we were looking at the other day."

The "film" was actually a digital video recording. Moshe inserted the DVD into the player and switched on the flat screen TV before leaving them alone again.

"Watch," said Ronan as he settled back into his chair and chain lit another cigarette.

On the screen a dim black and white image flickered into life. Ramsay recognized the inside of an airplane hangar and the shape of a large jet taxiing to a stop beside a waiting sedan. A hefty man whose features were hard to make out other than a walrus moustache exited the plane and consulted briefly with the sedan's driver before gesturing back toward the plane. A second figure, also impossible to recognize in the hangar's gloom came out and got into the car, after which they drove away.

It was evident that they were watching clandestine surveillance footage from a concealed camera. Ramsay cocked an eyebrow at Ronan, but the *memuneh* only said, "Keep watching. There's more."

The second segment was shot outdoors from an obviously moving platform. This time the video was in color, and in the bright sunlight the image was better defined. The camera travelled along a residential street lined with Spanish style houses and lush foliage. Half-way down the block a black Mercedes that Ramsay assumed was the same sedan they had seen in the hangar, turned and slowed to a stop at the gated entrance of one of the houses. The camera swiftly closed the distance and captured a clear image of the side of the car. The profile of the man sitting in the right rear could be made out behind the glass. The Mossad technicians had worked with this image, and the next thing that flashed on the screen was an enhanced still of the man in profile.

Beside him Ramsay heard Sasha's quick intake of breath.

"Is that Shurgin?" she asked.

"We think so," said Ronan.

"Where was that taken?"

"Paraguay, the airport in Asunción, several months ago."

"Is he still there?"

"Off and on. He comes to Asunción for occasional meetings, but he's been spotted in São Paulo living under an assumed name. And he's changed his appearance since this video was made."

Ronan pushed a button, and a photo of a trim man with shaggy black hair appeared on the screen.

"This is what he looks like now. Brazil is practically the world capital for cosmetic surgery."

Ramsay studied the picture.

"I didn't realize the Mossad was after Shurgin."

Ronan shook his head. "We're not."

"Then what's this all about?"

Ramsay waved a hand at the television screen that still held the image of the remodeled Shurgin.

The *memuneh* revealed large, square teeth in a shark-like smile that had been known to jelly the spines of enemies. Early in their relationship Ramsay had commented to Sasha that Ronan was intimidating even when he intended to look friendly. She'd responded that the big Israeli knew how to smile in only one way, and the recipient would just have to figure out where they stood with him.

"Learning Shurgin's whereabouts was the by-product of another operation. Does the name Rus Ismayilov ring a bell with you?"

Ramsay's reply was instantaneous.

"He's an arms dealer and drug smuggler, a big one. Law enforcement has tried to pin something on him for years, but he's slippery. What's he doing in Asunción with Shurgin?" He thought about the background investigation carried out on the orders of Ismayilov's front company.

Ronan sighed. "That's a very long story. Are you up to it?"

"We came a long way to see you, Eitan."

"You probably already know a lot of this, but it bears repeating. You know that the Soviets supported the Ayatollah Khomeini from the beginning, and Iran and Russia remain close allies to this day, thanks in no small part to Shurgin. It's a marriage arranged in hell, and the Russians aren't about to ask for a divorce so long as they see Iran keeping the U.S. off-balance.

"But Soviet Communist support for international terrorism began much earlier. They backed terrorist organizations in Western Europe, Northern Ireland, and elsewhere. In our own neighborhood, while Andropov was still the KGB Chief, he authorized arms deliveries to the PFLP. Its deputy chief, Wadi Haddad, was, in fact, a KGB agent. Yasser Arafat, may his worm-infested soul rot in hell, received his share of Soviet largesse, as well.

"To make a long story short, the Russians continue to do everything they can to keep the Middle East boiling. Their support for radical Islamists (except in their own territory, of course) is only the latest example of their meddling. It benefits the Russian energy sector and advances their global political objectives to keep the Americans off-balance and the Europeans frightened that they might lose their energy supplies. More importantly to me, everything they do threatens the existence of Israel."

None of this was news to Ramsay.

"And Rus Ismayilov?"

"Ah, Rustum Ismayilov. He's Azeri, you know, speaks Farsi like a native, as well as several other languages, a gifted polyglot. Former KGB, under Air Force cover as a major. When things began falling apart in the old Soviet Union, he saw an opportunity and took it ... evidently with Shurgin's financial assistance. When you stole Shurgin's financial records and almost put him out of business twenty years ago we got a lot more than money out of them."

Ronan referred to Ramsay's maiden operation with the Mossad.

"We also got a list of front companies and traced their connections. That's how we discovered that Shurgin owns Ismayilov's company, Rusavia."

"And he uses Rusavia to deliver arms to clients all over the world," interjected Sasha.

"Correct, and Ismayilov is very close to the Iranians, especially VEVAK. He deals almost exclusively in weapons he finds in former Soviet Bloc countries like Bulgaria and Moldova, but over the years he's acquired other suppliers, as well. He specializes in breaking arms embargoes and has sold weapons to some of the worst criminal regimes in Africa, and more recently he's made deliveries to the Taliban in Afghanistan. The Iranians use him to supply Hezbollah and Hamas. The Americans may even have used him on occasion."

"OK," said Ramsay, "so we've established his connection with Shurgin, but what are they doing in Paraguay?"

"More history," said Ronan. "It's becoming more difficult even for terrorists to set up bases in areas where terrorism flourishes, so they found someplace relatively quiet but sufficiently lawless and secluded to do their business – the so-called Triple Border in South America. We've had a special interest in penetrating terrorist operations in the region since 1992 when Hezbollah bombed our Embassy in Buenos Aires. Two years later they bombed the Jewish Center there. In all 114 people died.

"Ismayilov maintains a small operational base

and a house in Asunción, and we mounted a long term mission to find out what he's up to. The video you just saw is one of the fruits of that mission. We believe that Ismayilov is at the center of the supply and training network the Islamists have established in Ciudad del Este on the border with Brazil."

"I'm sure you didn't collect all of this information just for the archives," said Ramsay. "What are you planning?"

"We're going to take him down and hopefully his network with him. And we're preparing something for the nest of Hezbollah vipers he's keeping company with in South America," the big man rumbled.

"When?"

"We've had a setback. He has a base in the Emirates, and we were preparing for a mission there to snatch him, but the Prime Minister called it off because of recent events."

Ronan was being uncharacteristically delicate in his reference to the United Arab Emirates where a Mossad team had successfully assassinated Mahmound al-Mabouh, an influential Hamas official, in Dubai. The ensuing publicity, replete with videos of the Mossad team compiled by an unexpectedly capable Emirate security service, had been a major embarrassment for the Israeli government.

"So," said Ramsay, "you want to kidnap him. Then what?"

"Just taking him out of circulation will disrupt his organization and deprive Hezbollah of access to weapons, at least for a while. And with enough softening up, he could be a prolific source of information on the Iranians."

"Where else does he have bases besides the Emirates and South America?"

"Belgium and Spain."

"Can you track his movements?"

"Most of the time. He's filed a flight plan that includes an overnight layover in Madrid for next week."

"Then there might be a way. We have a good friend with contacts in Spain. But you'll have to trust me, and Shurgin needs to go down, too."

"What happened in Brussels and Washington has nothing to do with Israel. This is personal with you, and that could be a problem."

Ramsay looked him in the eye. "It should be personal for you, too, Ronan. Shurgin wants to kill Sasha."

CHAPTER 32

Madrid, Spain

Strachey set up bachelor quarters at his club, the *Gran Peña*, at No. 2, Gran Vía, one of Madrid's more picturesque thoroughfares, just west of the Plaza de Cibéles. The club had been established in the 19th century for the *grandees* of Spain and their sons. In the tradition of London's famous Pall Mall establishments it featured richly paneled reception halls, a billiard room, a library, gaming rooms, two bars (one for guests and one for members), and a large dining room. There were eight guest rooms on the third floor. On the wall of the cavernous reception hall above a curving double staircase that put Tara to shame was an ornate marble plaque listing the names of club members who had died in the Spanish Civil War -- fighting for the *Franquista* side, of course.

Strachey's room was typical – smallish with a single window, narrow bed, chair, writing desk, and a tiny TV attached to the wall with a bracket. The spare furnishings and the crucifix appended to the wall above the headboard lent the room a monkish air, but rumor had it that in the 19th and early 20th centuries the rooms had not been for lodgers, but rather for secret trysts with paramours and prostitutes who were escorted up the back stairs by the faithful and ever discreet staff.

He might have checked into one of the city's luxury hotels, but the tradition-soaked atmosphere of the club charmed him. Spain was a colorful tapestry composed of many threads, reflecting a culture inherited from the ancient Iberos through a succession of occupations by the Romans, followed by the Visigoths, the Moors, and on through the *Reconquista* to today's bustling, modern democracy.

Only three years earlier Strachey had found surcease here from a painful divorce, and more importantly, he found friends who introduced him to their country and its well-developed culture. He could almost physically sense his body re-absorbing the atmosphere and not for the first time toyed with the idea of establishing permanent residence here. Amy's work at the CIA was an impediment for the time being, and he would never ask her to abandon it, but retirement at some future date to a *finca* somewhere near Toledo was a definite goal.

He'd returned to the club after a late breakfast of strong coffee and a slice of Spanish *tortilla* and was chatting with Rodrigo, a tall, mournful-faced porter with a droopy black moustache, when his Blackberry vibrated in his pocket.

The screen told him the caller was Ewan Ramsay. He excused himself and walked through the reception hall toward the marble stairs as he answered.

"Where are you?"

"Here, in Madrid. My flight just landed. When can we meet?"

He gave Ramsay directions and returned to the entrance where he forewarned Rodrigo that he was expecting a visitor.

Forty-five minutes later he and Ramsay found seats in a corner of one of the large ground floor reception rooms, redolent with the aroma of furniture polish, and otherwise deserted.

Ramsay had been annoyed when Strachey informed him that club rules required a coat and tie, but he was quite presentable in a blue blazer and Hermés neckwear when he appeared. Strachey thought he looked more tanned than usual and suspected he had not acquired the tint in Ireland. The only witness to their conversation was a marble bust of King Alfonso XIII on the antique sideboard behind Strachey. In the center of the hall a large bronze figure of Generalissimo Francisco Franco mounted on a rearing stallion, sword raised in triumph, stood guard.

Ramsay gave a low whistle of appreciation as he took in their surroundings. "This place could be a museum."

"You can almost hear the sound of horse's hooves on the cobblestones outside, can't you? Unfortunately, a lot of the members can probably actually remember the horses. If they don't start attracting some younger people this place will end up being sold to the highest bidder. It would be a shame, but it's prime real-estate."

Ramsay produced a short cigar that Strachey recognized as a Monte Cristo No.4 from his inside pocket and held it up. "May I?"

Strachey swept his arm at the empty hall in a magnanimous gesture.

"This is God's country where a man can still do

as he pleases."

"Except not wear a coat and tie."

"Correct, but there are compensations."

Ramsay took his time lighting the cigar, first clipping the shoulders and holding its tip over the flame from a battered silver S.T. DuPont lighter until it glowed red and then taking a delicate first puff, like a *sommelier* testing a fine wine.

The ritual complete, he leaned back in the leather chair and said, "From your messages I take it you've had some success with your Spanish friends?"

"I thought about asking for some unofficial help from my police buddies, but decided against it. They might have been sympathetic, but they would have been hard pressed to agree to abet a Mossad kidnapping on Spanish soil."

Ramsay sank back into the soft leather of the chair, his face partially masked by the aromatic blue smoke of the Montecristo as he waited for Strachey to continue.

"But I have a way to get us into the airport. One of my old friends is the president of an air cargo carrier. He has an office out at Barajas Airport, and that gives him free run of the place."

"Do you trust him?"

"With my life." Strachey's reply was immediate and heartfelt. "What about your end?"

To tell the truth, he was more than a little irritated by the absence of regular communications from Ramsay.

"Some things are best transmitted by word of mouth, and this is one of them."

Strachey listened for the next thirty minutes as Ramsay outlined the Mossad's plans.

"... as you see," he concluded, "this is a major operation, the most important of its kind since Entebbe. With luck, it will lead us to Shurgin."

Strachey whistled softly.

"We'll get Ismayilov when he shows up. I'm surprised that the Mossad has his flight plan."

"So was I, but they've been watching him for years, and this time he's carrying an especially deadly cargo that he cannot be allowed to deliver. Eitan Ronan is a man not to be underestimated."

Strachey recalled that the fabled Mossad chief had excited both admiration and chagrin at Langley.

Ramsay had reserved a seat on an evening flight to Paris where he would connect with an El Al flight back to Tel-Aviv. This permitted enough time for the two to share a Spanish lunch at one of Strachey's hang-outs, *La Máquina*, a restaurant that specialized in Asturian cuisine, not far from the Plaza de Cuzco several blocks north of the *Gran Peña* just off of the Paseo de la Castellana.

Over coffee, Ramsay asked, "What do you hear from Amy?"

"I talk to her every day. Krystal Murphy is still with her at the house. A cop car will be stationed outside as long as Krystal is there."

"Maybe you should have brought Amy to Ireland."

"The baby's still too young to travel, and Amy would never go so far away from the pediatrician anyway, at least not now."

"I understand. How is she holding up?"

"OK, I think. Having Krystal there helps."

"Murphy's tough."

"Damn straight. She's the only victim to escape from that motherfucking Iranian."

"Speaking of whom, what's the latest? Any leads?"

"Given her condition, Murphy's no longer in charge of the task force, but she stays in touch with her FBI friend ..."

"Hatchet-face Whitehall?"

"That's the one. The CIWG is still on the case, but there've been no new developments since Krystal escaped."

"What's your opinion of Whitehall?"

"I think he's smarter than the average bear. Murphy said he connected the serial killings to the Brussels bombing from the get-go. So, he's no slouch in the brains department. I wonder how much he figured out about the Andropov Memo last year. There were a lot clues left lying about. It was impossible to conceal Sasha's involvement, and Krystal's former partner, Cogburn, described both of you pretty accurately."

"Cogburn was too scared to remember details."

"They at the least know Sasha wasn't working alone. They never figured out who killed those three Russians out in Fairfax County, but the cluster of events concerning the Russians made it fairly certain they were connected. Still, it's all anonymous. None of it can be connected to you by name."

"Do you think Vicky ever told them anything

about what really happened in Europe after she was abducted?"

"According to Krystal, Vicky stuck with the story you concocted with Lawrence and Nancy Nelson that omitted your part in her rescue. I couldn't probe too much because even Krystal doesn't know everything. She put two and two together fast enough when the Iranian mentioned your name and described Sasha, though, and she figured out that I knew who 'the blond Russian woman' was."

"Will you return to Virginia when we have Ismayilov in hand?"

"I'd love to see it through to the end with you, but that Iranian nut case is still on the loose somewhere. Until he's captured my place is with my family."

Ramsay nodded his approval. "Right you are."

They separated outside the restaurant where Ramsay boarded a taxi for the airport. It was nearing five P.M. and there was plenty of daylight left, so Strachey decided to walk the long blocks back to Gran Vía along the teeming Paseo de la Castellana. He needed time to think.

There still had been no sign of the serial killer.

CHAPTER 33

Charlotte, North Carolina is known as the "Queen City," named as it was for Charlotte of Mecklenburg-Strelitz, the wife of King George III. Once fading into genteel obscurity, these days the rejuvenated city is actually more like a southern belle, ambitious, beguiling, and attractive.

Thomas Jefferson Dawson had driven a bus the length and breadth of the city for the better part of thirty-five years and was proud of it. His father had been a sharecropper with eight children, and his grandfather had been one step away from slavery. The move from sharecropper to bus driver had been a gigantic step up in the world, and it had set him apart from his brothers and sisters who became jealous of his success and took to calling him "uppity."

But Thomas was determined to get on in the world. He married late in life, when he felt he could afford a family, to a slender, light-skinned girl with green eyes who had the wit to recognize him as a man of certain values. Although Thomas was eternally disgusted by the aimlessness of modern youth, the pride of his life was his daughter, Amy.

His wife passed away when the child was only five, and Thomas devoted his life to ensuring that his daughter had a future. He was both surprised and delighted when the school sent her home with a note that informed him she was "gifted" and eligible to take advanced courses. She'd continued on this trajectory with full-boat scholarships, first to the University of North Carolina and then to M.I.T. where she earned her Master's in Mathematics and Computing Science.

He'd been surprised and somewhat disappointed when she accepted an invitation to join the Central Intelligence Agency, an institution he viewed with distrust. But he'd raised her to be independent, and if that was where she wanted to be he would not object.

She'd surprised him again when she married a white man and moreover a white man whose name he recognized. A diehard Tarheel fan, Thomas recalled Robert Strachey's days as a football star and shook his head in bemusement at the strange ways of fate.

The wedding had been a small affair at Amy's insistence, and Thomas knew her reason was that her father was the only member of her family that would attend, and she didn't want to embarrass him. So the marriage had taken place in the small church in Charlotte in which Amy had been raised, and the numerous Strachey family had not displayed even the smallest discomfort as they welcomed a black girl to carry their name.

The times, Thomas reflected, had changed.

He'd been present at the birth of his grandson, Robert Thomas Strachey, and when he learned that his son-in-law had unaccountably left the country, he paid the full fare of $147.00 and rode the first available Greyhound bus to Washington, D.C. He took a taxi to the Strachey house in McLean, where he was surprised and alarmed to see a police car stationed in front.

A uniformed officer confronted him demanding to know his business.

Thomas carefully placed his suitcase on the sidewalk and said, "This is my daughter's house. Has something happened?"

The cop looked him up and down, and Thomas knew what he was thinking. *What is an old black man doing in this fine neighborhood?*

"May I see some identification, please?" asked the cop.

"What is this, Russia? Why do I have to show any documents to see my daughter?"

Thomas was getting his back up, and his anxiety was growing by the second.

The situation might have deteriorated further had Amy not come out of the house and joined them on the sidewalk.

"It's alright, officer. This is my father."

"I'm afraid I still have to see some identification, ma'am. Orders."

"Daddy, show him your driver's license, please. It's alright. I'll explain later."

Still grumbling Thomas displayed his license, which the officer examined carefully before returning it and waving him past.

On the way to the door, Thomas asked, "Amy, what in the world was that all about?"

When Amy ushered him inside he was startled again when they were met by a young red-haired woman in blue jeans with her arm in a sling, a badly bruised face, a swatch of hair missing from the side of her head, and a gun in a holster at her hip.

Amy introduced her as Krystal Murphy, a friend and also a police officer.

"Take a seat, Daddy, and I'll get you a glass of sweet tea from the kitchen."

A half-hour later the three sat together around the kitchen table. The story they told him didn't make a lot of sense, but the situation obviously was serious. His old reservations about Amy's involvement with the CIA returned.

"And Bob left you alone with all this going on?"

"I'm not exactly alone, Daddy."

"There's no man in the house. There should be a man in the house. Bob had no business gallivanting off and leaving you like this."

The young woman with the gun started to say something, but apparently thought better of it and clamped her jaw tight.

Amy and Krystal Murphy exchanged a look, one of those women's only looks he recognized as signifying that 'the old guy just doesn't get it.'

"Daddy, we are perfectly safe. There is a policeman on duty outside twenty-four hours a day, and Krystal is more than capable of handling any situation."

With a disbelieving look at Krystal, Thomas said, "Looks like she didn't handle the last one too well. You need a man here, and here I'm staying until Bob gets back. Then I'll give him a piece of my mind."

CHAPTER 34

The first break in the case of the "Arlington Ripper," as the media predictably dubbed the killer came about as the result of the new sketch that incorporated truck driver Donny Strickler's recollections of his confrontation. He'd gotten a good look at the man in the glare of his truck's headlights, and he had a good memory.

Two days after it appeared, a desk clerk at the Rosslyn Marriott hotel reported that a man answering the description had been a guest. A check of the hotel register showed that the man had identified himself as Mario Rodriguez of Los Angeles, California. He'd checked in several days before Vicky Kondratieva's murder and out the same day the first sketch, based on the Westin bartender's description, appeared in the papers. He'd made no reservations, and he paid in cash.

Until he was taken into custody there was no way of knowing whether Rodriguez and the murderer were one in the same person, but Enoch Whitehall was convinced he was on the trail of something bigger than the serial killings. The gruesome death of Vicky Kondratieva and the Brussels bombing were separated by geography and method, but the linkage was there if one knew where to look. Counterintelligence officers, if they are good, are intuitive, and Whitehall was exceedingly good at his craft. He'd raised a few eyebrows at the Hoover Building when he inserted himself into the investigation of a domestic crime, but the Director allowed him the latitude.

The findings of the ethnic DNA test were intriguing, and they established a second link to the Brussels bombing for which the authorities blamed Hezbollah.   The other killings in Los Angeles and Arlington were puzzling anomalies that blurred the picture like grease smeared across a lens.   But perhaps that was another clue.   It would not be the first time a criminal laid a smokescreen to confuse investigators.   The attempt on Krystal Murphy confirmed the killer's true targeting criteria.

Whitehall had caught a scent, faint at first but growing stronger, of something he had long anticipated – Iranian espionage agents operating in the United States under non-official cover.   But the apparent connection between the murders and the so-called "Andropov Memorandum" was confusing.   Why would the Iranians be interested in slaughtering these people?   Even more confusing, how would murdering all these women benefit the Mullahs in Tehran?   Was this the beginning of a new kind of terrorism?   He didn't think so.   The grotesque nature of the post-mortem mutilations bespoke a personal rage, a psychosis that was inconsistent with state-sponsored terrorism.

The doubters, the politicians, would seize on the anomalies to avoid repercussions from the revelation that an Iranian intelligence operative was killing women on both coasts. They would want to avoid the public opprobrium that could force a serious confrontation with the Mullahs.   Whitehall was a

Washington veteran. He knew how things worked in a capital more concerned with politics and posturing than the truth. Managing public opinion was not Whitehall's concern. His job was to catch spies. How the politicians chose to handle the consequences was their business.

The Los Angeles killings were a priority for the LAPD, and the day after the Rosslyn Marriott lead Whitehall received a call from the SAIC in Los Angeles.

"Director Whitehall." The SAIC's voice was deferential.

"What have you found out?"

"We searched the apartment. It's a modest place in a lower middle-class neighborhood, and it was Spartan clean. Nothing that would tell us anything about the occupant. Anyone could be living there. Except for one thing." The SAIC paused for effect.

"I don't appreciate artificial drama," Whitehall snapped. "Get to the point."

"We found a Quran concealed in the false bottom of a dresser drawer. It was printed in Farsi."

Whitehall drew a deep breath. "Anything else?"

"Rodriguez has lived here for about a year. Neighbors describe him as a good-looking Latino, but very quiet. Keeps to himself. Pays his bills on time. Nobody knows where he works, but he's absent for long periods. There's no trace of him before he rented the apartment."

"Have you uncovered any new trails?"

"Unfortunately, no. Rodriguez has a few hundred dollars in a checking account with a debit card, but he pays for almost everything in cash and he personally made all the deposits to the account in cash. The California driver's license he used as i.d. at the Rosslyn Marriott was a fake."

"He had to get the money somewhere."

"Yes, sir."

"You recovered DNA from the apartment?"

"It's at the LAPD lab now, and a sample is on its way to Quantico."

"Good work. Stay close with the LAPD and report any new discoveries."

"Will do."

Whitehall cradled the phone and leaned back in his chair, steepling his long, bony fingers under his chin and closing his eyes. He did not doubt that the DNA from the apartment would match that from the L.A. and Arlington crime scenes.

He wished Krystal Murphy were still on the case. He'd warned her that she, too, might possibly be a target, but either he'd been too subtle or she had rejected the idea. He wished he'd been more forceful. She'd very nearly lost her life and would be on medical furlough for another week at least. Murphy was a tenacious, stubborn investigator with real potential, but she'd not yet learned to think outside the box. A few months at Quantico and an apprenticeship under him and she would make a first rate FBI agent. He would pitch her again when the time was right.

Whitehall had quietly confirmed that the Arlington Police had assigned a security detail to Krystal. He feared that she still could be in the killer's crosshairs.

CHAPTER 35

Ghasem Esfahani now had a thick, dark beard, and he'd let his hair grow over his shirt collar. A half-hour at a Wal-Mart yielded a new wardrobe of jeans, work boots, T-shirt and a jean jacket. Sunglasses and a Pittsburgh Steelers cap completed the transformation from suave West Coast Latin lover to West Virginia normal.

Following the fiasco in Maryland he'd moved, again marveling at how easily one could lose oneself in this country. He ditched the rental car near Fredericksburg and stole a 10-year-old Ford pick-up that fit with the persona he intended to create. The Rodriguez identity he'd used to rent the car would have to be discarded.

After consulting the local papers and searching Google Earth, he found an isolated mobile home park several miles west of Martinsburg, West Virginia, where the proprietor was only too happy to accept cash payment in advance to rent a small, furnished mobile home. He was still within easy driving distance of Washington, DC, but in this rugged countryside, he might as well be on a different planet. The people here did not have internal tuning forks that vibrated to the rhythm of Washington's news *du jour*, and they weren't overly curious about people who kept to themselves.

The trailer had cable television, but no internet connection, and Ghasem searched out an internet café in Martinsburg that served his purpose. He'd not yet reported recent events to Tehran. VEVAK would want to pull him out, but he needed a victory before he could let that happen. If the murders he'd committed in Los Angeles were connected to him he was not certain he could explain to the mullahs. Success in his current assignment was vital if he wanted a future. Besides, it was personal now. He had been humiliated and frustrated, and he would even the score.

He had the female police officer's gun, a nice Beretta nine-millimeter with a full 15-round magazine, and he found that he could purchase extra ammunition without showing an ID at the same Wal-Mart where he'd bought his new clothes.

He needed more cash. His funding mechanism was simple and undetectable. It depended on a front company set up in Delaware. The company had a bank account into which funds were transferred from off-shore. Ghasem had a company debit card in an untraceable alias that he could use to withdraw funds from ATM's anywhere. So long as he was not connected with the card and kept withdrawals small, the method was foolproof.

He'd been forced to use the California debit card to rent the car in Washington, and it must already have been discovered. The media was reporting that the authorities had traced the identity of the "Arlington Ripper," and he had no doubt they had traced the Rodriguez alias. He destroyed the counterfeit driver's license, Social Security card and California debit card in that name and switched to his alternate set of documents.

He would have to leave the country which meant the job would have to be completed quickly before Tehran became too impatient. The mullahs would not be content with anything but complete success.

He drove east and then south on Interstate 270 and onto the Capital Beltway to cross over the Potomac into Virginia via the American Legion Bridge. His destination was the Strachey residence in McLean, the address of which had been supplied by Tehran. The plan was simple – take the man's wife hostage and await his return from work. He didn't doubt the American would break when his knife began to split his wife's skin.

Ghasem was prepared to put his plan into action immediately if the situation were propitious. He turned off Chain Bridge Road into a narrow, asphalted street lined with houses and mature oaks. The Strachey house should be several hundred yards ahead around a 90-degree turn in Meadowbrook Avenue. It was mid-afternoon, and activity was at a minimum. Ghasem reached his hand into the space between the driver's seat and the truck's center console to grasp the Beretta's butt. The solid feel of the weapon increased his confidence.

He turned the corner. The Strachey house should be at the end of the block at the cross street. Google Earth had shown it to be a one-story ranch on the corner to the left. So far, so good. The area was clear. Not a person was in sight. He slowed as he rounded the corner focusing all his attention on the house. At this time of day Strachey's wife would be inside attending to her chores -- an easy target.

To his chagrin a marked police car with a single occupant was parked in front. Ghasem turned into a side street and drove around the block before drawing to the curb when he had the police car in sight again. It was best to park and watch for a while than to circle the area several times and risk attracting attention. He waited for a half-hour before leaving. He would return tomorrow despite the risk. He would be ready if the cop car were still there.

Time was his enemy now.

CHAPTER 36

Madrid, Spain

Rus Ismayilov turned the yoke to swing the heavy Ilyushin-76TD in a wide circle to establish a glide path onto Runway 33R at Barajas International Airport. The Soviet-era behemoth carried a crew of four besides himself – co-pilot, navigator, flight engineer, and cargo master. He lined up on the runway five miles out, the complex of new highways and bypasses that surrounded Madrid spread out to his south. The weather was clear with only a slight crosswind, and he adjusted his flaps and air brakes as the engineer let down the landing gear sending a rumbling shudder through the aircraft as it lumbered out of the sky on final approach.

They had gained an hour with the time zone change after leaving Minsk three hours ago. On board was a very special cargo consisting of an R-17 "Elbrus" ballistic missile, designated the Scud-B by NATO, complete with its massive MAZ-543 "Uragan" launch vehicle. The missile and vehicle together with a combined weight of over twenty-five tons did not challenge the maximum load capacity of the massive Ilyushin workhorse, but it did occupy most of the cargo space. The weapon was destined for delivery to one of the Hezbollah launch sites deep in the Bekaa Valley of Lebanon. With a 300 kilometer range the missile could deliver its heavy payload all the way to Tel-Aviv.

The plane would spend the night in the restricted transit zone where it would suffer no Customs inspection. After a night's rest they would refuel and be back in the air in the morning on their way to Damascus where the cargo would be off-loaded for overland shipment to Lebanon. The crew were all Russian, former Soviet Air Force personnel and thoroughly professional. The cargo master would remain on guard with the aircraft through the night.

As was his custom, Ismayilov would use his alias Argentine passport to enter the Spanish capital. He could mimic the soft Patagonian accent to perfection and had been through Barajas enough times to be recognized by the passport control officer and waived through after a perfunctory examination of the counterfeit document.

Ismayilov was glad of the extra hour the time zone change gave them which made it possible to get into town in a courtesy van and check himself and the crew into a hotel in time for his appointment that night with a man who specialized in supplying explosives to the Basque separatist movement ETA to whom he would explain the finer points of pricing for Semtex.

The airport courtesy van dropped them at the Hotel Wellington, an elegant establishment on Calle de Velazquez not far from Retiro Park and the Prado Museum. The driver helped his passengers carry their light luggage through the revolving doors to the reception desk. Ismayilov handed him a twenty euro note and instructed him to pick them up the following morning.

*****

Strachey had set up a command center in Nico Villagas' office at the airport. A colorful figure and a bit of a wild man, Villagas ran a successful cargo airline company. He had been one of Strachey's best friends for several years. As a young Air Force fighter pilot stationed in Seville, he had fallen in love with a beautiful, raven haired gypsy girl and married her, a match that produced two daughters of incredible beauty and a son who was winning recognition as an artist. Strachey could never think of Spain without the memories of week-ends at the Villagas country house where the wine flowed freely and Nico's daughters danced to the *Sevillanas* sung by their mother. Nico's well-known penchant for adventure had guaranteed his immediate acceptance of Strachey's proposal, a proposal that would have given most men pause.

Besides Strachey and Villagas the office was occupied by a three-man Israeli Air Force crew that had arrived the day before. Each had flown into Madrid on a separate flight from a separate origin as tourists. Villagas provided passes for them to enter the protected free zone where his company had its offices. The Israelis were sprawled in chairs dozing as Strachey and the blond Spaniard stood at the window studying Ismayilov's Ilyushin parked in the transit zone below.

"Could you fly that monster by yourself if you had to, Nico?" he asked. Strachey had briefly considered the idea of he and the Spaniard taking the plane themselves. Had Ismayilov been flying his G-5 there would have been no question.

Villagas scrutinized the Ilyushin for a moment. "I could fly it alright. Any really good pilot can fly any airplane. It would be entirely illegal, of course, to lift off in that thing without a crew." He pointed out the window. "It's a complicated aircraft with lots of moving parts. The flight deck looks like the space shuttle. Normally, besides the pilot and co-pilot, the crew includes a flight engineer, a navigator, and a radio operator."

Strachey scanned the inert forms of the three Israelis and hoped they knew what they were doing.

*****

At six the following morning the courtesy van appeared at the gates of the transit zone with the returning Russian flight crew.

The day before in an out of the way café Strachey had met with Eitan Ronan's Madrid station chief to accept delivery of a package, and each man waiting in Villagas's office was now armed with a Heckler & Koch USB Compact pistol in a leather shoulder holster, along with two spare 13-round magazines. Strachey noted that the serial numbers had been filed off the German weapons. He removed the magazine and checked the mechanism one last time before replacing it and racking a round into the chamber.

He had never imagined himself as a hijacker

and wondered what Amy would say if she knew what he was up to at that moment. But he could not deny that after so long an absence from the CIA, it felt good to move into action again.

The van deposited Ismayilov and the other crew members outside the gate. Inside the duty free zone, the Israelis boarded an airport van. All wore one-piece jumpsuits supplied by Nico, emblazoned with his company logo. The Israelis would intercept the Russians as they crossed the tarmac and force them into the van at gunpoint.

In the meantime, Strachey and Nico approached the Ilyushin on foot. It was noisy on the tarmac, even at this early hour, and the smell of jet fuel and charred rubber permeated the air. Aircraft tractors zoomed across the expanse on the way to ferry planes to and from the runways. Men in hard hats were at work around the area. No one paid attention to them as they crossed to the giant Ilyushin.

A hatch on the right side of the fuselage was open with a ladder providing access. This was a piece of luck because it blocked the view from the Administration building.

Strachey waved Nico to wait while he climbed up and cautiously stuck his head inside. He caught the faint aroma of brewing coffee and heard the clatter of china from the rear of the hold. The cargo, shrouded in a tarpaulin blocked his view. He stepped through the hatch and made his way as quietly as possible through the narrow space between the cargo and the fuselage toward the sounds. The smell of fresh coffee became stronger, and he guessed someone was preparing for the return of his comrades.

Upon reaching the end of the cargo area he risked a peak around the edge and saw a well-equipped galley with a man in a flight suit placing heavy, steaming mugs on a tray. Strachey stepped into the open.

His Russian was rusty, but he gave it a try. "Good morning."

The man turned quickly at the sound of an unfamiliar voice, reaching for a pistol in a holster on his belt.

Strachey pointed the H&K at his chest. They were about ten feet apart. "Just raise your hands, please."

The man complied, a baffled expression on his face. "What is this?"

"This, my friend, is a hijacking. Please turn around and keep your hands in the air or I will shoot you where you stand."

The man complied, and Strachey disarmed him and secured his arms behind his back with handcuffs provided by Eitan Ronan. He called for Nico to come aboard, and a moment later the Spaniard's blond head appeared around the edge of the cargo.

"I've got it under control here, Nico. Better head for the flight deck and wait for me there."

The Spaniard smiled broadly and gave Strachey a jaunty thumbs-up before disappearing toward the front of the aircraft. Turning back to his captive, Strachey struck him on the temple with the pistol and left him unconscious on the floor while he headed back for the front hatch to wait for the van, which soon appeared around the Ilyushin's nose.

One of the Israelis leapt from behind the wheel, ran around to slide open the side panel to reveal the other two standing over four men who were hunkered on their knees, hands cuffed behind their backs, their heads encased in black hoods. The four were ordered out of the van and shoved roughly up the ladder one by one. It was difficult for them to climb with their arms bound, and they had to be steadied from behind. The last to board was sloppily overweight. Strachey pulled the hood from his head and recognized Rus Ismayilov's shaggy head and walrus moustache.

The last to board was the Israeli pilot. "We have to move fast," he said.

Strachey turned back to the group now crowded inside the hatch at the foot of the stairs up to the flight deck. "Let's get them all to the rear of the plane and secure them. They have a long day ahead, and I don't want them getting loose."

Ismayilov's face was beet red. "What's the meaning of this? Who are you?"

Strachey took a good look at this man who was allegedly Vitaliy Shurgin's trusted agent. Ismayilov was surely no older than he, but his face and body were bloated from years of overindulgence in food and drink. He would no doubt experience a radical change in Israeli hands.

"You can be certain we're not your friends, Mr. Ismayilov. Now get back to the galley."

Ismayilov gasped when he saw his crewman sprawled on the deck.

"Don't worry about him," said Strachey in

Russian. "He'll recover. But I won't guarantee the same for anyone who causes a problem. Here is what is going to happen. My colleagues are going to immobilize you, and you will remain nice and quiet throughout the flight. If you try to escape or cause any other problem whatsoever, you will be shot."

"Who are you?"

Ismayilov was still indignant, his face red.

"You'll know soon enough. For the moment it's enough that I know who you."

One of the Israelis began methodically trussing the hooded prisoners and securing them to O-rings attached to the deck that were normally used to tie down cargo. Strachey replaced the hood over Ismayilov's head and shoved him in the direction of the Israeli to be secured.

Strachey headed back to the hatch where Nico Villagas waited in the van on the tarmac. The entire operation had consumed less than ten minutes. Strachey scrambled down the ladder to join Villagas and return to the office where they watched as the Israeli pilot, now wearing a Russian flight suite, completed his external pre-flight check of the Ilyushin and finally boarded and closed the hatch.

A half-hour later the Ilyushin trundled down the runway and was airborne carving a wide, ascending arc through the brightening morning sky as it turned to the east. They watched until it was a tiny speck and finally disappeared from view.

Villagas broke out a bottle of Spanish brandy and poured them each a generous helping. Grinning broadly, he lifted his glass.

"I know it's early, but that's the most fun I've had in a long time. When can we do it again?"

CHAPTER 37

Just a little over an hour later the Ilyushin ascended to altitude as it crossed the coast of Spain north of Valencia on a course that would take it over Palma de Majorca, now just visible on the horizon, and the southern tip of Malta following the seven-hour flight plan to Damascus Ismayilov had filed. The Israeli pilot took the plane to its 42,000 foot cruising altitude as Spanish Air Traffic Control bade them farewell and handed them off to the Maltese controllers.

The crew settled back for the long flight, one of them remaining in the tail with the four Russian prisoners who remained silent beneath their hoods, still unaware of their final destination.

Five hours later they passed through airspace controlled by the air control center in Lefkosa, Greek Cyprus, and finally were handed off to Damascus control.

After ten minutes the pilot raised Damascus on the radio to report he was experiencing difficulties with the Ilyushin's oxygen system and requested permission to descend below 18,000 feet and switch to visual flight rules. Permission was granted immediately, and the pilot brought the aircraft down to below 10,000 feet.

Fifty miles off the coast of Lebanon, he descended further until they were at the Ilyushin's minimum safe altitude and changed course sharply to the southeast as the co-pilot switched off the plane's two transponders. In Damascus the Ilyushin disappeared from the controllers' screens.

Several minutes later the coast of Israel appeared, growing larger by the second, and the pilot switched to a pre-arranged cloaked frequency that put him in contact with the tower at Sde Dov Airport, just northeast of Tel-Aviv. The Ilyushin banked left to parallel the coast, approaching the main runway from the south and touched down. Fifteen minutes later it was in a secure holding area controlled by IDF troops.

Mossad operatives boarded immediately to take charge of the prisoners. Black hoods still over their heads, they were escorted into a waiting van. The team leader informed Eitan Ronan by phone as soon as the van was rolling.

*****

Strachey had a seat booked on the noon flight to Dulles and was packing his bags when there was a knock at the door of his room. The wiry Deputy Director of the Spanish National Police Alberto Macías standing outside with a look on his face Strachey could not quite decipher.

Without ceremony Macías walked past him into the cramped room and sat on the side of the bed.

"We need to talk," he said. His narrow, bearded face was grave.

Strachey's heart sank. He would probably miss his flight.

Macías was a resourceful and daring Spanish cop. Strachey had worked closely with him during his tour in Madrid, and the two had become close friends.

In planning the hijacking with Ramsay,

Strachey had considered and then discarded the idea of asking for Macías's assistance. Relations between the Mossad and the Spanish services were almost non-existent, and with considerable Spanish equities at stake in the Maghreb, successive Spanish governments had gone out of their way to avoid offending the Arabs. Doing Strachey a favor was one thing, but assisting in a Mossad operation on Spanish soil would put his friend's career in jeopardy. Macías likely would have agreed to help, but in the final analysis Strachey just could not ask him.

Macías lit a cigarette and squinted at him through the smoke. "You've been here almost a week, and you haven't called. Should I feel insulted?"

Strachey groaned inwardly and resigned himself to one more night in Madrid. He'd call Amy later to tell her he'd be a day late.

"You should be grateful," he said to Macías.

The Spaniard's eyebrows climbed toward his hairline.

"Did you think you could be anywhere in my country without my knowing?"

"I had reasons, Alberto."

"Such as reasons having to do with stealing an airplane?"

"I should have known that Nico couldn't keep a secret. Are you going to arrest me?"

Strachey asked the question only half in jest.

Macías's face was unreadable.

"I'd have to arrest Nico, too. You should have come to me."

"I didn't want to place you in an awkward

position."

"You doubted I would help you?"

"I doubted you could survive the political shit storm if anything went wrong."

"Are you going to tell me about it now?"

Just as he had said to Ewan Ramsay, he would trust his Spanish friends with his life. There was no reason he could not share what had motivated his attempted deception.

It took an hour to lay out all the facts, omitting any mention of Ewan Ramsay and Sasha. Macías agreed that the attempt on Krystal Murphy's life on the heels of the deaths of the Nelsons and Vicky Kondratieva was good reason to conclude that Shurgin was somehow was behind the murders. The suicide bombing in Brussels seemed to affect Macías most, and Strachey knew it brought to the surface memories of the death of the Spaniard's own son when the commuter train he was riding was bombed by Islamist terrorists on March 11, 2004. There was no ambivalence in Macías about how to deal with terrorists and those who support them.

When he chose to display it, Alberto Macías's smile was infectious. He stood and laid a hand on Strachey's shoulder while he leaned close.

"Actually, *amigo mío*, Nico told me all about your plan before it happened. I decided to pretend it was just another of his dubious stories. Purely by coincidence, however, we learned that a certain Russian arms dealer was in town using an Argentine alias. Our surveillance saw him meeting with a man we later picked up. It turns out he supplies explosives to ETA."

Strachey had to laugh at his own foolishness. Deputy Director of the Spanish National Police Alberto Macías could not be topped on his own turf.

"Congratulations, Alberto. I hope you forgive me."

"Well, the fact that you have been in my city for so long and we have not had a meal together is unforgivable. But I've arranged to make up for it this afternoon."

*****

It was nearly seven in the evening before Strachey returned to his room. Alberto had arranged for a reunion of Strachey's friends, including a sheepishly smiling Villagas, and the meal had gone on for hours, followed by whiskey and cigars.

He'd changed his reservations to the next day's two o'clock flight and notified Amy, who had been disappointed.

The fear still lived in his gut, and he knew it wouldn't go away until the serial killer was caught or killed. So far, so good, although Amy was unhappy about his injunction not to leave the house until he returned, especially with her father trying to give orders to everyone.

Krystal was mending well, and the swelling had gone down in her face. The detective, too, was chafing at her confinement and exclusion from the case, and Strachey was certain she was NOT getting along with the irascible Thomas Jefferson Dawson.

Krystal checked in regularly with the task force, but no new leads had turned up, and the media had turned its attention to yet another Congressman who couldn't keep his pants zipped.

Strachey knew all the tricks of going to ground in hostile territory and was certain that was exactly what the killer had done. If he hadn't cut and run, his mission still pointed him at the Strachey family.

CHAPTER 38

Ciudad del Este, Paraguay

Ciudad del Este, Paraguay, sits on the banks of the Paraná River opposite its Brazilian counterpart, Foz do Iguaçu. The city is known for its unsafe streets and generous supply of contraband and counterfeit goods. Not far to the north the land is smothered under the thick, green canopy of the nearly impenetrable Mato Grosso, the gigantic jungle of southern Brazil.

Hamid Mahmoud Sayed suffered in the sticky climate. He longed for the cool of Brussels or even Beirut with its refreshing Mediterranean breezes. Despite the devastation of war and ethnic divisions, Beirut was preferable to this backwater. There at least he could fight directly against those children of apes, the Israelis.

Hamid surveyed the lush countryside from the second story window of the barracks that was his temporary refuge. The Belgian police had somehow traced the Grand Place bombing to Hezbollah, the Army of God, and Hamid, the leader of the Brussels cell, instantly became a wanted man throughout Europe. VEVAK, which had ordered the suicide bombing in the first place, facilitated his escape to South America. He wasn't ungrateful for the help, but the destination displeased him.

Hamid was the youngest son of a prosperous Lebanese family that had immigrated to Belgium soon after the troubles began in their native land. Brussels, they discovered, was not so different from the cosmopolitan Beirut they had known years in the past, and the family settled in contentedly.

But in 1992 Lebanese Christian Phalangists massacred hundreds of Palestinian refugees in Sabra and Shatila camp while Israeli IDF troops stood by. For Hamid's family it was an outrage, but for the young man it was more – it was a radicalizing event, and despite his family's wishes, he'd returned to Beirut where it was a simple matter to link up with radical Islamists.

A native Lebanese with a Belgian passport was very interesting to Hezbollah.

The barracks sat on one side of a lightly guarded compound several kilometers northwest of Ciudad del Este near Lake Yguazú at the very edge of the green immensity of the Mato Grosso. It served as a training and logistics center for Islamist warriors from around the world. Some, like him, were in hiding while others enjoyed a respite from war while they received additional training.

Hamid specialized in explosive ordnance, and he spent mornings training jihadis in the fine art of constructing IED's and suicide vests. Everyone knew him as the organizer of the Brussels bombing, and he enjoyed a certain exalted reputation among the younger jihadis. Hamid had made several instructional videos using the camp's recording facilities to encourage suicide bombings.

The Tri-Border area made for strange bedfellows. The compound housed nearly 100 men, and he found himself sharing quarters with Sunni Muslims as well as fellow Shiites. Jihad united them all against the infidels. According to rumor, even the Sunni Sheik Usama bin Laden had passed through here in the years prior to his spectacular attack on the Americans.

The ten hectare compound hummed with other activities revealing a side of jihad Hamid had never seen, nor even imagined. Trucks moved daily through the gates bearing loads of processed drugs to be stored for transport by Rus Ismayilov's planes into Mexico and later smuggled into the United States to poison its decadent population. In exchange, large bails of cash found their way into the accounts of Muslim businessmen in Asunción, Ciudad del Este, and Foz do Iguaçu, Brazil, to be laundered through shopping centers, auto dealerships, and the like, and ultimately scattered around the world to fund the jihad. There was even an operation to print counterfeit American dollars that the Iranians had moved here years ago from the Bekaa Valley.

Despite his dislike of the locale, he knew the support provided to his cause was irreplaceable. The location, an area long dominated by corruption, lawlessness, and smuggling, provided safe haven, and a population that included tens of thousands of Muslims promised a benign environment.

The kingpin of Hezbollah's financial network was a Lebanese businessman, Assad Ahmad Radawi, who lived across the Paraná in Foz do Iguaçu, Brazil, where he was immune from Paraguayan and Argentine prosecution, although these days he spent a lot of time in Lebanon. The man and his sons had contributed over fifty million dollars to Hezbollah over the years in the guise of humanitarian assistance. Recently he'd returned to Foz do Iguaçu, and sent word that he wanted to meet fellow Lebanese Hamid to personally congratulate him on his success in Brussels.

Hamid was driven from the compound to the city's commercial center. It was bustling with shoppers anxious to find the latest bootleg DVDs, counterfeit designer clothing, and electronics, and possibly receive their change in counterfeit currency.

At the Galeria Page, a shopping center in downtown Ciudad del Este, owned and operated almost entirely by Hezbollah sympathizers, he was fitted with a new suit, a clean white shirt, and shoes to make him presentable to the great man.

In the late afternoon, Hamid was driven across the Puente de Amistad, the Bridge of Peace, to Foz do Iguaçu on the opposite bank. He'd bathed and trimmed his beard in preparation for the meeting. Despite his nervousness, he was mildly surprised at the pleasure he derived from wearing western clothing again. He had been too long away from the comforts of Brussels.

CHAPTER 39

McLean, Virginia

Ghasem Esfahani turned the pick-up into the quiet McLean side street. The trees that canopied the neat yards were beginning to flaunt their autumn colors, and the lawns were dappled yellow where the sunlight penetrated. It was nearing four in the afternoon, and a school bus was just depositing children at one of the intersections.

This time he was prepared in the event a police car still was parked in front of the Strachey home. He'd concluded that the police presence could only mean they had discovered the pattern in the deaths he had meted out and identified his targets. This was a problem, but it was not insolvable.

The police car was still there. As before, there was only one uniformed officer. To Ghasem's mind this did not connote a serious attempt at security. Far more disruptive to his plan would be a casual observer or a group of children that might see his approach. Danger came from the unanticipated, not from anything for which he had prepared.

He turned away from the intersection, circling the neighborhood and eventually glided to a stop in the same spot as the day before, where he could observe the house and the police car. He would remain here until twilight if he could escape attracting attention.

He slumped behind the steering wheel to wait.

At this time of day, the woman should be alone in the house, perhaps preparing dinner for her husband. If the husband returned before Ghasem was inside, his plan would change only slightly.

He checked the pistol once again, removing the magazine and replacing it, then racking a round into the chamber.

All he needed now was darkness, just enough to conceal his approach until it was too late.

Three hours later the shadows under the trees had grown deep and the streets were deserted. He could see television screens glowing through windows. He'd watched as one car after another entered driveways as residents returned home from work, but there had been no such arrival at the Strachey house.

Ghasem slipped out of the truck and walked slowly toward the house keeping to the shadows. He'd traded his West Virginia clodhoppers for rubber-soled running shoes that were silent against the pavement, and he wore dark clothing.

The policeman had the driver's side window down, probably to take advantage of the cool evening air, and this changed Esfahani's plan slightly. He pocketed the pistol and drew the small, razor sharp knife. He was at the side of the car before the policeman had time to react and in a practiced movement buried the point of the blade just behind the man's jaw and then slashed forward to sever the carotid artery and windpipe. An inarticulate gurgle escaped the dying man as one hand shot to his mangled neck. He reached for his sidearm with the other, but slumped forward against the steering wheel as he passed out from loss of blood and oxygen. He would be dead within ninety seconds.

Ghasem scanned the vicinity. Seeing nothing that might present a danger, he opened the car door and shoved the body onto the floor on the passenger side before walking to the house.

He rapped on the door briskly three times and stood back, pistol at the ready as he heard stirring within.

As soon as the door opened a crack, Ghasem shoved it roughly aside and was surprised to see a slight, elderly black man staggering backward. The man steadied himself, and a curse of protest was cut short when he saw the gun in Ghasem's hand.

For a moment Ghasem feared he'd entered the wrong house, but then a small, pretty woman with café au lait skin emerged from a doorway carrying a baby.

"Daddy, what's ..." she began, then stopped short with a small shriek when she saw Ghasem.

So this was the woman's father. Two surprises in as many seconds, but fortuitous ones. The woman matched the description he had been given of Strachey's wife. The old man and the baby would provide excellent leverage to force the woman to talk before he killed them all. He sensed victory.

"Don't move," he ordered, tracking the pistol between them.

The old man did not obey, but rather stepped back to place himself between Ghasem and the woman with the baby. He balled his hands into fists, and his eyes glowed with the anger and desperation of a trapped animal.

"You're not going to hurt my baby," said the old man in a determined but high-pitched voice that cracked with age.

This was as good a moment as any to exert the first piece of leverage. It would be easier to work on the woman with the querulous old man out of the way. Then he would wait for the husband.

Ghasem smiled as he raised the pistol to take careful aim at the center of the old man's narrow chest.

CHAPTER 40

Strachey raised his Business Class seat back to the upright position and watched the jigsaw landscape that marked northern Virginia passing beneath the Boeing 757. They were on final approach into Dulles International Airport after a nine-hour flight from Madrid, and he was anxious to get home.

As soon as they were wheels down he punched the speed dial for home on his blackberry.

Amy answered before the second ring. "Are you back?"

He'd called her just before leaving Madrid and given her his estimated arrival time.

"I am," he said. "Is everything OK there?"

Amy's voice dropped to a whisper. "It'll be better with you back. Maybe my father will go back to Charlotte then. He's driving Krystal around the bend."

Strachey had to chuckle. Thomas Jefferson Dawson was a handful, but he'd become one of his favorite people. He hoped he was half as animated when he was Thomas's age.

"OK, I'll try to make peace between them. I picked up a bottle of Spanish brandy at the Duty Free Shop at Barajas. I'm sure that will mellow your father out."

Amy sounded doubtful. "Maybe, but get ready for an earful about 'leaving the women-folk alone.'"

The plane drew up to the mid-field terminal, and the flight attendants began opening the doors.

"Hey, gotta go now. It'll be dark by the time I get there. Leave the outside light on for me."

"I sure will. R.T. will be happy to see his daddy."

Strachey recognized the relief in his wife's voice at his return and had to admit he felt the same himself. He slipped the phone into his jacket pocket and rose to retrieve his carry-on bag from the overhead bin and joined the other passengers shuffling their way out the cabin doors.

They were herded down a long, narrow corridor to board one of the unique Dulles mobile lounges, long ago dubbed "people movers," for the familiar ride across the tarmac to the main terminal with its gracefully curved roof and soaring glass walls that reminded Strachey of a cathedral dedicated to flight.

How many times had he been in and out of Dulles International Airport during his CIA career? Upon departure the shiver of anticipation always pitched one's thoughts forward to the destination, but always on the return the sight of the terminal meant one was once again home and safe.

He queued for Passport Control and then retrieved his checked luggage from one of the carousels and cleared customs. By the time he reached his BMW in the multi-level parking garage the sun was nearing the horizon. He glanced at his watch. It would be around seven by the time he reached home.

It was already dark when he turned into his street and drew to a stop behind the police cruiser in front of the house. There were only a few widely spaced street lights in the neighborhood, common enough in Northern Virginia where suburbanites thought the absence of street lighting preserved a rustic air that had long since disappeared.

Amy had not turned on the outside light as he had requested. Strange.

Strachey was already out of the car before it occurred to him that the policeman on guard should have challenged him. Maybe Amy had forewarned him of his pending arrival.

He peered at the cruiser but in the darkness could see no one inside. Closer inspection confirmed this. Maybe the policeman was patrolling on the other side of the house. He placed his hand on the window sill of the car door and felt something sticky and wet that he recognized instantly as blood.

Shocked into momentary immobility he was startled into action by the distinct crack of a gunshot from inside the house followed immediately by a second.

He sprinted for the front door. He had no weapon, and the only chance was to surprise the intruder before he could react.

The door was not closed all the way, and he crashed through it prepared for the worst, trying to make sense of what he saw, searching for a target.

*****

Just moments earlier when the knock came at the door Krystal Murphy was in the kitchen helping an overjoyed Amy prepare snacks for Robert Strachey's arrival. Thomas was in the living room.

"I'll get it," he called.

"I think I'm going to have more words with your father," said Krystal. "I've told him never to answer the door unless I'm there."

"I know," said Amy, "He's incorrigible. But it must be Bob or the policeman outside would ..."

She was interrupted by a loud bang and an inarticulate exclamation from Thomas.

"Daddy!"

Amy had just lifted the baby from his high-chair next to the kitchen door, and before Krystal could stop her she rushed into the living room. There was a frozen second's strange silence followed by Amy's shriek before she heard the order, "Don't move."

Her skin prickled at the sound. Only two words, but she knew that voice. She had heard it before when she was locked in the trunk of the killer's car.

She drew her pistol and stepped to the kitchen door. Amy and her father were to her left with Thomas between his daughter and a dark-clothed man with a beard and long hair who stood a few paces inside the door. He was smiling, displaying a row of perfect white teeth as he aimed a pistol at Thomas.

The intruder saw her at the kitchen door and began to bring his pistol to bear on her at the same instant Krystal fired. She had a clear shot and pulled the trigger twice seeing every detail as her bullets struck the man center mass. Afterwards she could not recall having heard the sounds of her own gunshots.

Within seconds the front door burst open, and

Krystal trained her sights on the figure that entered.

*****

Strachey burst into the living room and saw a dark-clothed figure sprawled on the floor in a widening puddle of blood. Beyond, in the direction of the kitchen stood Thomas Jefferson Dawson, his eyes round as saucers and his mouth shaped into a small 'O,' for once in his life entirely speechless. Behind him was Amy, holding little R.T.

Krystal Murphy stood just behind and to one side of them at the kitchen door. Her left arm was still in a sling, but her right was extended as she pointed her pistol at Strachey.

She recognized him, lowered her weapon and walked over to the man on the floor. Strachey for the first time noticed the pistol that was lying about a foot from the man's outstretched right hand. Krystal kicked it away and prodded the prone figure with the toe of her shoe.

He didn't move.

The spell broken, Strachey rushed to encircle Amy and the baby in his arms. She was trembling violently and R.T. had begun to wail. He led Amy back out into the kitchen and helped her into a seat at the breakfast table before drawing a glass of water for her.

"It's ok now, baby," he said. "It's all over."

"We thought it was you, and when Daddy opened the door that man just burst in. He was going to shoot Daddy and then Krystal just came out of nowhere. Is he dead?"

"I don't know, but he's no longer a threat. Will you be alright here while I go check on Thomas and Krystal?"

"Daddy was so brave. He stepped right between me and that madman."

Strachey returned to the living room. Thomas still had not moved. Strachey put a gentle hand on his shoulder. The old man might be in shock, and at his age anything could happen. They didn't need any more tragedy this night.

"Thomas," he said soberly and deliberately, "why don't you go into the kitchen and take care of Amy? She shouldn't be left alone now."

Thomas seemed to come to himself as his eyes focused on Strachey.

"What did you say?"

"Go to the kitchen and take care of Amy and R.T. They need you."

Thomas nodded slowly.

"My God. I've never seen anything like that in my life."

"I know. But it's alright now."

He took the old man by the arm and led him into the kitchen. Thomas felt as brittle as a dried twig to his touch. He and Amy would comfort one another.

Moments later Strachey was bending beside Murphy to help her roll the man onto his back. There were two profusely bleeding holes not six inches apart in the middle of his chest. He wasn't breathing.

She looked up at him.

"I damn near shot you, Bob. I thought you were with him."

"You saved my family, Krystal. I'll never be able to thank you."

"We were in the kitchen preparing snacks to celebrate your return when there was a knock at the door. We all assumed it was you, and Thomas went to let you in.

"Then we heard a sort of crash and Thomas cried out, and Amy went out with the baby still in her arms to see what had happened before I could stop her.

"Then I heard that voice and knew it was HIM. I rushed out as fast as I could and shot the bastard. He had his gun on Thomas and Amy."

Strachey nodded. She'd put two large caliber bullets into the man center mass with a one-handed shot, and now she couldn't stop talking as the adrenalin ebbed.

"This is the same guy that abducted you?"

"It sounded like him, but I never really got a good look at his face."

"The cop outside is dead."

"Oh, my God. I've got to call this in."

"Are you OK?"

Murphy had replaced her sidearm in its holster, and her hand had begun to tremble.

"I think so."

"Have you killed anyone before?"

"I tried to once, Strachey. You were there. I missed that time. You didn't."

Strachey remembered the night the year before when they had been set upon by Russian thugs intent on recovering the Andropov Memorandum at Vicky

Kondratieva's house.

"Why don't you sit down for a few minutes? I can make the calls."

Murphy rose to her feet and tightened her jaw. There was the hint of a tear in the corner of one eye that she blinked fiercely away.

"I'll make the call, Strachey. I'm the cop."

The kid has a lot of steel in her, he thought.

"May I make a suggestion?"

She gave him a baleful stare, waiting to hear what he had to say.

"Call Enoch Whitehall first. If this guy was an Iranian agent, the FBI has to be put in the picture. Call Whitehall first, and then do what he says."

"The cop outside was from Arlington. That's where the first call is going. We take care of our own first." She paused. "Then I'll call Whitehall."

CHAPTER 41

Murphy stared at the photos spread across Whitehall's desk a few moments longer. They could be termed morbid. The subject was the face of an obviously dead man, front and profile, first with a beard and long, unruly hair, and a second set of the corpse shaved and barbered.

It was two days after the shooting, and FBI Executive Assistant Director Enoch Whitehall had summoned the two of them to his office for mid-morning chat.

Murphy had done as Strachey suggested and called Whitehall, but only after she'd reported to the Arlington Police that one of their own had been killed in the line of duty. Whitehall arrived in time to settle a squabble between the Fairfax County Police and the Arlington Police by asserting that the FBI would take the lead in the investigation.

The photos of the corpse's shaven visage closely matched the artist's drawings of the "Arlington Ripper" that had been released to the public.

"So both the hotel bartender and the truck driver made positive i.d.'s?" Murphy asked.

"Yes," said Whitehall, "there's no doubt this is the man we were looking for. We have DNA confirmation, as well, linking him to the murders here and those in California."

"Good. I never got a good look at him, but I remembered his voice."

It was the second day following the attack at the Strachey home, and Robert Strachey sat beside her in Whitehall's austere office in the Hoover Building. Strachey, she noticed, was in a particularly foul mood. He had said nothing since the meeting began.

"We're not releasing the fact that he was Iranian to the public," said Whitehall.

Strachey at last entered the conversation. "Why not?"

"It'll give us time to investigate his activities more deeply and discreetly. He was carrying an excellent set of forged documents, as well as a debit card in a completely different name for a business account we've traced to the Bahamas."

"And this contributes to the view that whoever he was, he was working for VEVAK."

After a couple of beats Whitehall replied, "Yes."

"What's VEVAK?" Murphy was unfamiliar with the term.

"Iranian Intelligence," said Strachey. "In English it's known formally as the Iranian Ministry of Intelligence and Security, MOIS."

Whitehall concentrated his attention on Strachey.

"And why, Mr. Strachey, do you think VEVAK might have come after your family and Detective Murphy?"

Uh oh, thought Murphy, *Here we go into spooky la-la land again.* Despite earlier misgivings she'd had to admit that there was, after all, validity to the speculation the two Feds had shared with her earlier. Those conversations seemed so far in the past after all that had happened. She decided to keep quiet and see where the spooky conversation led.

"I think you know," said Strachey. "There's no reason the Iranians would come after me, or any of the other people connected with the Andropov Memorandum that have been killed. I think there's a Russian hand inside the Iranian glove."

The words kindled a cold fire in Whitehall's deep-set eyes.

"As do I, Mr. Strachey. But not an OFFICIAL Russian hand, eh? You're thinking of Vitaliy Mikhailovich Shurgin."

Strachey said nothing.

After a moment Whitehall said, "I'm afraid we have little chance of proving it."

"Something might turn up."

"There's nothing we can do but follow the leads from the dead man's documents," said Whitehall. "But there is something more to consider."

Strachey raised his eyebrows in inquiry, but his tight smile told Murphy that he knew what was coming."

"And that is?"

"If we're right and Shurgin is doling out revenge on the people who orchestrated his downfall, he's not likely to stop now."

Murphy kicked herself mentally for not having thought the matter completely through. She'd naively believed the death of the Iranian killer had put an end to the affair. But she could not ignore the conclusions these two men had drawn.

It was not over.

She recalled Robert Strachey's words just before he left the country. He'd said he was going "to find Shurgin." What the hell had that meant?

Given what had happened, they'd not had a chance to discuss his trip, and she intuited that this was not the time to raise it, just as she'd acceded to Strachey's plea not to mention the name Harry Connolly or the blond woman. She hated concealing anything from Enoch Whitehall, but if Strachey had something to share with the FBI it was his decision to make. She bit her lip and waited.

"I think you're right," said Strachey. "Does the FBI have something in mind?"

"Unfortunately in this instance, the FBI can act only on the basis of solid evidence. Unless the present investigation turns up a connection to Shurgin, there is little that can be done … officially."

Murphy wondered if Whitehall knew more than he was saying about Strachey's recent travels. The man had a way of making one feel that he always knew more than he revealed.

"I'm no longer with the CIA, Director Whitehall, officially or unofficially. All I can say is that I'm uncomfortable just sitting around waiting for the other shoe to drop."

Whitehall's expression betrayed nothing of his thoughts.

"I would advise against any rash actions, Mr. Strachey. Something will break eventually."

Strachey met Whitehall's gaze evenly.

"I never act rashly, Director."

CHAPTER 42

Tel-Aviv, Israel

Two men, one tall and lean and the other broad, bald and grizzled, and a blond woman stood at the edge of the tarmac where they had an unobstructed view of the bustling activity surrounding the Russian transport aircraft. They were in a section of Sde Dov Airport that had been quietly appropriated for this purpose and was now alive with preparations for the plane's imminent departure.

Two canvas-covered troop transports already had been driven up the rear ramp and secured inside the cargo bay, followed by two dozen men and their commanding officer, a Major. Besides these soldiers and their equipment the plane carried two three-man flight crews and a medical officer.

Over the past several months they had undergone intense practice for the mission. They had been aided by a full-scale mockup of a five square hectare compound located thousands of miles from Israel's shores. The mockup was based on satellite reconnaissance, as well as close-up ground level photography clandestinely collected by Mossad agents on the ground. Each man had memorized the lay-out and the purpose of each of the structures at the site.

The soldiers belonged to *Shayatet* 13 (Flotilla 13), the Israeli Navy's elite commando unit, the Israeli equivalent of the U.S. Navy Seals. S-13 members are known as "Bat Men" because of the bat wings on their unit insignia. Those hoping to become members of this unit have only a five percent chance of making it through training.

The mode of insertion would be unusual, and there had been some dispute over whether S-13 or the *Sayeret Matkal* should be tasked with this operation.

In 1976 the *Sayeret Matkal* rescued over one hundred Air France passengers whose plane has been hijacked by Palestine Liberation Organization militants held Uganda. One hundred *Sayeret* were flown 2,500 miles to Entebbe airport and successfully rescued all but three of the passengers. During the action three hostages died and the Israelis killed fifty-two hostiles. The Israelis suffered only one loss, their commander, Lieutenant Colonel Yonatan Netanyahu, the brother of a future Prime Minister who had been himself a unit commander in the *Sayeret Matkal.*

On this occasion the plan was even more daring and relied on a troop contingent one quarter the size and a journey of many more thousands of miles. Unlike Entebbe, this was not a rescue operation. Its purpose was to collect intelligence, destroy the objective and kill as many of the enemy as possible. They would rely on good reconnaissance, surprise and superb training to compensate for their relatively small numbers, just as Israel itself must rely on cunning and intelligence to survive in a sea filled with man-eating sharks.

The diplomats from the Foreign Office opposed the operation in the belief that such a drastic action on sovereign foreign soil could not succeed and the blame inevitably would fall at Israel's doorstep, isolating her even more than she already was in an increasingly hostile world. The intelligence and military side presented their analyses and concluded that the plan had a 60/40 chance of success, and the capture of the Ilyushin had increased the odds a bit in their favor. The after-action escape and evasion plan, the subject of heated discussion in the Prime Minister's office, was the reason the mission was entrusted to S-13.

The raiding party had to achieve a clean getaway that left behind no evidence of Israeli involvement – no one left behind, and no trail back to Israel. The Prime Minister reasoned that if this could be accomplished the world could speculate all it wanted. Israel was not the only country capable of such force projection. The Prime Minister would simply follow the old dictum: admit nothing, deny everything, blame others.

*****

Ronan put a hand on Ramsay's shoulder, breaking into his thoughts.

"I recognize that look, Ewan."

"I thought I was hiding it pretty well. But you're thinking the same thing, aren't you?

Ronan sighed. "Of course. I wish I were going, too.

The *memuneh* leaned close and rumbled loudly enough for Sasha, standing behind them, to hear.

"But this is work for the young, my friend, not for two old dogs such as you and I."

The comment did not sit well with Ramsay. He knew Ronan, a good ten years older than he, was prodding him. Charitably, he surmised that the *memuneh* was making a feeble attempt to alleviate the tension of the moment. Ronan, he recalled, had always had a weak grasp on the concept of humor. In any event, Sasha's hand on his shoulder stifled any riposte.

There was a roar from the tarmac as the pilot spun up the Ilyushin's massive engines. Several minutes later, they covered their ears as the volume increased and the plane moved forward onto the access ramp leading to the runway.

They watched in silence as it trundled to the end of the runway and turned around. The pitch of the engines increased until the pilot released the brakes and the plane started forward, slowly at first, then gathering speed until it finally became airborne and traced a low trajectory out over the sea until it faded from sight.

"You might think you want to be with them," Sasha said to them both, "but I don't envy those men."

Later as their car sped along the Ayalon Highway Ronan said, "If this were purely a Mossad operation the *memuneh* would be with them, just like Isser Harel when we grabbed Eichmann in 1960, but the military is in charge of this one."

"That's a big job for so few men," said Ramsay. He'd been surprised at the small size of the contingent.

"God willing, they'll have surprise on their side."

"You already have people on the ground," said Sasha.

"Oh, yes. Our man who got that video of Shurgin and Ismayilov has been there some time already, and we sent five more operatives to join him a couple of weeks ago, including your old friend Michael Mossberg. They're all our people, of course. The targets have all been reconnoitered. The groundwork has been laid. I think the operation will succeed. It's what happens after that worries me."

Ramsay agreed.

"You mean your exfiltration plan."

"With so many people on the ground the likelihood that all could escape clandestinely overland is practically nil even if they split up, once local governments put out the alarm. And the terrain out there is not particularly hospitable."

The best bet for the raiders escape was to return to the Ilyushin and be airborne before the authorities could organize a response. The only problem was that in short order the plane and its passengers would be identified as the culprits. They would be unable to land anywhere for refueling after leaving Paraguay. Without refueling stops, the Ilyushin's maximum flight range was woefully inadequate even for them to make the African coast. The distance from Israel also made in-flight re-fueling all but impossible.

"Are you two going to stand watch with me?" asked Ronan.

"Of course," said Ramsay.

"Nothing is going to happen for several hours. If they can keep to the schedule, they'll land at Ciudad del Este around midnight local time. That will be five

A.M. tomorrow here. Why don't you get some rest and come by the office sometime after midnight?"

Ramsay knew that Ronan would get no sleep, at all, but would fill his office with a dense fog of Gauloise smoke as he followed the mission's progress.

Shayalet 13 would be far from home, and their safe return would depend on skill, precise timing and luck.

CHAPTER 43

Foz do Iguaçu, Brazil

At one P.M. Sergio Blanco drove across the Friendship Bridge from Ciudad del Este into Foz do Iguaçu, Brazil. It had taken him five hours to drive from Asunción, and he did not expect ever to return.

Michael Mossberg, a seasoned Mossad field operative, had driven up from Iguazú Falls, the region's major tourist attraction. Two days earlier, using a German alias, he had checked into the Iguazú Grand Resort and Casino on the Argentine side of the falls. Except for a few moments to cross the border, the drive into Foz do Iguaçu had taken only twenty minutes.

Mossberg had rented a Mercedes sedan at the resort, reasoning that a Mercedes would get him past border controls more smoothly than a Renault. He rendezvoused with Blanco, and they left the Mercedes parked on a side street and continued in Blanco's less conspicuous Fiat.

Their destination was the home of Assad Ahmad Radawi, wealthy Lebanese supporter of Hezbollah and Hamas. Radawi, along with his sons, owned several shopping centers, automobile dealerships, and restaurants. These enterprises were useful for money laundering, and they brought in a lot of money, but not as much as the smuggling and drug trafficking they ran out of the Hezbollah training camp on the other side of the river.

Radawi was wanted by the authorities in Paraguay and Argentina, but enjoyed complete immunity in Brazil, a peculiar country that does not provide for extradition.

Blanco had painstakingly cased Radawi's house and neighborhood over the past several months and knew that the household included three Brazilian servants, a cook, a gardener, and a maid. Whenever one of the Radawis was in residence two armed guards patrolled the grounds inside the high, adobe wall that surrounded the property. Tel-Aviv had confirmed that Radawi had returned to Brazil from Beirut a week and a half ago.

The neighborhood was affluent and busy during the afternoon while they observed the entrance through binoculars from a block away. Just after nightfall, a black Mercedes passed them, and Blanco recognized one of the Radawi sons as the driver. He had a bearded passenger. The car turned in at the gates that were opened manually by a guard.

"He has a guest for dinner," said Blanco.

"I wonder if there will be others," worried Mossberg.

If there was a crowd their orders were to abort the mission.

But by nine P.M. no one else had entered the house. Everyone inside should be sitting down to the evening meal at this hour. The narrow, blacktopped street was deserted and not well lit.

Their first task was to silence the guards.

Blanco and Mossberg carried only light weapons, silenced Glock-17's that had been issued to

Mossberg by the Station in Buenos Aires, and commando knives. They would be no match for an alert guard with an AK-47.

Blanco put the car in gear and drove slowly to a point few hundred feet from the entrance. Mossberg got out and melted into the shadows before moving forward with his back against the wall.

Blanco drove on and turned into the driveway, stopping a few feet from the wrought iron gates and flashed his lights. The Mercedes they had seen earlier was parked just inside the gates.

Within seconds a guard emerged from the darkness and peered through the gates' wrought iron bars into the headlamps' glare. He carried the ubiquitous AK-47 with a folding stock.

Blanco stuck his head out the window.

"*Salaam Aleikhum,* brother. I have a message for Mr. Radawi from the camp."

Blanco's Arabic was perfect.

The guard lowered the AK slightly, suspicious, but not yet alarmed.

"We had no notification that you were coming."

Blanco stepped out of the car keeping the door open to conceal the Glock in his right hand.

"Those idiots were supposed to call. Look, I don't want to disturb Mr. Radawi. May I just hand the message to you?"

The guard hesitated a moment before saying, "OK, bring it over."

He lowered the AK in his right hand and reached with the left for a walkie-talkie that was holstered at his belt. He undoubtedly intended to notify the other guard or someone inside the house.

He was less than eight feet from Blanco and clearly illuminated by the headlights. The wrought iron gate with vertical bars spaced eight inches apart made it a tricky shot. Blanco made up his mind.

He stepped around the door, closing the distance by a few more feet, and raised the Glock in both hands. The pistol bucked only slightly as he placed two silenced rounds into the guard's brain.

The body slumped to the ground, landing with its face grotesquely supported through the iron bars by a crossbeam at the bottom of the gate. The sightless eyes stared at eternity with terminal surprise as Blanco rushed to the gate and took a quick look inside to make sure no one had seen what happened. He returned to the car and backed it into the street along the curb so it would not attract attention, switched off the lights, and then clambered over the gate.

He dragged the body to the side of the Mercedes away from the front door and unclipped the walkie-talkie from the man's belt before beginning his search for the second guard who should be patrolling in the rear. He began a clockwise circle around the house, keeping low and treading carefully. Mossberg would continue watching the street until he gave the all-clear.

Tonight would see the culmination of a year's arduous work, and he would be glad when it was over. That he had been selected to be the instrument of his country's vengeance on these killers of innocents, the murderers of his parents, gave him no particular joy.

Nothing would fill the void left by the deaths of his parents. Dealing out mortal retribution was not a joyful endeavor. But neither did he feel pity for those who would die this night. He was not the first operative to be called upon to dispense final justice on behalf of the Israeli nation, and he doubted he would be the last.

He heard the clatter of dishes and rapid Portuguese conversation through one of the side windows and assumed this was the kitchen or a serving area. Radawi was treating his bearded guest to dinner.

It would be their last.

He ducked under the window and continued toward the rear of the house, finally stopping to peek carefully around the corner. There was a lush garden with several palm trees, a pool, and a large patio with an assortment of lounge furniture. The man who owned this house had funneled more than fifty million dollars to Middle Eastern terrorist organizations and had put up the money for the Buenos Aires bombings. That he should enjoy such luxury in the safe haven of Brazil deeply offended Blanco.

Over eight minutes had elapsed since he'd killed the man in front and he still had not located the second guard. Time was running out.

There was a squawk, and a voice speaking rapid Arabic froze him in place until he realized it was coming from the walkie-talkie confiscated from the guard's body.

The voice had a Lebanese accent. "Muhammad, where are you? You're supposed to be in front."

This was not good. It sounded like the second guard had walked round to the front of the house to find his comrade. He must not be allowed to find the body and raise the alarm.

Keeping low, Blanco raced back along the side of the house to the front and crouched behind the Mercedes where he had dragged the body of the first guard.

"Muhammad, where are you? I don't see you."

There was the beginning of alarm in the man's voice.

Blanco grabbed the walkie-talkie, pressed the transmit button and whispered, "I'm here by the Mercedes. I hurt myself."

"What happened?"

Blanco could hear the approaching footsteps of the second guard. He counted two more seconds then rose, resting arms across the car's trunk to steady his aim, hoping he had timed it right.

The guard was about fifteen feet away hurrying toward the car, and Blanco had only a split second to acquire his target and fire. The only light was cast by the gibbous moon and a lamp over the front door that silhouetted his target. The chances of connecting with a head shot were slim, so he fired at the man center mass -- two quick shots that knocked him down.

The guard coughed and tried to rise, but Blanco covered the distance between them quickly and silenced him with a bullet to the head.

He dragged the body around the car and left it in the shadow beside the first before opening the iron gates and signaling Mossberg to join him.

They donned balaclavas, and Mossberg headed for the rear while Blanco carefully opened the front door which miraculously was unlocked. It swung silently inward on well-oiled hinges. After living there so long with impunity, Radawi apparently felt safe in Brazil and put a lot of faith in his guards.

He would soon regret it.

Blanco stepped inside a large foyer with rustic decoration and heard the sound of voices speaking in Arabic from deeper within the house.

Alert for the appearance of another guard or a servant he padded through the main part of the house. Judging from the voices he had heard from the kitchen there were at least two women present in addition to Radawi and his two guests. In planning the operation Blanco had reasoned that the cleaning lady and gardener should not be present in the evening. Besides the guards, that left the cook and the maid.

The conversation grew more intelligible as he neared what must be a formal dining room. Mossberg already would have entered and begun clearing the rear of the house. It would take him a few more minutes, and this gave Blanco an opportunity to listen to what Radawi and his guests were saying.

Radawi was speaking.

"Hamid, once again we must congratulate you on the success of your operation in Brussels. It was masterful, absolutely masterful, and will not soon be forgotten. I understand you are quite the hero at the camp."

"I but follow the Word of the Prophet, peace be upon him," answered another, younger voice. "But I long to return to our beloved Lebanon and fight the Jews."

Blanco was always bemused by the flowery Arabic of bloody-minded terrorists.

Radawi said, "Spoken like a true patriot. You are highly regarded in Beirut, let me assure you. The brothers are in awe of your achievement. It will not be long before you can return."

"*Insha'Allah.*"

Mossberg's two minutes were up.

Blanco walked through the double doors into the brightly lit dining room. All three men seated at the table turned wide eyes toward the balaclava-masked intruder, and the older man cried out in alarm.

"Don't move. Don't attempt to escape," said Blanco in Arabic. "Place your hands on top of the table."

Nervously eyeing the silenced pistol in his hand, the three complied.

"Who are you?" asked Radawi in a voice somewhere between outrage and terror.

Blanco pronounced the words in precise Arabic.

"I bring you justice from Israel."

It required but an instant for expressions of horror to appear on the three faces, and the younger men started to rise before Blanco cut them down. He killed Radawi last, the hollow point bullets crashing him backwards onto the floor along with his chair.

Blanco administered a *coup de grace* to each of them.

Although their pistols were silenced, the old

man's cries and the clatter of falling furniture and broken china had alerted the house's other occupants. A woman in a maid's uniform appeared at the service door and screamed.

Then another figure appeared behind the maid - - Mossberg. He clapped a hand over her mouth to stifle the screams.

"There's another one in the kitchen," said Blanco.

"You handle that one. I've got my hands full here."

Ten minutes later they left by the front door. The two women were left bound and gagged on the kitchen floor. With luck it would take them a while to free themselves.

The escape plan was simple. They would switch back to Mossberg's rented Mercedes and drive across the border into Argentina where Mossberg already had paid for two guests at the resort. They would return to Buenos Aires by tourist bus the next day and fly out of the country to a neutral destination the next.

They arrived at the resort just after ten-thirty P.M.

CHAPTER 44

Shayatet 13

The Ilyushin sliced a low arc across a perfect azure sky until well away from the coast of Israel before climbing to set course for Njamena, Chad, 1,540 miles away in central Africa. The flight plan would show that it had originated in Malta, something the Maltese authorities later would vehemently deny. After refueling at Njamena, the second leg took them to Conakry, Guinea on the west coast.

The men inside the cargo bay alternately baked on the ground and froze at altitude in the cavernous cargo hold. Like all Soviet-era Russian aircraft, this one stank of oil and leaking hydraulics fluid.

On the plus side, they had plenty of room to move about and a well-equipped galley. They had been supplied only normal rations, but the coffee was fresh, hot and good.

Two hours after leaving Conakry Staff Sergeant Yael Sharanksy stood and stretched to work out the kinks, his breath hanging in the air. The blankets provided for the long flight provided barely adequate warmth. Harsh training in the Negev had prepared them for heat, but the men were less accustomed to cold.

He spotted the trim figure of Major Barak, the unit commander, at the coffee urn and walked over. Barak, like Yael, was the ideal size for S-13 -- 5'8" and 155 lbs. soaking wet. Yael poured a steaming mug, inhaling the rich aroma before raising it to his lips.

The previous year Yael had been a corporal. His promotion was due in large part to the fact that he was the S-13's best sniper. Using a yacht "borrowed" from a millionaire as cover, he and his men had set anchor one night a mile off the coast of Syria with line of sight to the villa of a certain affluent General known to be in charge of arms sales to Hezbollah and the North Koreans. While his target was sunbathing in his back garden, oblivious to any danger, Yael put a 250 grain .338 Lapua Magnum projectile through his brain, launched from a custom built Accuracy International equipped with a suppressor. Even though not perfectly silent, considering the extreme range the noise was covered by the sound of waves and wind. The yacht was away long before the General's family discovered the body.

"Where are we now, Major?"

"About mid-way across the Atlantic. We have a couple more hours before refueling and another two thousand miles or so before we reach the objective. How are the men doing?"

"Well, they're happy we're carrying M4's instead of paintball guns on this one."

In 2010 a group of highly publicized "peace activists" attempted to break the blockade of Gaza and an unwilling S-13 had been dragooned into intercepting the flotilla armed with paintball guns, a brilliant idea dreamed up by some genius to "avoid unnecessary casualties." They had listened in disbelief to a briefing by lawyers on the legal aspects of the operation. They were assured by these wise men that there would be no resistance, but as soon as they repelled to the activists' ship from a helicopter they were attacked by Turkish Islamist militants armed with knives and makeshift weapons. The S-13's were forced to defend themselves with their sidearms, and in the end nine of the "peace activists" lay dead. The event was filmed and broadcast the world over. Every member of S-13 strongly resented the assignment, the ridiculous restrictions, and the embarrassment. They were, after all, soldiers, not policemen.

Barak grimaced at the reference.

"This should make-up for that disaster."

"And no one will ever know about it, sir."

"God willing."

Yael glanced across the bay. All but a few of the men were taking advantage of the space to stretch out on the deck, each under several blankets. The deck itself was cold, which required insulated pads for both comfort and thermal protection. The smart veterans had clambered into the troop carriers secured to the deck cleats shortly after takeoff. Four of the men from his squad were playing cards to pass the time.

"The men are trying to keep warm for the most part. Some have managed to get some sleep. There's certainly plenty of room in this behemoth to stretch out."

For a moment Yael envied the six members of the flight crew the warmth of the bi-level flight deck until he remembered how uncomfortable executing the escape and evasion plan would be for them. They were, after all, just flyboys.

Major Barak suggested, "You'd better get some

rest yourself, Sergeant. We'll have some chow just before we land for refueling, and on the final leg everyone will be busy checking weapons and equipment. Spread the word when you've finished your coffee."

Their mission gave them the advantage of stealth and surprise and their weapons had been chosen to enhance those factors. Each carried a Glock 19c sidearm. Yael and the other squad leader carried silenced H&K MP5SD2 9mm submachine guns loaded with sub-sonic ammunition, while the rest of the men carried suppressed M4's, body armor, and transceivers. Their BDU's were without insignia, and none of their weapons or equipment was traceable back to Israel. Deniability was always a concern.

Humidity seeped into the plane during refueling at Recife, soaking them with sweat as they endured in silence. Only one hop remained to the target zone.

Yael watched the medical officer setting up his station at the front of the bay. In recent years S-13 had suffered more killed and wounded in combat than any other Israeli Special Forces unit. Yael prayed the doctor would have little to do this night.

0000 Hours, Ciudad del Este, Paraguay

The IL-76 lumbered out of the night sky descending like some terrible, roaring dragon over the darkened green canopy of the *Mato Grosso* toward Guaraní International Airport at Ciudad del Este. The flight plan from Recife had been filed only hours earlier. The late arrival did not surprise the

Paraguayan air controllers. This was not the first time a RusAvia plane had landed on short notice at midnight.

In the cargo bay the S-13 contingent and their commander checked their weapons and strapped on gear. As soon as the plane landed they would board the two troop carriers with canvas stretched over metal ribs covering cargo areas with long benches along the sides. One truck would have sufficed to carry them. The second was for insurance.

The ramp dropped, and the trucks drove into the night and through a gate in the perimeter fence. No one challenged them. The airport authorities ignored RusAvia flights, their questionable cargoes and passengers and irregular schedules. Rus Ismayilov's generous contributions to their bank accounts guaranteed the absence of inquisitiveness.

The Israeli Air Force flight crew remained with the plane to see to its immediate refueling.

There was no need for Yael to remind the men of their individual tasks. Each man knew his job and was deep in his own thoughts. The best Arabic speakers from each squad, dressed in mufti, drove the trucks.

Soon after leaving the airport they turned onto narrow dirt roads cut through the thick growth at the edge of the *Mato Grosso* that eventually became narrow, rutted tracks. The fresh air felt good, and Yael recalled that Spring would soon begin in this part of the world where people still lived in thatched huts and women did their laundry along the banks of muddy rivers.

The drivers knew each twist and turn of the satellite-mapped route. Within a half-hour of leaving the airport Major Barak held up two fingers to signal that they were two minutes out from the compound entrance. Four of the Mossad operatives who had joined Sergio Blanco in-country over the past several weeks already waited in place around the compound's perimeter. Upon Major Barak's radioed command they would silently dispatch any guards stationed around the periphery.

The compound consisted of a loose collection of buildings circling a large clearing of packed earth with no perimeter fence. Although he couldn't see them, Yael knew that six S-13's already had left the rear-most truck to link up with the Mossad operatives around the perimeter. They would first silence the sentries assigned to guard the weapons cache and move to positions to prevent any stragglers from escaping through the jungle.

Thanks to Radawi's bribes, the compound had operated for years with impunity, and the Mossad's months' long months-long close target reconnaissance and surveillance had revealed lax security with the exception of the weapons and explosives cache.

Yael pulled on his balaclava and secured the chin strap of his helmet as the trucks pulled to a stop at the wide spot in the rutted dirt road at the entrance. He was in the first truck and he could hear the compound sentries arguing with the driver. The unannounced arrival had raised their suspicions, and they insisted on seeing what they were carrying.

Yael took a position in the rear of the truck bed,

legs spread wide, weapon at the ready. Fortunately, the two guards stayed together, and when they lifted the back flap, Yael's silenced M4 spat four times at point blank range. The only sound was the click of the ejector and the clink of spent shell casings landing on the bed of the truck.

Two vapor lights set on tall poles cast harsh cones of light over the hard-pack at the center of the compound. The halo around the lights teemed with flying insects that provided a rich feast to the bats that darted in and out of the swarm. The trucks rolled to a stop, and the drivers killed the engines. Yael could hear the calls of the night birds in the surrounding forest.

Three clicks transmitted through his earpiece signaled to Yael that the guards at the weapons cache no longer posed a threat.

Yael and his men clambered to the ground and trotted toward their objective, a large two-story wood building at the right rear corner of the compound. It would be instantly recognizable to any soldier as barracks. There were doors at each end and exterior stairs leading down from the second story doors. The barracks and another structure that might once have been a farmhouse were the only solid structures besides the weapons and explosives bunker and a barn that they would discover held processed cocaine intended for shipment to the United States.

Two battered pick-up trucks of indeterminate make and a new Land Rover were parked in front of Major Barak's objective, the farm house that served as a command center and media studio. In the basement of this building the Israelis would be surprised to find all the equipment needed to print U.S. $100 bills. Classes were conducted in an open-sided structure on the other side of the clearing.

While Major Barak and the men remaining of the second squad prepared to clear the command center, Yael and his squad would cover and handle the barracks. When they were in place Yael keyed his radio twice to signal the Major.

Firing an M4 with a suppressor makes a noise, and when Yael heard the first shots from the Major's attack on the farmhouse he signaled his men, who began tossing high explosive HE fragmentation grenades through the barracks windows. The grenades created immediate chaos as the sleeping warriors of Allah awoke to thunderous explosions, the cries of the wounded, a deadly hail of shrapnel, fire and thick smoke. Their first panicked instinct was escape. With the compound's weapons secured in the cache, there was no chance for them to mount an effective defense.

As they poured out through the doors of the burning barracks, Yael and his men switched their M4's to full automatic and methodically cut them down with short controlled bursts. Those who realized what was happening clustered inside the doors to make a stand, trapped between the growing fire and continuing explosions within and the certain death that waited without.

Yael and his men closed in. Some of the remaining terrorists brandished knives and put up a brave front with bared teeth, wild round eyes, and imprecations. But within two minutes they, too, lay dead. The S-13's stepped across the bodies and cleared the barracks, killing stragglers and the wounded wherever they found them.

When he was certain that there were no survivors, Yael re-grouped his men. Standing amid the carnage he was gratified that none of them had suffered injury. As for the *jihadis* they had just killed, better they died here, far from Israel, than to have detonated a suicide vest on a busy street corner or a bus in Jerusalem. These men were no innocents. Each had been a sworn enemy of Yael's country who felt no compunctions about killing defenseless men, women, and children. As far as Yael was concerned, S-13's actions this night was pre-emptive and would save countless lives.

Yael joined Major Barak at the command center while his squad re-grouped around the trucks. The Major's assignment had been sensitive site exploitation, i.e. to clear the building and collect documents, hard drives, CD's and any other items that might contain useful intelligence.

Barak radioed the order for the men stationed around the perimeter to join them at the trucks, and ten minutes later they were rolling back toward the airport.

When they were a mile out from the compound, the night sky behind them lit up with an orange glow, and the thunder of multiple explosions reached them seconds later as the charges they had set destroyed the weapons and explosives bunker, shattered the printing press, and left the structures in flames. By the time the sun rose the "safe" jihadist training camp would be a smoldering ruin strewn with the charred corpses of zealots who would never harm an innocent victim.

By the time they reached the airport, passed through the perimeter fence, and rolled up the plane's ramp the pilot had filed a flight plan for Medellin, Colombia, and already spun up the engines. At 0200 hours they were back in the air. Fifty miles out they would descend to below 10,000 feet and change course eastward for the coast. Within an hour they would be over the open sea.

No alarm had yet been raised. Ciudad del Este was not Asunción. The inhabitants did not expect anything of the authorities beyond accepting bribes and protecting special interests.

The destruction of the Hezbollah compound would not be discovered until the following morning when a curious local was drawn by the pillar of smoke in the sky. By then, the Ilyushin was no more.

CHAPTER 45

Word spread quickly to those arriving for work that morning that the *memuneh* had spent the entire night in his office. Everybody in the non-descript building on the low hill in northern Tel Aviv surmised that something big must be happening. Those who knew said nothing.

The mission wheels-up signal came just after eight thirty. Ronan, Ramsay, and Sasha had followed the action in Paraguay via a secure link with the Ministry of Defense.

With Phase One of Operation Longshot complete, Phase Two got underway.

The name assigned to the operation suggested that someone in the IDF had a morbid sense of humor.

Ramsay and Sasha had arrived before sunrise and endured the Gauloise-charged atmosphere in Ronan's office for the past three hours as the operation unfolded in Paraguay.

"I think I'll get some air," announced Sasha. She made her concern for his health clear when she chided Ramsay about his long-held penchant for Cuban cigars. But he'd never heard her utter a word of admonishment to Ronan about his foul French cigarettes. Ramsay suspected this was because Ronan and all his habits had been an unchanging, reassuring part of her life since childhood. It would not occur to her that anything about him could be improved or changed.

Ramsay rose to join her. His back was stiff as he stretched, feeling his joints pop.

"How long before things start happening again?"

Ronan sat behind his desk in the same position he'd held for hours, having stirred occasionally only to pour himself another cup of black coffee.

It was a second or two before the question found its way through the barrier of his concentration. He blinked slowly and turned to face them, his face as rumpled as his shirt.

"The ship was in position long before the plane landed in Ciudad del Este."

He referred to a Liberian flagged container vessel that belonged to Capricorn Maritime Agency, a London subsidiary of Israel's largest shipping group. This would not be the first time the group's owner, a patriot and one of the world's richest men, had lent his support to one of his country's clandestine operations.

The 50,000 ton Cap Halston had picked up cargo in Buenos Aires five days before the Operation Longshot aircraft took off from Tel Aviv. Next, it spent two days in the port of Montevideo before setting sail for the Mediterranean. It now circled in a dark and deserted part of the Atlantic at a pre-arranged rendezvous four hundred miles east of the Brazilian coast.

"First contact should be sometime within the next hour," Ronan concluded.

He looks tired, thought Ramsay, he really is getting old. He was feeling the strain himself in the ache that began between his shoulder blades and radiated up the back of his neck.

"Why don't you take a break, too, Eitan?" asked Sasha. "We could all use some breakfast."

The corners of Ronan's mouth lifted in a small, tired smile as he recognized the concern in her voice. In the past he would never have permitted his fatigue to show.

"The *memuneh* doesn't leave until the operation is over. It's bad form."

"It's an IDF mission, Eitan."

"There are four of my men on that plane. When they are safe, I'll have breakfast."

In the cafeteria people shot covert glances toward the mysterious pair who had been closeted for days with the *memuneh*. Whispered speculation about their identities was rife. Ramsay, whose identity and nationality was a closely guarded secret, had never before been inside Headquarters. He ascribed his presence now to the fact that he was retired.

Ignoring the attention, Ramsay contemplated his tray of pastries, fruit, and cottage cheese. How could cottage cheese possibly have become an Israeli breakfast staple? He would have preferred bacon, eggs, and hash browns, but the cafeteria was kosher.

Switching his attention to Sasha, he said, "You and I have always been at the pointy end of the stick. Until I saw the way Eitan was suffering in there I don't think I ever realized what it must be like at the other end. I don't think I could do it."

*****

"We have visual contact." The voice crackled

through the ether from the Cap Halston, across thousands of miles to Ronan's office via the Ministry of Defense connection. The Ilyushin had arrived at the rendezvous.

The plan was simple in concept but difficult in execution. The Cap Halston's two motor dinghies already rode in the water at the ship's side. On deck, the first officer supervised the breakdown of a specially designed container to reveal a UH-60 Blackhawk helicopter whose rotors were quickly deployed. The flight crew boarded and began their pre-flight check as the Ilyushin made its first pass overhead, the roar of its mighty engines clearly audible.

It was at this stage that the reason S-13 had been tasked with Operation Longshot became manifest. Jumping from a plane into the ocean was not something the *Sayeret Matkal* spent a lot of time on in training.

S-13's preferred mode of mission deployment was from sea-launched helicopters inland to the target site, but in this instance the objective had been well beyond the helicopters' range, ergo the Ilyushin. S-13 training, however, ideally suited them for the planned mission recovery.

Major Barak's men were already in wetsuits, UDT life jackets, and parachutes, masks around their necks and swim fins and dangling from their utility belts. They assisted the four Mossad operatives into wetsuits and life vests. Four of the S-13's would tandem jump with them to ensure their safety. Three of the S-13's would jump in tandem format with watertight containers holding the intelligence materials retrieved from the Hezbollah camp snapped to the D-rings of their harness. Although theoretically unnecessary, tradition dictated they never make a jump unarmed, and each S-13 carried his Glock 19c in a low draw leg-holster, along with a K-bar knife, IR chem-lights, and a day-night flare for emergencies only. No one wanted to be lost at sea in the dark. They would regretfully leave the M4's behind, but they were no longer needed. In addition, each man was equipped with an infrared strobe light and a high-frequency acoustic homing beacon. All the men carried waterproof radio transceivers.

The pilot brought the plane back around toward the ship and opened the rear cargo ramp. The roar of the wind filled the plane. As soon as his instruments indicated the proper coordinates, the green light above the ramp gave the signal to jump. The men with containers went first, followed by the seventeen other S-13's and their Mossad tandem passengers.

On most operations this would have been a high altitude high opening (HAHO) jump, but because of the low altitude the jumpers would have only 5 seconds of freefall to get stable and pull their ripcords. This was less than optimum for their sterile MT1X military freefall rigs but at least there would be minimum dispersion. Once under canopy they would turn towards the lights set by the Cap Halston's tender boats, marking their drop-zone, or in this case their splash-zone.

After the first drop, the pilot set the autopilot to bring the big transporter around in an extended oval over the designated drop-zone. This gave him and his crew the time to clamber down to the cargo bay and, with the help of Yael and five of his remaining men, snap into their tandem harnesses. The flight crew was already wearing inflatable life-vests but they would have to forego the comfort of wetsuits. There was simply not enough time. Even though they had all jumped before during flight training, at night into the ocean was something new and frightening. Fliers did not like to jump from perfectly good aircraft unless they had to, and on this night they had to.

Yael, with the pilot on his chest, was the last to leave the plane. Just before they jumped Yael activated the timer set to detonate a series of explosive charges five minutes later. Stepping off the ramp into the night was terrifying for the pilot, but the freefall and canopy deployment went perfectly. As they floated toward the surface of the Atlantic Yael watched the flashing navigation lights that marked the location of the big aircraft dwindle into the distance.

He punched his three-ring quick release as soon as they hit the water, and the chute billowed away before sinking beneath the surface. After unsnapping the pilot, he put on his fins and oriented himself. They were lucky. The famously tempestuous Atlantic had welcomed them into a cold, but calm embrace under a cloudless sky. He had just spotted the lights of the cargo ship across the water some 500 yards away when he heard the motor of a tender boat approaching.

CHAPTER 46

The Israeli Prime Minister was pleased and the IDF was pleased, which meant that Eitan Ronan, also, was pleased. Aside from scattered press reports by a few especially enterprising reporters, the annihilation of the Hezbollah compound and its inhabitants had not aroused the curiosity or the ire of world governments. Paraguay was unlikely to complain publicly about a raid on an illegal, unacknowledged training camp for terrorists that had been allowed to exist for years on its soil. The authorities in Asunción quietly ordered that the site and all it contained be bulldozed into the earth.

The Argentines were quite content to be rid of an existential threat so close to their border.

The unexplained violent deaths of Ali Ahmad Radawi, his son, and an unidentified man at his home in Foz do Iguaçu attracted more attention. The perpetrators left no clues and no witnesses other than two hysterical female domestics who could report only having seen two men in balaclavas. The Brazilian authorities, well aware of Radawi's activities even if they had seen no reason to arrest him, chalked it up to an internecine feud among jihadists in which they had no interest.

Speculation was most animated in Lebanon's Bekaa Valley and other Hezbollah strongholds, as well as VEVAK Headquarters in Tehran where the dual loss of Radawi and Rus Ismayilov, only weeks apart, represented a serious blow to the terrorists' cause. They concluded that only the Americans had the resources to mount such an ambitious operation, probably with Israeli intelligence support. There were oaths of vengeance to be visited upon the big and little Satans.

The international intelligence community and a few astute reporters correctly connected Radawi with the Hezbollah camp. They made polite inquiries and held quiet chats about who might be responsible. Eitan Ronan himself had instructed his station chiefs to make inquiries of their liaison contacts. Months later when some intelligence analyses inevitably leaked to the press, the world gained another wave of conspiracy theories to contemplate.

But there was one person who could not accept these events with equanimity. Vitaliy Mikhailovich Shurgin was stuck in a country that was foreign to him, far from his accustomed climes, and he realized belatedly how isolated he had allowed himself to become. He had placed too much reliance on Rus Ismayilov as his lifeline to the outside world, and that had been a terrible mistake.

He'd lost contact with the wily Azeri, and the system of emergency communications they had devised produced no results. That Ismayilov was intimately connected with the slain Radawi and the covert Hezbollah activities in Brazil was not lost on Shurgin, and he suspected that his right-hand man might also have met a bloody end.

At the same time, press and television reports reached him of the death of the so-called "Arlington

Slasher" at the hands of one of the very people on the target list he had supplied to the Iranians. His plan for vengeance was stalled, perhaps forever. The mullahs would certainly never again run such a risk with one of their precious assets.

He should never have re-located so far from his power base in Europe, he now realized. What was left of his old Moscow *Voskreseniye* network lay dormant, and the criminal side was controlled by Ruslan Lomonosov who had replaced his slain brother, Zhenya, in Zurich.

What was worse, his ex-KGB bodyguards reported signs of discreet surveillance of his residence in São Paulo. Like a game animal about to be flushed out of a thicket, he decided the time had come to fly. He knew where he had to go first.

CHAPTER 47

Caesarea, Israel

The three of them sat around a glass-topped table on the veranda of what Ramsay believed must be the Mossad's most luxurious safehouse. A few paces from the beach on the outskirts of Caesarea, the villa fit in well with its neighbors, with the exceptions of its state of the art perimeter security system, ubiquitous CCTV cameras, bullet proof windows, and the wide-ranging arsenal in the basement.

Ramsay and Sasha had first made love in this same house twenty years earlier while he convalesced after a nasty encounter with a Russian assassin and his name was still Harry Connolly.

Several months later, when the liaison came to the attention of Eitan Ronan he hadn't ordered them to end it, as would have been his prerogative as head of the *Kidon* unit. Sasha was the only soft spot anywhere in the hard-bitten Israeli's make-up, and he would never risk alienating her affection. He assumed the affair would run its course. Instead, it grew stronger, and Ronan was forced to accept Ramsay, much in the way a jealous father must accept a future son-in-law about whom he has doubts.

Over a week had expired since Operation Longshot, during which Ramsay and Sasha enjoyed a respite in the sun before their planned return to Ireland where the harsh winter gales would be pounding the walls of their house in a few months.

The hospitable Mediterranean was in sharp contrast to the violence the North Atlantic so often displayed. The villa and its memories of their time there kindled their passion, and Ramsay had achieved a level of contentment not felt for some time, so much so that he didn't even mind Ronan's intrusion.

The *memuneh* arrived mid-afternoon in a chauffeured BMW followed by a chase car with his bodyguards.

Ramsay came out to greet him.

"You travel incognito these days."

Ronan grunted as he hefted his bulk out of the back seat and shook his head in mock solemnity.

"It's a burden of office. They send these poor boys with me so I can look after them in case there's trouble."

Ramsay almost laughed out loud.

One of the bodyguards remained outside on watch, and Ronan sent the others to the kitchen for refreshments provided by the retired Mossad couple who served as safehouse keepers. On Sasha and Ramsay's first visit the keepers had been Moshe and Marnie, whom Ramsay immediately dubbed Mickey and Minnie. They had long since been replaced, and Ramsay had been slightly horrified to discover that the new people were younger than he.

He ushered Ronan to the wide veranda at the back of the house where Sasha waited with a fresh pitcher of lemonade and a tin of Ronan's favorite tea cookies. Ronan accepted his usual hug and kisses on each cheek from Sasha and dropped heavily into one of the chairs.

He brought news that would bring their idyll to an abrupt end.

"The bird has flown."

He meant Shurgin. At their request, Ronan had expended some effort to find the man at the root of so much misery. With the Nelsons and Vicky Kondratieva dead, Krystal Murphy wounded, and Robert Strachey's family threatened Shurgin had to be stopped before he caused any more grief.

Rus Ismayilov had proven intractable. It had not been the kind of interrogation he might have suffered at the hands of Ronan in the old days. He would talk eventually as day after endless day of isolation in a cell wore him down, and the information would add to Israel's target list. Ismayilov would be tried *in camera*. He would never escape confinement.

In any event, thanks to the efforts of Sergio Blanco, they already knew Shurgin's location in São Paulo even before the local Mossad surveillance team investigated.

"You mean he's left Brazil," said Ramsay. "Do we know where he's gone?"

Ronan swirled the ice in his lemonade. He hadn't touched the cookies, a sure sign that he was worried, and Ramsay suspected his hesitation had to do with not wanting to see Sasha march off into another dangerous situation at this point in life. He'd already offered them the villa as a permanent residence as an enticement, if only they would remain in Israel.

"Come on, Eitan," urged Ramsay, "Sasha and I are on his list, too. He even knows my real name."

"But not your new one, and he can't find you, especially not here." The old man dug in his heels, and Ramsay knew he was hoping he could keep them close.

Sasha reached across the table and squeezed the *memuheh's* large, calloused hand.

"This is something we must do," she said. "He's finally out in the open, and I owe him something personal."

She seldom mentioned the savage rape and torture to which she had been subjected by Shurgin's men. They had waylaid her in London and taken her to Zürich where Ramsay and Ronan, along with Michael Mossberg managed to rescue her, but not before she had been in the Russian's hands for two days.

Just as they entered the room where she was being held one of her attackers slashed her face with a scalpel, costing her an eye. That act of savage and wanton cruelty turned Ramsay into a merciless destroyer of his enemies. He'd plunged a knife deep under the man's rib cage until he felt it enter his beating heart, and then he'd twisted it and watched with satisfaction as life disappeared from the man's eyes.

Sasha required months to recover, both physically and emotionally, and there were moments when Ramsay feared her spirit would not return. When she'd regained enough strength to travel he took her to the house in Ireland, and it was there that she at last agreed to become his wife.

Ronan's brow creased at the painful reminder,

and he placed his other hand over Sasha's.

"I'm against this," he said, "and you know it. I would take care of it myself, but the powers that be in Jerusalem will not sanction killing a former Russian president, not even Shurgin. I do, however, have the means to find him. He left São Paulo yesterday on a commercial flight to Paris. A Paris Station team was at Charles DeGaulle to pick him up, but he didn't leave the airport. He transferred to another flight at the domestic terminal."

"Destination?" asked Ramsay.

"Nice."

Ramsay's reaction was immediate.

"He's going to check on his money."

One of the things the Mossad had discovered after disrupting Shurgin's clandestine *Voskreseniye* funding network, and in the process stealing billions of dollars from it, was that his considerable personal funds remained under the control of Edmond Salmen, the international money man. It had been Ramsay's first operation with the Mossad, and his heroics at the time had convinced Ronan that the *Kidon* unit could use his talents.

Sasha asked, "Did our people in Nice pick him up?"

Although the Mossad was a small service in a tiny country, the Israeli Government expected much of it all around the world. To meet such demands the service augmented its personnel with a network of informal cooptees, some former Mossad, some ex-pat Israelis, and others simply sympathetic to the Israeli cause. They might be shopkeepers, academics, or doctors who were ready to support operations whenever called upon. Some were accomplished surveillants.

"They're looking for him now."

"We know where he'll go," said Ramsay.

He was thinking of a palatial estate in Villefranch-sur-Mer, a few miles east of Nice.

CHAPTER 48

They caught the evening flight out of Tel Aviv to London where they would switch documents. On their rare visits to Israel the couple always used alias documents permanently held for them at London Station. On this occasion they would use Canadian passports and fully backstopped credit cards authorized off the books by Eitan Ronan, which was not their normal practice. Ramsay and Sasha had traveled in and out of France countless times using their own names, but given their intentions on this occasion, they would need cover.

After a short layover at Charles DeGaulle, they caught an internal flight to Nice. They had debated whether to enlist the help of old friend Alain DeBlottière but decided it would be unfair to involve him in an unsanctioned assassination in his own country. Robert Strachey demanded to be a part of it and would not take no for an answer. They appreciated that the former CIA man's reasons were as deeply personal as their own. They would link up in Nice the following day. Otherwise, they were on their own.

It was still early afternoon when they landed, and a short taxi ride later they checked into a suite at the Grand Hotel Aston on the Avenue Felix Faure and ordered a late lunch from room service. Both were fatigued after the long trip and the quick London turnaround. The hoops spies must jump through can be exhausting.

They instructed the bellman to set the plates on the table on the terrace where they could take advantage of a view of the Place Masséna just across the street and the panorama of the Mediterranean beyond the picturesque city center. The afternoon sun washed the terrace in yellow warmth, reflected from the hotel's façade. The half-bottle of perfectly chilled Montrachet Bâtard that accompanied the sandwiches and *salade niçoise* improved their mood.

"Would you mind if I had a cigar out here?" Ramsay perceived that his wife was just mellow enough not to scold.

She assumed a squinty-eyed expression that he'd learned meant either that she was displeased or feeling mischievous.

"I very reluctantly agree, so long as you keep it out here and not in the room, and providing you order up another bottle of this wonderful wine."

"Your wish is my command, *Madame.*"

He re-entered the suite to make the call to room service and retrieve an *Hoyo de Monterey* double corona from his travelling humidor. He clipped the end of the cigar before re-joining Sasha.

The cigar would help him think. They needed a plan and didn't know how much time they had before Shurgin disappeared again. Ramsay's meeting with the leader of the local Mossad surveillance team was scheduled for seven P.M. at a bar in the old town. Events would move forward from that point, and things could happen fast.

Strachey would not arrive before noon the next

day, and there was no guarantee that the operation could wait until then. The American was travelling in true name, which complicated things. Ronan had firmly refused to provide documents for him, and Ramsay could appreciate how far the *memuneh* already was sticking his neck out.

The Montrachet arrived, and he poured them each a balloon of the rich amber liquid. Sasha swirled hers and took an appreciative sniff before setting her glass back on the table.

"Here we are on the Côte d'Azur," she sighed, "All these people enjoying this wonderful place, and we're here planning to kill someone."

He was puzzled. Was she having second thoughts?

"It has to be done," he said.

"I'm not saying we shouldn't do it. I'm saying I had hoped we had left all this behind."

Ramsay studied her from behind a gauzy cloud of blue smoke from the *Hoyo*. Her mood had changed in an instant.

"Shurgin is an old ghost that must be exorcised if we're ever to have any peace."

"Is peace what you really want?"

"Of course."

"I'm not sure I believe you. I think if you could, you'd go on doing this forever."

"This is the last one, Sasha."

"You need to find something else that makes you happy."

"You make me happy."

"I'm not so sure anymore. You're never content

when we're at home."

He couldn't argue with that. He'd been hard-pressed of late to hide his restlessness. Was it like this for everybody, he wondered? Was there such a thing as a happy retiree? He supposed there was. He'd seen them taking the sun on the pub veranda in Cleggan, playing golf, whatever – old men; they may have found new pastimes, but he suspected they all were dreaming of when they were young and vigorous and life had some purpose other than trying to make the best of the time left before senility or death claimed them. Of course, some men toiled their whole lives at jobs they hated or that were backbreaking. Maybe they were the lucky ones. They could look forward to when those jobs tasked them no more.

Was it possible to be more than the sum of one's experience? Ramsay supposed that academics had it best. The life of the mind went on. They could write books, create new ideas, and continue to build upon their life's work. But what book could he write? His life had been defined by intermittent lacunae of inactivity between operations that required the skills of subterfuge and deception, as well as the deadlier arts he had mastered.

Even the name he carried was not the one he had been born with. The only permanent thing in his life was the woman sitting across the table. She was his anchor, his refuge, and the cocoon of dissatisfaction he had wrapped around himself was breaking her heart, giving birth to doubts when there should be none.

"I'll tell you what," he said.

She'd been staring across the city toward the sea and now turned to face him, a quizzical look in her eye.

"We'll travel. We have more money than we can ever spend, so let's see the world. There are places we've never been, foods we haven't tasted, wines we haven't tried, and beds we haven't made love in. It would make going home to Cleggan all the more pleasant, like in the old days when we couldn't wait to get back there."

He could read the doubt in her face and knew he deserved it. He'd been a selfish pig.

"Do you really mean it?" she asked.

"Cross my heart."

"How much longer will that cigar last?"

For second her question confused him. Then he carefully placed the barely started cigar in the ashtray and picked up his wineglass.

"You know," he said as he stood and held out his hand, "we should finish this bottle while the wine is cold. And if I'm not mistaken, there's a bed inside that we've yet to make love in."

CHAPTER 49

The bar was one street away from Nice's open air market on the south edge of the old city near the beach. *Les Trois Diables was* a modest establishment with a deteriorating façade that might once have been white and scabrous green doors and shutters. A balcony of uncertain resistance to gravity clung stubbornly to the second floor over the entrance. Motor scooters lined the walls of a near-by pedestrian tunnel.

Across the street was a Thai restaurant that looked right at home in the seedy neighborhood. A tall man in a flat, cloth cap, slouched, head down, with a cigarette cupped in his fist in a shadowed niche next to the restaurant where he could observe the bar's entrance. He wore jeans, a black t-shirt, and an old leather bomber jacket. Had anyone seen him in the light without the hat they would remark his resemblance to the actor Clint Eastwood.

Five minutes before seven P.M. just as the last of the evening light was fading a man carrying a black leather valise emerged from the pedestrian tunnel and paused in front of the bar before entering. On his head was a red baseball cap. Ramsay waited five minutes to make sure his contact had not been followed before crossing the street and pushing his way through the green door.

Inside, a bar extended along the wall on his right to the rear of the smallish room. To his left a half-dozen sparsely populated tables covered with checkered cloths filled the rest of the space. The lighting was dim and red, an excellent color for camouflaging shoddy decor and improving the looks of older women of uncertain virtue. An old Johnny Hallyday song from the Sixties throbbed from hidden speakers.

> *Je ne crains plus rien*
> *J'ai mon cœur sur tes mains*
> *Je te crie ouais dans la nuit*
> *Reste ici …*

The man with the baseball cap sat on a stool at the far end of the bar. Ramsay took the stool next to him and ordered a *demi*, a half pint of beer.

"Are you a Cardinals fan?" he asked his companion, referring the the red baseball cap.

"No, I prefer the Yankees."

Their recognition *parole* complete, Ramsay extended his hand.

"That's one of the strangest *paroles* I've ever used," said the man, introducing himself only as "Damian." "Did you think of it?"

"It's inside baseball," Ramsay replied, eliciting a small frown of incomprehension from Damian.

"I have what you wanted in the bag there."

He nudged the leather valise on the floor with the toe of his shoe.

"And our target?"

"Still viable, but not easy."

"Where is he?"

"He arrived yesterday and took a suite in the

Orangerie at the Hôtel Royal Riviera in Cap Ferrat."

Ramsay's surmise that Shurgin was going to meet Edmond Salmen was correct. The hotel was not far from the banker's estate. They may already have met, which lent even more uncertainty to their chances.

"How many bodyguards are with him?"

"None. He took a taxi from the airport, alone."

This made no sense. How could Shurgin risk travelling without security?

"You're certain it's him?"

"He matches the surveillance photos from Brazil."

The change in Shurgin's physical appearance was a complicating factor. The absence of bodyguards meant they could be looking at the wrong man. Surveillance reporting on the ex-president's residence in São Paulo said he had guards. Why would he be traveling without them?

Ramsay could only hope that an up close and personal look at the man would confirm his identity.

"Your people are there now?"

"Of course."

"How many?"

"Just two. They'll switch on and off throughout the night."

"Has he come out of his room?"

Damian shook his head. "So far, he's having his meals sent in. Not a normal tourist, for sure."

"So he's not left the hotel since he arrived?"

"That is correct."

He could not imagine why Shurgin would not

have met with Salmen immediately. It didn't make sense.

Ramsay said, "We'll relieve your people at seven tomorrow morning, Damian, and take it from there. Eitan Ronan sends his personal regards."

They agreed on tomorrow morning's rendezvous, and Ramsay left the bar carrying the valise.

CHAPTER 50

Night had fallen over Nice, and the lights from the ships and yachts anchored off-shore reflected across the water in compliment to the brightly lit by-ways of the city. It was warmer than usual for this time of year, and the streets teemed with strollers out after an evening meal or just a promenade and a *limón glacé* from a sidewalk vendor.

But on the top floor of the Grand Hotel Aston on Avenue Felix Faure a man and a woman who were contemplating the opposite of pleasure had just spilled the contents of a valise across the king-size bed: three pistols (one for Robert Strachey), extra magazines and ammunition, silencers, and a pair of good quality binoculars with night vision capability. The pistols were old Walther PP's and the serial numbers had been eradicated. They would be tossed into the sea when the operation was over.

Professional assassinations are planned carefully after weeks or months spent collecting information on the location. The habits of the target are studied. Suitable operational sites, weapons types, and escape routes are selected and memorized. Like a ballet, the choreography must be perfect.

Sometimes even the best laid plans can go wrong. The recent Mossad operation in Dubai to assassinate Hamas terrorist Mahmound al-Mabouh had involved a large, well-rehearsed team of operatives plus many more support and logistics personnel, flawless execution, and escape via pre-arranged routes. But still, Emirates security had compromised the identities of eleven of the operatives. Tradecraft would have to adapt to the new realities of electronic monitoring.

For Ramsay and Sasha there had been no time for such painstaking preparation and rehearsal, and they had only the barest minimum of support. Less that twenty-four hours had elapsed since they learned of their target's departure from Brazil. They had guessed the destination correctly, but they had only just learned where he was staying, and his plans were unpredictable. Shurgin could disappear again just as quickly as he had appeared.

Ramsay said, "I'm worried about the absence of bodyguards. It's not like Shurgin. And why would he have come all this way only to stay cooped up in his hotel room?"

"It could be a bit of luck, I suppose. Maybe he doesn't want to attract attention."

"Of course not. But he had guards in Brazil, and he should have felt safer there than in France."

"His relationship with Salmen is virtually unknown. It would probably be worth it to him to run the risk of travelling alone to protect the secret."

"That may well be correct. Ismayilov's disappearance must have spooked him. If there's one thing that fox would want to be sure of, it's that his money is safe."

"Or he could be planning something. Damian said he's kept to his room since he checked in to the hotel. Maybe he's waiting to link up with someone before he sees Salmen."

"It's possible. We have no choice now but to tend to practical matters, do what we can and hope it's enough. What does the terrain look like?"

Sasha had studied maps and Google Earth photography on her laptop while Ramsay was meeting Damian.

She said, "Salmen's estate occupies a huge chunk of hillside above Villefranche-sur-Mer, and without a lot more work than we have time for, there's no way we can even hope to get inside. It must be well guarded. We might hit Shurgin between the time he leaves the hotel and arrives at the estate. The vehicular entrance is off of a narrow street named Leopold II that essentially runs around the western boundary of the property. One of us will have to case the area. If there is no good ambush site, we'll have to go mobile."

Damian would have motor scooters waiting for them in the morning. The local team would then break off. Ronan was willing to task them with an off the books surveillance, but could not risk their participation in an unsanctioned assassination.

"That's a lot of flying by the seat of our pants, and with only two of us it would be risky. Things could well come down before Strachey can get here. We'll do a hit and run if we have to, but what about his hotel suite?"

"That would certainly be less risky than the Villa La Leopolda. Damian will know about hotel security."

He said, "It may be our best shot, no pun

intended. Casing will have to wait for morning. It's too risky to try sneaking around in the dark on the grounds of a five-star hotel we know nothing about. You scout the route to the estate first thing while I look over the hotel."

"You realize this plan depends on his returning to the hotel after leaving Salmen," she said.

"If he leaves with luggage, we both follow and make the hit on the street before he reaches the entrance to the estate."

Sasha had another thought.

"Damian said nothing about Shurgin having a car. Isn't it likely that Salmen will send a car to pick him up? A man like that probably uses an armored car. We'd be screwed."

She was right. Their best chance of success was a hit at the hotel.

"Too many variables; too little time," he said.

*****

Cap Ferrat is a richly bejeweled finger that dips into the sparkling Mediterranean immediately south of Villefranche-sur-Mer. It contains some of the world's most prized real estate and was famously described by Somerset Maugham as "the escape hatch from Monaco for those burdened with taste."

For over a century the five-star Hôtel Royal Riviera at the base of the finger on the eastern side had been a preferred destination for the privileged classes. It offered two ways in and out: the entrance to the hotel proper at No. 3, Avenue Jean Monnet, and a dead end drive leading around the side to a parking lot in the rear with direct access to a separate building known as the Orangerie. The hotel swimming pool lies between the Orangerie and the main building.

Ramsay and Sasha wore jeans and light cotton shirts, untucked to conceal the pistols in their waistbands. Motor scooters were common, and they had no trouble fitting in. Both wore helmets with visors that covered their faces.

When he was still with the CIA, Ramsay had relished solo operations with no Headquarters superior looking over his shoulder. But this was different. CIA operations in his day seldom had fatal outcomes. Much had changed. This was the most primitive operation he had mounted since beginning work with the Mossad. The severely constrained time for preparation meant they possessed insufficient knowledge of the turf. He'd planned an escape route, but Nice was a small area with a police force alert to protect the moneyed visitors and inhabitants.

His spirits were lifted by a call from Robert Strachey whose flight had landed at Nice at eleven A.M. He instructed the American to take a cab to the Royal Riviera and try to get a room, preferably in the Orangerie. This was not the high season, and there was a chance that something would be available.

Just before noon Sasha, stationed along the incongruously narrow Avenue Jean Monnet watched as a heavy Bentley glided through the gate at the side of the hotel. She alerted Ramsay who was in the rear parking area. He was within twenty-five yards of the car when a slim man with shaggy black hair walked with quick, nervous steps out to it from the Orangerie. Ramsay did not miss the fact that the man was alert to his surroundings.

He punched the speed dial for Sasha on his mobile phone.

"It's him, or at least he matches the photos we have. Same build, but with long, black hair that must be a wig. He's wearing sunglasses."

The Bentley swung smoothly into a U-turn and headed back out.

"Got him," said Sasha.

Keeping two or three cars between them, she followed the Bentley onto the Boulevard Napoléon III and began the climb toward the winding Avenue Leopold II, staying with it until it turned into the entrance of the Villa La Leopolda. It took only a few minutes to traverse the short route.

"We were right about the destination," she reported to Strachey over the phone. "When he leaves, it will be only minutes before he's back at the hotel.

She rode past the entrance and took up a position higher on the hill with a view of the gate and settled down to wait.

*****

Unlike the pink exterior of the hotel proper, the Orangerie's two-story stucco façade was golden yellow with a Mediterranean red-tiled roof. It had been completely re-modeled in 2006 and boasted fourteen rooms and two suites, including Shurgin's two bedroom suite on the top floor.

Ramsay stripped down to the swim trunks he wore under the jeans and switched the sneakers for leather sandals from the scooter's saddlebag. He traded the Casio G-shock wristwatch for a showy gold Vacheron Constantin which would advertise to those who noticed that he was a member in good standing of the well-heeled clientele of the Hôtel Royal Riviera. He sauntered from the parking lot into the swimming pool area with the leather satchel tucked under his arm. There was a rack of thick beach towels available for guests, and he grabbed one and draped it over an empty lounge chair under a white umbrella before diving into the water and swimming a lap as if he belonged there.

He dried off, settled onto the lounge chair, and ordered a gin and tonic from a passing waiter who was pleased to keep the change from a fifty Euro note. Ramsay settled back to await Strachey's appearance while studying the area from behind his RayBan's.

There had been no activity at the Villa La Leopolda for three quarters of an hour. Given the time of day, he suspected Shurgin was having a long lunch with Salmen. There was a risk that Shurgin would return before Ramsay could get inside, but Sasha would forewarn him. If need arose, he and Strachey could overpower the Russian before he reached his room.

His phone vibrated, and he recognized Robert Strachey's number. The American reported he was in the lobby and had been successful in securing one of the deluxe rooms in the Orangerie.

"That's the best news I've had all day. I'm at

the pool. Call me when you're in the room, and I'll join you."

He didn't want the two of them to be seen together.

Five minutes later Strachey called with the room number. Ramsay threw a towel over his shoulder and left the pool area. Within minutes he knocked on the stout wooden plank door which opened immediately to reveal a broadly smiling former CIA officer.

"I rented a car, a fast one, in case we need it," he said. "I didn't fancy relying on a motorbike while being chased by cops. We had some luck. There was a cancellation, so I could get into this building."

"We needed some luck," said Ramsay.

He closed the door behind him and scanned the room. It was on the second floor with a view of the sea, and that was fortunate because it did not face the hotel proper and the pool area. He had noticed something in the hallway, and a plan already had begun to form, a plan that should work.

Beside him, Strachey said, "Shurgin likes to live well. This room cost fifteen hundred Euros a day."

With Strachey following, Ramsay went to the French doors and opened them onto the balcony drenched with the late morning sun. The Mediterranean stretched away to the East toward Monaco, dotted with large yachts and the brightly colored sails of smaller boats rising and falling with the sea's gentle undulations. The larger than usual number of yachts was a sign that Monaco's impending annual Yacht Week would again be a success and reminded Ramsay that he had a twenty-six foot whaleboat waiting to be reassembled in Ireland.

The large balcony was furnished with a table with four chairs and two lounge chairs. It was enclosed on both sides by a stucco wall that separated it from the adjoining balconies. Ramsay leaned out and peered on the other side of the wall on their left.

"Nothing is cheap on the Riviera," he said. "Shurgin rented a suite at twenty-five hundred a day. And speaking of luck, I think it's right next door." Damian had informed him of the location of Shurgin's suite.

"I'll be damned," said Strachey. "As my father used to say, 'Even a one-eyed hog finds an acorn once in a while.'"

"It's still broad daylight. There's a risk we'll be seen, but it's the easiest way into his room, and there are no closed circuit television cameras covering the balconies."

CHAPTER 51

The chauffeur held the door of the Bentley for Vitaliy Mikhailovich Shurgin. The seats were of soft, creamy leather, and the interior was decorated in rich, tropical woods, but Shurgin did not notice. He settled into the seat and tried to collect his thoughts as the car slid quietly away from the hotel. He didn't feel safe, and he was uncharacteristically apprehensive. He was used to being in control and missed the feel of the reins in his hands.

Adding to his discomfort was the unexpected reception he had received from Salmen. A call to the banker the day before had not resulted in the immediate agreement to meet that he had expected. Instead, Salmen had begged off, claiming a previous engagement and suggested they meet over lunch at the Villa La Leopolda the following day.

He was not interested in lunch and nor did he care to listen to Salmen's inevitable recitation of the history of the renowned estate. What he wanted was a full accounting of his holdings and above all to assure himself that they were safe.

He had lost enormous sums to thievery in the past. The American Harry Connolly and that accursed woman had somehow managed to drain a number of the accounts he and Morozov had set up and entrusted to a Russian banker for *Voskreseniye* operations with the Brotherhood. They'd lost billions, and their banker had been killed. That had been in the early Nineties, and they had been forced make withdrawals from the personal accounts he had set up with Salmen.

Now, after all that had happened, he was uncertain how much he still could trust the Lebanese Jew. He suspected Salmen of using the funds for his own ends, despite the exorbitant ten percent "handling fee" the banker charged to protect Shurgin's stolen treasure from prying eyes. The man was greedy, but for the time being there was no one else. Later, he would look for an alternative. There was no shortage of avaricious bankers who would be eager to work with him.

Fearful of being recognized despite the changes to his appearance, Shurgin had cooled his heels in the hotel for the past twenty-four hours and had his meals sent up. He had not hesitated to demand the best suite, but his preoccupation left no room to appreciate the exquisite furnishings and soft Mediterranean colors of the décor. The pale tangerine and lavender shades were intended to promote relaxation, but Shurgin was unable to calm his nerves, and this condition shamed him.

In his younger days he had been an exemplary officer of the KGB who relished the most complicated and risky operations. To venture into enemy territory had provided the greatest satisfaction, both personal and professional. He had been fearless.

The coup he and Morozov pulled off inevitably changed all of that. Morozov remained with Russian Intelligence where, as the Head of Department "S," he maintained control of the SVR's illegals operations all around the world. This position gave him enormous latitude to pursue *Voskreseniye* goals in league with the Brotherhood. Shurgin abandoned the intelligence world to pursue a political career aimed at winning supreme power in post-Soviet Russia.

He became a puppet master, the secret arbiter of who lived and who died, who won what contract, which foreign companies were awarded licenses to do business in the new Russia (so long as he received a hefty percentage of the profits).

He worked his way upward through the political ranks, aided by generous bribes and the occasional murder, until he reached the pinnacle of Kremlin power. The climb had not always been smooth. The terrain was strewn with boulders, and he had nearly slipped and tumbled back down the slope.

To survive an incident that could have cost him everything it had been necessary to sacrifice his loyal comrade, Morozov. He was certain the General understood. It was the way things had always been done in Moscow.

The Kremlin was a den of wolves constantly on the prowl for wounded prey, and the pack had set upon him mercilessly when they sensed he could no longer defend himself. They brought him down and savaged him when his efforts to prevent the exposure of a more than half-century old Soviet crime failed spectacularly.

The irony was that the reason for his "crimes" had been so noble. A naïve American Administration had signed an arms control treaty that guaranteed the deterioration of their own military might while permitting Russia to continue to modernize its own strategic forces.

The disgraced former CIA officer Harry Connolly and his woman had risen out of the mists of the past to strike at him yet again. They had hounded him for years, stolen his money decades earlier, and they had even precipitated the crisis that cost Yuriy Ivanovich Morozov his life. Connolly had viciously killed Zhenya Lomonosov, as well.

Were Morozov still at his side things might have been different. Without him, Shurgin's enemies had conspired to bring about his disgrace and have him tossed out into the cold.

Wretchedness hung over his thoughts like a foul miasma that light could not penetrate. It was not the wretchedness of regret, because he felt no regret for anything he had done. It was as though the loss of power had left him weightless, like a leaf falling from a branch, subject to the caprices of the wind.

"We're here, sir."

Shurgin was jolted out of his reverie by the chauffeur who stood holding the car door open. They had arrived at the Villa La Leopolda.

CHAPTER 52

Edmond Salmen waited to greet Shurgin under the portico looking like a smooth skinned, well-fed seal. In contrast to the brightly colored bougainvillea that enthusiastically wreathed the entrance, the banker wore a somber, chalk-striped suit and silk tie. He had chosen the formal banker's uniform rather than the chic informal attire of the proper Riviera host.

Perhaps he means it as a sign of respect, thought Shurgin, who also had chosen to wear a suit. Unlike Shurgin, the banker had grown stout with age, and the narrow fringe of white hair contrasted sharply with his well-tanned pate.

Shurgin thought he detected a hint of unease in the way the banker shifted his weight from foot to foot and attributed it to nervous anticipation of a meeting with his most important, and notorious client. Salmen had his greedy fingers in many less than salubrious financial dealings, but he strove to maintain a clean public image. He would never have agreed to meet Shurgin anywhere but behind the thick walls of the Villa La Leopolda.

"The change in your appearance is remarkable, Monsieur Shurgin."

The banker's hand, when Shurgin shook it, was as limp and clammy as a dead fish.

Salmen offered up a fatuous smile as he led his guest inside and fussily ushered him into an extravagant dining room where a table that could easily accommodate forty was set with two places. Floor to ceiling windows and French doors, open to a wide, tiled *terrasse*, provided a privileged view of the Villa La Leopolda's gardens as they stepped down the hillside, with Villefranche-sur-Mer and the sea at its foot. This was a view reserved for the very few, the rich and famous, fortunate enough to be invited to the estate by Edmond Salmen.

The opulence served only to remind Shurgin of the gilded halls and rooms of the Kremlin where he had once ruled supreme. He couldn't wait to finish his business and be out of this place, though he still had not decided where he would go to ground.

Salmen invited him to sit and took his place at the head of the table with Shurgin on his right.

Their conversation was in English.

"It is good to see you again after so long an absence, Monsieur Shurgin." Salmen's tone was unctuous. "When you dropped out of sight I became quite concerned."

"I'm sure you did, but I'm here now."

"I assume you've been covering your expenses out of the numbered account we set up for you in Zürich?"

The account was considerable, holding over one hundred million dollars. Shurgin had ordered it established years ago in case of emergency. But, in fact, most of his expenses since going to Brazil had been covered by Rus Ismayilov and RusAvia profits. It was only since Ismayilov's disappearance that he had been forced to draw on the Zürich account. One of the reasons he was seeing Salmen was to establish easier and more direct access to the assets still held in Monaco.

"You are correct, but I'm here to discuss my other holdings."

Salmen waved his hand in the air as though shooing a fly.

"Of course, Monsieur. All in good time. Shall we discuss it after lunch?"

He rang a small bell that sat atop the snowy white tablecloth, and a servant appeared instantly with a silver ice bucket containing a chilled bottle of wine. Another followed with a tureen and ladled a rich gazpacho into porcelain bowls.

Salmen skillfully deflected his attempts to broach business during the meal, pouring more darkness into Shurgin's mood. He sat mostly in stony silence as the Lebanese prattled on about his plans for the social season.

Halfway through the main course, he had had enough and slammed his silverware to the table.

"Salmen, remember that you work for me. I'm not asking a favor of you; I'm ordering you to provide an accounting of the assets you hold for me. Why are you so reluctant?"

The banker was startled and gulped his wine before answering with an air of injury.

"I was just being polite, Monsieur. It has been so long since I saw you last, I thought you would enjoy sharing a meal."

"That's not what I came for, Salmen."

A servant interrupted them to whisper something in Salmen's ear. The banker looked strangely at Shurgin for a moment before standing abruptly and placing his napkin over the unfinished main course of grilled sea bass with carrots and zucchini.

"I fear you will miss a superb dessert. Please follow me."

His manner had turned decidedly brusque.

He led Shurgin to a darkly paneled library off the main entrance. On a fine, Louis XV desk several folders with leather covers had been stacked. Salmen invited him to sit.

The banker waved a hand over the folders as though he were a magician performing a conjuring trick.

"These are the account books for the holdings. I am sure you will find them in order."

"Give me a general précis."

"Of course. We put most of the cash and bearer bonds into the American securities market, and the interest over the years has been steady and considerable. As for the gold, you yourself must be aware of the appreciation in value, especially over the past year. The value of the bullion you brought to me in 1991 hovered at around $350 an ounce. As of this morning the price was over $1,700 per ounce. That is nearly a five hundred percent increase in value, M. Shurgin."

Shurgin made a mental calculation. He and Morozov had deposited 350 tons of gold bullion with Salmen twenty years ago. At the time it's value had been roughly four billion U.S. dollars. According to the banker, it was now worth 20 billion."

"Of course," said Salmen, avoiding the Russian's eyes, "there is the question of ownership."

Shurgin's head jerked up. "What's that supposed to mean," he snapped, suddenly wary.

"Oh, I'm not talking about the ORIGINAL owners, of course. I'm talking about General Morozov."

It was true, Morozov had been an equal partner with Shurgin on the money side.

"Morozov is dead." Shurgin enunciated the words carefully.

"True, but there is the question of his heir."

Morozov had had a child, but there had been no agreement concerning heirs. Besides, in this matter there was no question of "rights," or legalities. The funds were now his alone to do with as he pleased.

"There was no agreement ..."

His words were cut short by the intrusion of another presence into the room, a heavy, dark presence that Shurgin sensed before a new voice joined the conversation.

"Hello, Uncle Vitaliy. You really look quite different."

Shurgin spun around and stared at the figure in the doorway. It was a young man of perhaps thirty-five. He was tall, over six feet, and broad. He was dressed casually in light wool slacks and a blue blazer with a cream-colored shirt that did little to conceal his muscularity.

He thought he recognized the face until the realization slammed home that it was another face he recognized reflected in this one.

Shurgin stood and turned to face the intruder.

"You are Yuriy Ivanovich's son."

"Dmitriy Yuryevich Morozov, at your service, sir," said the young man.

General Morozov's son had been about fifteen at the time of his death. Shurgin had provided a generous stipend for his widow and child and later pulled strings to ensure the boy's acceptance in the SVR. He had seen him but rarely since Morozov's funeral and didn't know how to treat him now. The young man's unexpected appearance put him off balance.

"You see," said Salmen who remained seated behind his desk, "the question of an heir is quite real."

Shurgin was still trying to comprehend what was happening, but he could not think clearly.

"How did you know I was here?" he asked Morozov, and shot a venomous glance at Salmen who had clearly betrayed his trust.

A second figure appeared behind Dmitriy Yuryevich, a thin man of average height with blond hair and a bad complexion. Shurgin did not recognize the coarse features until he stepped through the door into the light. And when he did the vague apprehension that had plagued him all day coalesced into prickly fear.

What was Ruslan Lomonosov doing here?

The *vor v zakonye's* eyes were like two blue marbles, empty of any emotion.

"Twenty billion dollars in gold bullion is enough to attract anybody, Vitaliy Mikhailovich." As empty as his eyes, Lomonosov's voice carried no intonation.

Shurgin sat back down, suddenly weak. The reason for Salmen's procrastination in seeing him and the time wasted over a meaningless lunch was now clear. The banker had been stalling, waiting for Lomonosov to arrive. It was not a long flight from Zürich.

"Did you think we didn't know about the money, my mother and I?" asked Dmitriy Yuryevich Morozov. "That night before they dragged him away to Lefortovo my father told her everything, but even after I came of age I didn't dare approach you. I used my time in the SVR to discover the truth about my father's death. Even then there was nothing I could do. You had become too powerful, Vitaliy Mikhailovich, and I had to bide my time.

"But you finally stumbled, and it was just a matter of time before you were stripped of power and disappeared, and sooner or later you would have to come out of hiding to check on your assets. That's when I approached Mr. Lomonosov, who was quite interested in the story, as you might imagine. He agreed to help me claim my inheritance."

There was a roaring in Shurgin's ears. How could this be happening to him?

"You want half of everything?" he managed to ask as he deeper into the chair, his knees suddenly weak.

Lomonosov answered.

"No, Vitaliy Mikhailovich. I think we'll take ALL of it."

Shurgin turned to Salmen and switched to English.

"You can't permit this. It's illegal." He appealed to Salmen, but he already knew it was futile.

The banker sat with his arms crossed over his paunch, like a Buddha without the smile. His visitors had been speaking in Russian, a language he did not understand, and a fact for which he was grateful. He had no desire to know what these people were saying. He remained silent, as he had been ordered.

Lomonosov put his hands on the back of Shurgin's chair and leaned over, placing his head inches from the former president's.

"Mr. Salmen and I had a conversation some weeks ago. With only a little persuasion, he agreed that 'ownership' of the assets implies the right of inheritance. Our young friend here has every right to expect his share. As a matter of fact, should anything untoward happen to you, he would inherit everything. Should such an eventuality come to pass he's agreed to share equally with me." He smiled at Shurgin and tilted his head. "So you see, Vitaliy Mikhailovich, it's all quite legal."

Lomonosov stepped away and at a signal from him the two bodyguards each grabbed one of Shurgin's arms and jerked him roughly to his feet.

Salmen was visibly alarmed now.

"Monsieur Lomonosov, you promised nothing would happen here.

Lomonosov switched his attention to the banker who shrank back from the *vor v zakone's* poisonous gaze.

"Yes, Salmen, and I always keep my promises, including those concerning what happens to those who try to cheat me, especially bankers."

At another signal from Lomonosov, the guards hauled Shurgin outside to a waiting Mercedes saloon. They placed him in the back seat and took up positions on either side.

CHAPTER 53

From her vantage point Sasha had seen the long Mercedes pass through the gates into the estate and surmised that whoever it carried was there for a meeting with Shurgin and Salmen. She settled down, expecting a long wait, and was surprised when less than twenty minutes later the same car emerged back onto the Avenue Leopold II.

She had counted four men through the smoked glass of the Mercedes when it entered, two in front and two in back, but saw that it now carried three in the rear. The person in the middle was much smaller than the other two and had shaggy, black hair. It had to be Shurgin.

This was the unanticipated factor they had feared from the beginning, the manifestation of something Ramsay called "Murphy's Law." Shurgin could well be heading to the airport with these men, whose presence made a hit and run attack impractical, or they might be accompanying him back to the hotel.

She decided to follow. If they were going to the airport they would continue west along the D33 and cover the 15 kilometers in around twenty minutes. If they were going to the hotel, they would be there within five minutes.

*****

Before swinging over to Shurgin's balcony, Ramsay had pulled on the jeans and shirt that he'd earlier stuffed into the valise along with the pistols. It was a simple matter to jimmy the lock on the French doors that opened into one of the bedrooms of the suite.

Ramsay had insisted that Strachey not accompany him. The American was using his true name, and the propinquity of his room to Shurgin's could well make him suspect. For that reason Strachey succumbed to the suggestion that he take up a position at the bar on the other side of the pool area where he would be seen by the maximum number of people. At the same time he would be in position to observe the target's arrival and alert Ramsay, who would be waiting inside the suite. There would be no more contact between them until they all were outside of France. Strachey would remain for a few days so that his departure would not appear hasty or associated with the death of the man in the suite next to his room.

Ramsay had just settled down to wait when his phone vibrated. When answered he heard the whine of the motor scooter and the sound of traffic. Sasha's voice was urgent.

"You've got to get out of there now! I'm just a few blocks from the hotel, and Shurgin's in a car with four other men."

"Who are they?"

"I don't know. They arrived at the villa about twenty minutes ago, and Shurgin left with them. I couldn't get a good look at them."

"I'm going to wait until they get here," said Ramsay. "There's a chance they won't come inside with him."

He wasn't willing to abort the mission yet, but he had a sinking feeling. They'd known from the beginning that it would require an extraordinary amount of luck for them to succeed.

"Be careful, Ewan. I'll be outside."

"Strachey is out there, too. There'll be plenty of warning."

Precisely five and a half minutes later his phone vibrated again. It was Sasha.

"Ewan, they're all getting out and going in. Shurgin doesn't look happy."

Ramsay swore under his breath.

"I'm out of here."

He slipped out into the corridor and swiftly entered Strachey's room, using the American's key card. Moments later, he heard the passage of several feet outside the door, and then Shurgin's door opening and closing.

His phone was vibrating again, and this time it was Strachey.

"Where are you?"

"I'm back in your room."

"Thank Heaven, when I couldn't get through I hoped Sasha was warning you."

"Did you see them?"

"Yes. There are four guys with Shurgin, and they weren't smiling. It doesn't look like a friendly group."

"Russians?"

"They could well be, especially the two big guys without necks that were holding onto Shurgin. He's definitely not a happy camper. What do we do?"

"Sasha should be back in the parking lot with the scooters. You stay where you are. Do you have a good view of Shurgin's suite?"

"Give me a sec while I move to the other end of the bar."

"I'm going to link up all three of us on a conference call." He punched the appropriate buttons on his Blackberry.

No sound penetrated the thick walls of the Orangerie, an establishment dedicated to the comfort and privacy of its guests. But five minutes after the men entered Shurgin's suite, the sounds of a scuffle reached Ramsay's ears clearly through the open balcony doors. The scuffle came from Shurgin's balcony and the noise ended suddenly with a sharp scream that was cut short.

Simultaneously, Strachey's voice burst from Ramsay's Blackberry.

"Holy shit!"

CHAPTER 54

"We'll continue our chat in your hotel room, Vitaliy Mikhailovich."

Lomonosov turned in the front seat to look squarely at him, and Shurgin read nothing but menace in his face. He had known Lomonosov's brother well, and they had the same dead, blue eyes, as though the life had been sucked out of them by the gulag.

What more did they have to say to him? He had that feeling again, like a leaf drifting zigzag to earth with no control over where he might land.

Throughout his years in office Shurgin had staged numerous public displays to demonstrate his fitness and strength to an adoring public. There were films showing him throwing opponents in a *Jiu-Jitsu* dojo, he'd been photographed bare chested on horseback and fishing in wild Siberian streams. Even now, in his sixties, he was in superb physical condition, but it would do him no good against the two men seated on either side of him whose combined weight almost quadrupled his own. If he were to escape he would have to rely on his wits, but the bizarre events of the day had left him dazed. He feared losing touch entirely with reality. Perhaps none of this was really happening.

But the strong arms that pulled him out of the car and propelled him to the entrance of the Orangerie were real enough. What more could they want to "chat" about? Lomonosov's intent was to divest him of his riches with the help of that ungrateful dog, Morozov's son. He would still have the personal numbered account which would see him comfortably through many years. Perhaps it was time to retire from the world, find a young Brazilian mistress, to concentrate on the carnal rather than the political.

Lomonosov strode ahead and used Shurgin's key card to open the heavy wooden door of the suite and then held it as his goons half carried the former Russian president inside. Morozov the younger trailed the group.

The goons pushed Shurgin into a chair.

Lomonosov took a chair opposite and snapped his fingers in Shurgin's face.

"You are unusually silent, Vitaliy Mikhailovich," he said. "You would not have been so docile in the old days."

"I'm old," said Shurgin, ashamed of the piteous quaver in his voice. "I surrender. You can have the gold. I'll go back to Brazil, and you'll never hear from me again."

The statement evoked no sign of compassion from Lomonosov. He sat for a moment staring at Shurgin in the way one might study a curious specimen through a microscope.

The silence in the room was laden with menace, and tendrils of fear inserted themselves into Shurgin's numb confusion. As the fear gained ground it brought with it an awful clarity.

With his part in Shurgin's passion play complete, Lomonosov stood and retreated to lean against the door, arms folded nonchalantly as he observed the scene with bored detachment.

Shurgin's unwilling attention now was diverted from Lomonosov to the young Morozov who approached him with an odd expression on his face, something between rage and joy. Alternately hot and cold waves washed over Shurgin as he realized he had seen this before. It was the nightmare of General Morozov coming to his cell in Lefortovo. As had his father in the nightmare, young Morozov held something in his hands that he now dangled in Shurgin's face. He was saying something, but the words seemed to float in the air and burst like fragile bubbles before they could be fully comprehended.

"I know how my father died, Shurgin. I thought this was only fitting."

Lomonosov's goons roughly lifted him from the chair and tied his hands behind his back. Shurgin could not remove his eyes from the object Morozov's son now held toward him.

*****

Strachey had moved from his original vantage point overlooking the Orangerie entrance to the end of the bar where he had clear view of the northeastern corner of the building where Shurgin's suite was located.

He'd just ordered a G&T when a form that was instantly recognizable as a man hurtled over the balustrade of Shurgin's balcony like it had been launched from a catapult. His outward trajectory was jerked into a sharp downward arc by a rope around his neck, and the shriek that had shattered the air above the holiday-makers in the pool came to an abrupt end as the rope snapped tight. Under the horrified gaze of the onlookers, the man gave a few futile kicks before his entire body spasmed and then hung limply at the end of the rope, swinging like a macabre pendulum.

Something dark floated from the man's head to the ground. Investigators would later discover that it was a well-made toupee.

"Holy shit!"

"What the hell is going on?" Ramsay responded to Strachey's exclamation.

"You'll never believe it. There's a body hanging from Shurgin's balcony, and I'm pretty sure it's him. I suggest you stay put in my room until I can get you out cleanly."

While the attention of the public was riveted on the body, four men hurried out of the Orangerie to the Mercedes in the parking lot and sped away.

*****

Sasha had listened to the exchange between Ramsay and Strachey and realized the men who had accompanied Shurgin would be coming toward her, probably in a hurry. She found a place to hide with a view of the big Mercedes and turned on the video camera of her Blackberry. Sure enough, seconds later, the men rushed into the lot and tumbled into the car as she recorded the scene.

The Mercedes was at the airport on the other side of Nice at nearly the same time the police arrived at the Hôtel Royal Riviera in response to a frantic call from the hotel manager. A Gulfstream IV was waiting with the engines turning and already was airborne when the police were lowering the lifeless body of the former President of the Russian Federation of States to the ground.

*****

French investigators would be at a loss to identify the dead man for some time, which was an embarrassment for them, but manna from Heaven for the local press that fed for days on the juicy story of a mysterious death at a venerable and renowned Côte d'Azur hotel. The dead man had checked into the hotel as a Brazilian national, but the South American country's authorities had no record of his passport. Also leaked to the press were the facts that the man had worn an expensive custom-made wig, that his natural hair color was red, and he had worn brown contact lenses to conceal his blue eyes.

When the autopsy results became public the media went into frenzied overdrive, this time including the international media. The medical examiner concluded that the corpse was that of a Russian male around sixty years of age and that his face had been altered within the past year by plastic surgery.

A very few trusted reporters were alerted by a certain small intelligence service from a small country in the Middle East that the dead man was none other than Vitaliy Mikhailovich Shurgin, disgraced former president of the Russian Federation, and that he had been murdered by a well-known Russian criminal who resided in Switzerland. A video recording of the alleged killers entering a Mercedes saloon in the Hôtel Royal Riviera parking lot accompanied the tip.

The Russian Government denied all knowledge and refused to provide any information that might confirm or deny the corpse's identity.

In a rare spirit of cooperation, the American Central Intelligence Agency responded favorably to a quiet request from the French *Direction de la Surveillance du Territoire*, the DST, and provided samples of DNA that had been collected clandestinely from Shurgin during official visits to the United States. The subsequent confirmation of the dead man's identity was never shared with the public, although the information did make its way to the desk of the FBI's Executive Assistant Director for Counterintelligence, Enoch Whitehall.

Several months later the privileged enclave of Villefranche-sur-Mer would be shaken by another mysterious death, that of billionaire philanthropist Edmond Salmen, who died in a fire at the Villa La Leopolda that destroyed the entire library where Salmen did business. Security tapes from the estate's state-of-the-art surveillance system were nowhere to be found, and there was no explanation for the fact that the banker's entire security detail had been given the night off. No connection was ever made publicly between Salmen and Shurgin.

The day preceding Salmen's death a small,

Panamanian registered freighter received a cargo that had been transferred from vaults in the banker's bonded storage facility in Monaco. The attention of alert stevedores was attracted by the Cyrillic lettering and seal of the former Soviet Union stamped on several steel bound crates.

CHAPTER 55

Robert Strachey checked out of the Hôtel Royal Riviera the day after the incident with the plausible explanation that he was too upset to remain in the room next to the dead man's. He achieved a small triumph when the manager in a gesture of rare Gallic penitence cancelled all room charges in view of the unfortunate circumstances. The manager would not regret his generosity because the hotel would soon be filled with curious members of the idle rich hoping for osmotic acquisition of material to add spice to their dinner table chatter.

Back in Virginia Strachey was greeted by a relieved wife and a still-disgruntled father-in-law. He quietly informed recuperating Krystal Murphy that she no longer had to look over her shoulder for assassins sent by Shurgin. The detective, of course, was curious about how he could be so certain, and was disappointed when a full answer was not forthcoming. The imprecise responses to her questions undoubtedly provoked silent imprecations upon all spooks, but she had learned to accept that Strachey usually had good reasons for not sharing certain information.

Life returned to normal until he received an invitation to a meeting he could not refuse.

"My sources inform me you recently paid a visit to France, Mr. Strachey."

There was no use denying it. FBI Executive Assistant Director Enoch Whitehall would have impeccable sources. Strachey was in the man's faultlessly impersonal office. Several weeks had passed since the events in Villefranche-sur-Mer, and he had begun to hope there would be no repercussions from his presence at the scene. That hope had been dashed by the summons to the Hoover Building.

In a way Whitehall embodied the FBI: cerebral, gray, enigmatic, and the man could be menacing. The statement had been pronounced in a neutral tone that conveyed no hint of accusation, an effective tactic for fishing expeditions.

"Yes, I did," Strachey replied.

He resolved to provide no more information that necessary to answer the questions. Although ultimately he had had nothing whatsoever to do with Shurgin's death, there were things he could not reveal, especially concerning Ewan Ramsay and his wife. He would obfuscate if he had to, even if it was a Federal crime to lie to the FBI.

"I find it interesting that you would have travelled again so soon after the intrusion at your residence. I recall that we discussed the fact that the danger was not yet at an end."

Whitehall clearly preferred to conduct interrogations by making statements rather than asking questions.

"Yes." It was the minimal safe response.

Whitehall regarded him for a moment before proceeding in his carefully neutral tone. "In fact, you were a guest at the Hôtel Royal Riviera when a man died there. Your room was next to his."

More irrefutable statements. No questions.

"Yes."

"You're not being very communicative, Mr. Strachey."

Silence.

"Were you in any way involved in that man's unfortunate death?"

At last, a direct question, and one he could answer truthfully.

"No."

"You will recall I warned you against rash actions."

"I was at the hotel bar far away from the action, Director Whitehall. There are lots of people who will testify to that."

"Yes, I've already confirmed that. Nevertheless, it would have been a difficult feat to carry off on one's own."

Another question in the form of a statement.

"I can't disagree with you about that."

"And yet the man we all had reason to believe was behind the deaths of Vicky Kondratieva and the others, as well as the armed invasion of your residence ends up at the end of a rope, tossed from the balcony of the room next to yours."

"A remarkable coincidence."

"I don't believe in coincidences, Mr. Strachey."

"And yet, here we are. Is there a point to all this, Director Whitehall?"

It was several moments before Whitehall replied.

"It appears not, other than to commemorate the death of one of the world's first class villains and remark upon inexplicable turns of fate. Whatever it was that brought you to that particular hotel at that particular time, Mr. Strachey, I hope it was worth it."

Whitehall stood to signal the meeting was over. Strachey followed suit and was surprised when the FBI man extended a pale, long-fingered hand across the desk. The grasp was firm and dry.

"You will not be questioned further about this matter," Whitehall intoned, "and if you will accept one more word of friendly advice, please be careful of similar coincidences in the future." It was possible that the FBI man smiled as he said this, but Strachey could not be sure he had interpreted correctly the momentary shift in the man's features.

On the way home Strachey tried to puzzle out Whitehall's real reason for wanting to talk to him. Had it been to make certain there were no loose ends and to reassure him that there would be no personal repercussions, or was it to congratulate him?

*****

When they left Nice Ramsay and Sasha rented a comfortable Citroën sedan and drove at a leisurely pace in the general direction of Paris. For once they were not pressed for time. They enjoyed a two-day lay-over in the Loire Valley where they sampled the goat cheese and silky red wines of the area around Chinon. Upon reaching Paris, they contacted DeBlottière and filled him in on the facts. A day later, they switched documents in London, handed over a short report to be sent to Eitan Ronan along with the video from

Sasha's Blackberry, and caught the afternoon flight to Shannon where their Land Rover awaited them in long term parking.

Three hours later, after a leisurely drive across the rolling landscape of County Galway, the sea and home came finally into view, and when they passed Little Lake the black slate roof of their house was clearly visible. Mrs. Reilly, whom they had alerted from the airport, already would have aired out the house and deposited their Scottie, Angus, in his basket beside the fireplace. Mrs. Reilly, a local widow of uncertain age, helped Sasha clean the house and was Angus's favorite dog sitter. She spoiled him terribly, and he would require many romps in the moor to reduce his girth.

They had remained mostly silent during the trip through the familiar Irish by-ways, each of them reflecting on the events in France. The manner of Shurgin's death had been nothing less than anticlimactic after the desperate gamble they had planned, but it was nonetheless a relief. The spectacular demise of their most prominent foe of two decades signified a kind of closure, especially for Ramsay. He already had vowed to abandon the quests of his youth, and now the dragon he had fought for so long was dead. It did not matter that it had been at the hands of others. An unanticipated tranquility had settled over him, and he found to his astonishment that he welcomed it.

For the first time in years the sight of the stone house on the bay lifted his heart.

They had come home.

THE END

The Author

Michael R. Davidson was raised in the Mid-West. Heeding President Kennedy's call for more young Americans to learn Russian he studied the language, and military service took him to the White House where he served as translator for the Moscow-Washington "Hotline." His language abilities attracted the attention of the Central Intelligence Agency, and following his military service Mr. Davidson spent the next 28 years as a Clandestine Services officer. Seventeen of those years were spent abroad in a variety of sensitive posts working against the Soviet Union and the Warsaw Pact. In the private sector he worked as a business owner and security and economic development consultant before devoting full time to his writing.

Also by Michael R. Davidson

Did the Cold War end or did the KGB find a way to retain its power and dominate the new Russian Federation? "Harry's Rules" is an espionage thriller set against the backdrop of post-Soviet Russia in the early 1990's.

Who killed President John F. Kennedy? A long buried secret that could change the course of history draws murder to a quiet Washington suburb. Only an exiled CIA officer can solve a mystery that both the White House and the Kremlin will protect at all costs.

Find them at: www.michaelrdavidson.com
All books also available via Amazon.com

Deposed Russian president Shurgin is desperate to punish those who brought about his downfall, and nothing will get in his way. A suicide bomber and a serial killer are his chosen instruments. A quiet afternoon in Brussels is shattered by unspeakable horror, and a madman leaves a trail of blood in Washington. But his targets are anything but helpless, and Harry Connolly vows to put an end to Shurgin once and for all.

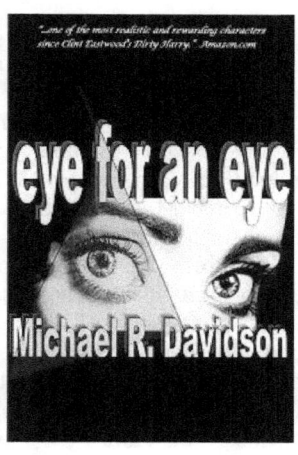

The Russians set a trap, and Harry Connolly's aka Ewan Ramsay's beloved Sasha falls into it. Captured by the sadistic and cruel Russian mafioso Zhenya Lomonosov and his henchman, Sasha will soon be secretly transported to Moscow into the hands of Vitaliy Mikhailovich Shurgin. The Mossad and Ewan Ramsay are faced with the necessity to mount a bold rescue operation against Zhenya's nearly impregnable stronghold.

Find them at: www.michaelrdavidson.com
All books also available via Amazon.com

Disillusioned by Spain's failing fortunes in the 30-Years-War, Eduardo Macías leaves the Army of Flanders and sets out for home. Eduardo's reputation as a valorous soldier leads to his being named Captain of the Santa Hermandad, a Spanish force charged with protecting the people and maintaining the law. He is forced to accept a mission by officials of the Holy Inquisition to investigate an alleged case of heresy involving a nobleman with ancient royal ties. What Eduardo discovers places him in a dangerous situation at odds with the Inquisition, and he must choose between upholding his honor. and excommunication.

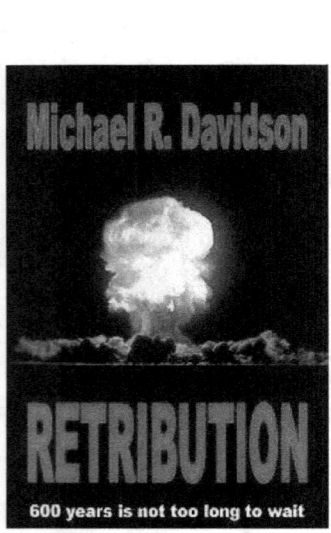

In 1492 victorious King Fernando of Aragon forces the daughter of the last Muslim ruler in Andalusia to become his concubine as a gesture of "reconciliation." The product of their coupling, a secret Muslim with an abiding hatred for his father, founds a line that nurtures the flame of vengeance through the centuries. Now, with the assistance of Iranian Intelligence his descendant threatens a nuclear holocaust if the ancient lands of Andalusia are not returned to him. Facing insurmountable odds resourceful Spanish cop Alberto Macías and CIA officer Robert Strachey must risk their lives and careers in a desperate race against time.

**Find them at: www.michaelrdavidson.com
All books also available via Amazon.com**

A controversial Miami judge is murdered in a Washington hotel room. Homicide detective Krystal Murphy identifies an ideal suspect, a person with motive and opportunity. Following the suspect's trail to Miami, she is confronted by an unspeakable tragedy. Convinced her initial instincts were wrong, she teams with a Miami detective. When more people associated with the case begin turning up dead, Krystal finds herself in a race against time before she herself becomes the next victim of an increasingly desperate killer.

Find them at: www.michaelrdavidson.com
All books also available via Amazon.com

COMING SOON !!

Michael R. Davidson teams with Russian author Kseniya Kirillova to pen a tale torn from the realities of today's Russia.